THE CRIMSON HARVEST

A serial killer reaps revenge in
this Welsh murder mystery

CHERYL REES-PRICE

Published by The Book Folks

London, 2024

© Cheryl Rees-Price

This book is a work of fiction. Names, characters, businesses, organizations, places and events are either the product of the author's imagination or are used fictitiously. Any resemblance to actual persons, living or dead, events or locales is entirely coincidental.

All rights reserved. No part of this publication may be reproduced, stored in retrieval system, copied in any form or by any means, electronic, mechanical, photocopying, recording or otherwise transmitted without written permission from the publisher.

ISBN 978-1-80462-199-8

www.thebookfolks.com

The Crimson Harvest is the ninth title in a bestselling series of standalone mysteries set in the heart of Wales.

Chapter One

I'm so cold. I've been standing in this spot for what feels like hours. My fingers are numb, and my toes are curling in pain. I'm on a grassy bank looking down at the house. It's in darkness apart from one downstairs window that has a weak light. Memories like shards of glass stab at my chest. They lodge in my throat so it feels like I can't breathe. Fear has frozen me in time.

At the side of the house is an old oak tree. The winter winds have stolen the last of its leaves. Now its branches stretch out to the house like gnarly fingers waiting to pluck out the occupant. A giant stick doll. I don't want to think about the stick dolls now. It's not the trees I should be afraid of.

The wind ruffles my hair and stings my cheeks. Beyond the house and tree is inky darkness. The rest of the world is hidden. I pull up my hood and dig my hands into my pockets. I feel for the lighter and twist it around. At my feet is a petrol can. I'd like nothing more than to see flames chase away the darkness that surrounds me and the darkness within. It's what I came here to do. To eradicate the place that haunts me.

I let the memories come now. At first, they overwhelm me, but I don't fight the panic. Then a spark of anger ignites. I feed it until it grows and turns into a burning rage. No one is going to help me. I'm alone. I've always been alone. I know what I have to do.

I leave the petrol can and walk down the bank to the pitted track. Ice that has formed over puddles breaks beneath my boots and makes a satisfying crunching noise. I pause for a second to look at the broken fence that once stood proud and erect. Like the rest of the house, it has fallen into disrepair. I move through the gate. It creaks on its hinges. I stop again and listen. There's no sound from within the house. I press on and, without hesitation, I open the door and step inside.

It's funny that so many people in this area don't lock their doors. They think they are safe here. Isolation has made them complacent. It never occurs to them that a stranger could walk in. Then again, I'm not a stranger.

I'm standing in the kitchen. There is no warmth here. The stove has gone out and damp clothes hang from a rack above. There was a time when this kitchen was the heart of the house. The aroma of stew and hot buttered bread would fill the air. There's another memory here. It lurks like a ghostly shadow, and I can't grasp it. Perhaps it's because I don't want to. A shiver runs through my body and it has nothing to do with the temperature. I turn away from the kitchen and push open the door that leads to the sitting room. There he is in the armchair. His face is illuminated in the lamplight. His legs stretched out. His head to one side, mouth open, and snoring. Revulsion crawls at my skin and shame burns a hollow in my stomach.

The air in here is pungent. It is a mix of stale sweat, alcohol, and smoke. Empty lager cans and an overflowing ashtray litters the table next to him. The carpet is worn and dirty, like the rest of the furniture.

I feel strangely removed from myself. It's like I'm in a dream, but in a dream you have no control. I should turn away and run from the house, but this is my only chance to face him. I may never have the courage again. He looks harmless sleeping in the chair. I know different. I know the danger I am in if he wakes up. I am standing here, exposed and vulnerable. That much hasn't changed. I wish I didn't feel so weak and pathetic. I should have stuck to my plan.

I move slowly backwards and keep my eyes on him. I'm afraid to turn my back. In the kitchen, I let my eyes once again adjust to the darkness. Something pulls me towards the staircase. I know what it is. I want to know if it is still there. It's strange what memories stay with you. If you asked me what I did a week ago, I'd struggle to remember, yet something from years ago can be so clear. All it needs is a trigger: a sound, a smell, or even a drawing.

I move up the stairs and wince at the creaking of the bare treads. I keep looking behind me, afraid he'll appear. He doesn't come. I make it to the bedroom. I know that this is his room. I can smell him. I get down on my hands and knees and crawl under the bed. I reach out my hand and my fingers touch the cold metal of a shotgun. Some people never change their habits. I pull out the shotgun then go back under to retrieve the box of cartridges.

I stand up and feel the weight of the gun. I run my hand down the smooth barrel. I pull on the end. It's stiff and it takes all my strength to cock it. I feed in the cartridges and snap it back. Now I feel powerful. Now I can take care of myself.

I walk back down the stairs. I don't care about the noise I make. Let him come and face me. I march into the sitting room and see he hasn't moved. I raise the gun and jam it against my shoulder. I creep closer and point it at his face before I kick his shin. His eyes snap open. He looks disorientated for a moment then jumps forward. The gun is almost touching his cheek.

'What the—'

'Shut up! You don't get to talk.' I jab the gun at his face. 'You're going listen to me.'

I talk and talk. My voice gets louder until I'm shouting. The gun shakes in my hand. When I stop to draw breath, I expect to see some sign of shame. There is nothing. It's like he's devoid of any feeling. He doesn't look sorry. He doesn't even try to beg for my forgiveness. I put the end of the gun to his mouth then trail it down over his chest and to his groin. I see a bead of sweat trickle down the side of his face. I want him to feel fear. Be powerless. Vulnerable. I squeeze the trigger gently. I want to drive terror into him. I want him to lie awake at night and relive this moment.

'You gonna pull the trigger?'

I see defiance in his eyes. It's like he senses my weakness. Without warning he propels himself from the chair and tries to grab the gun. I'm caught off guard and stumble backwards. One second we are both standing, the next he is thrown backwards by the force of the blast. It feels like I have been lifted off my feet and I'm falling. I land with a thud on the floor. My ears are ringing, and the gun lies beside me. I'm frozen. He makes a horrible gurgling sound which brings me to my senses. The first thing I notice is the feel of blood on my face. I look down and see that blood covers my hands and clothes. Something snaps within me. A memory, like a bolt of lightning. It's not his blood I'm seeing. I hear someone screaming. It takes a while to realise that it's me.

I jump up and start tearing at my clothes. My hands are shaking so much, it's difficult to get the zipper down on my coat. I keep pulling until I yank it down. I strip until I'm down to a T-shirt and underwear. He's silent now. I don't look at him. I run to the kitchen and scrub at my face with cold water then run from the house.

I don't feel the cold or the icy ground on my feet. I keep running until I reach my car. It's only then that I realise I've left my keys in my coat pocket. I lean against the car. I feel like sliding to the ground and letting the cold take me, but I don't want to die here.

It takes all my strength to go back to the house. I keep my eyes down and search my coat pockets. The smell of blood fills the air and mixes with other fluids that I don't want to think about. The screaming inside my head won't stop. It's the blood. I've never liked the sight of blood, but this is something different. A lid has been taken off a box and I'm terrified to look inside. Whatever lies in the recesses of my mind is something so terrible it steals the breath from my lungs.

I find the keys and bolt from the room. I grab a coat that's hanging on a hook by the door, slip it on, and run. I make it back to the car and drive home. I don't remember the journey. I go straight into the shower and turn up the temperature until it scolds my skin. After, I sit in a dark room. I'm in shock. This wasn't supposed to happen. It wasn't my plan. I just wanted to burn down the outbuildings, destroy the places that my memories hide. All I can do now is wait for the police to come.

* * *

There is nothing more for me to write. I move the cursor to the post icon. One click and it will be out there for the world to see. I can't change what happened and now I see he was meant to die. They all have to die. Too late to stop now. The police never came. It's been three days. I watched the news every day to see if he had been found. Nothing. He's still just lying there in a pool of blood. I'll have to go back and move him from the house. It's a sign that I'm meant to carry on. Finish what I started. I click the icon and the post goes live.

Now the world will know what I did and why. More importantly, everyone will know what *he* did. I've sent out a message to all those who have inflicted suffering on another. No matter how much time has passed, you can't get away with it. *You* could be next. I wipe the tears from my eyes and look down at the stick doll lying on the table. The next one has been chosen. So it begins.

Chapter Two

DI Winter Meadows walked into Ystrad Amman police station. It was a crisp, dry morning in the Welsh valley, and he was thinking about his upcoming wedding. He couldn't help smiling.

The first person to greet him as he entered the office was DS Tristan Edris. The sandy-haired detective was Meadows' partner. Edris had a quirky sense of humour and a dislike of dirt. Over the years, they had formed a close bond.

'Tea is on your desk,' Edris said. 'I thought a nice cup of ginger would warm you on this cold morning.'

Meadows moved to his desk and picked up the steaming mug. 'What's got you in such a chirpy mood this morning?'

'Nothing.'

'Oh, come on,' Meadows said. 'I know you too well. For a start, anything other than black tea or coffee, you call, "That crap you drink." Now you're serving up herbal tea.'

'I found your stash in the kitchen. Thought I'd give it a go. Start looking after myself. It works for you.'

Meadows smiled. 'What's brought this on?'

'Nothing. Well, I met this girl last night.'

'Another one of your Tinder dates?'

'Yeah, but this one is different.'

Meadows took a sip of his tea. 'You say that every time, then you find something you don't like.'

Edris perched on the edge of Meadows' desk. 'Not this time. All this talk of weddings has got me thinking. Maybe I'm being too judgy. Time is moving on.'

Meadows laughed. 'You're only in your thirties.'

'Yeah, well I don't want to leave it too late like…'

'Like me?' Meadows asked.

'You got lucky,' Edris said. 'It's hard enough to find someone in your thirties but when you reach forty.' He shook his head.

At that moment DC Reena Valentine walked in. She took off her bobble hat and shook her sleek black hair. 'What did I miss?' she asked.

'Edris is looking for a wife,' Meadows said.

Valentine laughed. 'Good luck with that.'

DS Rowena Paskin came in behind Valentine and handed her a mug of coffee. 'Are we talking about Edris' love life again?' she asked. 'There can't be many women left in the Amman Valley that you haven't dated.'

'I've not been out with that many,' Edris said.

Valentine raised her eyebrows. 'Oh, come on.'

Edris sighed. 'I just haven't found the right one yet. Anyway, you're still single. How about we make a pact? If we haven't found someone in, say, five years, then we get married.'

'Hell no!' Valentine said.

Meadows laughed. 'Setting your goals a bit high there, Edris.'

'I don't know. She's getting on a bit.' He turned to Valentine. 'You don't want to end up spinster of the parish.'

Valentine's eyes widened in mock horror. 'I don't think you're allowed to say that to me.'

'Definitely not,' Paskin said.

'I think that warrants a disciplinary,' Meadows said. A smile played on his lips.

Valentine laughed. 'I'm living my best life as a single lady. I tell you what, if you really want to find someone to settle down with, I'll help you. I know a few friends I can set you up with.'

'Yeah, great,' Edris said.

'What about the one you met last night?' Meadows asked.

Edris smiled. 'Gotta keep my options open.'

DS Stefan Blackwell sauntered in, completing the team. He mumbled a good morning and went straight to his desk.

'You look cheerful this morning,' Valentine said.

'My boiler broke down again,' Blackwell said. 'It's bloody freezing and I had to have a cold shower.'

'If you need some time to sort it out, it's not a problem,' Meadows said. 'It's quiet at the moment.'

'Let's hope it stays that way,' Paskin said. 'Only twenty-two days to go.'

Blackwell rolled his eyes. 'I hope we're not going to have another day discussing what everyone is wearing to the wedding. It's in a bloody field.'

Meadows sighed. The wedding was being held at his childhood home, a commune nestled in a remote valley in South Wales. All the team had been invited and he worried about how they were going to mix with the residents. He wasn't sure that Blackwell was going to come. His default mood was miserable. The people Meadows called his family would welcome him, even though the last time he had been there, he had arrested a member of the community.

The chatter fizzled out as they all took a seat at their desks and started work. The office filled with the clattering of fingers on keyboards which was only interrupted by the arrival of Sergeant Dyfan Folland. When Folland came into their office, it was usually to bring bad news.

'Got one for you,' Folland said. 'Body, male, found in the grounds of St Tyfi's Church.'

'Where's that?' Edris asked.

'Dinefwr Park estate,' Folland said.

'I know the one,' Meadows said. 'Looks like the quiet spell is over.' He turned to Edris. 'Grab your coat.'

* * *

Meadows drove while Edris sat in the passenger seat. He kept up a constant stream of chatter. They moved in and out of villages until they came to a long stretch of winding road. Hills and fields could be seen through the naked trees and sheep huddled in groups.

'Daisy get off alright?' Edris asked.

'Yeah, dropped her at the airport this morning.'

'That's the way to do it,' Edris said. 'I don't know why you won't agree to a stag night. There's still time for us all to go away for a weekend.'

Meadows smiled. 'Yeah, not my thing. Daisy's just going with a few friends for a bit of R&R.'

'That's what *you* think. It's going to be party all the way. How long is she away for?'

'Just till the end of the week.'

'Nice. Then the two of you will be off sunning yourselves. Wouldn't mind getting away from this cold myself.'

'I don't think it's going to be that hot,' Meadows said. 'It's autumn in New Zealand.'

'I'd love to go. I've never been out of Europe.'

'Well, now you've got a goal.'

They reached Llandeilo and drove over the old stone bridge that crossed the River Tywi. Blue, yellow, and pink-painted housed lined the hill. It gave the small town an all-year-round welcoming feel. They arrived at the Dinefwr Park estate and followed the long driveway that twisted past fields. On the right stood Newton House, an ivy-clad Gothic mansion, and on a hill directly in front of them, Dinefwr Castle rose from the low-lying mist. The impressive twelfth-century ruin still retained its towers and battlements.

'So, where's this church?' Edris asked.

'Erm, from what I remember, you walk through a field then take a pathway down through some trees. Then you cross another field. It's not far.'

'You've got to be kidding me,' Edris said. 'I suppose I better put my boots on if we're going to be traipsing through damp grass. They could have opened a gate for us.'

Meadows laughed. 'Yeah, and we'd get stuck halfway across.'

'Maybe you should get a Land Rover.'

They changed into boots and made their way across the field. Meadows breathed in the cold air and drank in his surroundings.

'Those cows have their beady eyes on us,' Edris said. 'Imagine that on your death certificate, "Death by cow".'

Meadows chuckled. 'Is that what's going through your mind? Look around at the trees. Take a moment to let the calmness of your surroundings wash over you.'

'Calmness? We're in a field, freezing cold, and being hunted by cows. Look, they're coming.' Edris picked up the pace.

PC Abbey Taylor was waiting at the other end of the field. Clouds of vapour rose from her mouth.

'You must be freezing,' Meadows said.

'Just a bit,' Taylor replied. 'I'm making sure no one tries to go down this way. There are a few cars left in the car park. We're working on securing the whole park but there is more than one entrance. I've taken information from a few walkers.'

'Thanks,' Meadows said. 'Once the park is secure, go and get yourself a cuppa and warm up.'

They followed the trail that led through trees and down into a clearing. A white van was parked in the field.

'They managed to drive down,' Edris said.

'CSI have to have off-road vehicles,' Meadows said. 'Stop bitching. Can you imagine walking down here and carrying all that equipment?'

'Fair point,' Edris said.

'How are you going to manage the wedding at the commune?'

'I won't be wearing a £500 suit.'

'You got yourself a pair of wellies?'

Edris laughed. 'Yeah, you did say dress down.'

Halfway across the field, they met up with PC Matt Hanes. The burly officer looked peaky, and his skin had a clammy appearance.

'You look a bit rough, mate,' Edris said.

'Yeah,' Hanes said, 'it's grim. Murder, no doubt about it.'

Meadows didn't want to ask for details. He could see that Hanes was struggling. 'We got an ID?'

'Yeah. The victim is a Mr Huw Jones, community councillor. Sixty-nine years old. Still had his wallet on him with his driving licence. He was found by a Mr Paul Berresford. The call came in at just after half past nine this morning. Mr Berresford is part of a group of volunteers that are restoring the old church. Poor guy was in a hell of a state. I took his statement and sent him home.'

'Did you get anything of interest?' Meadows asked as they started to walk towards the church.

'He didn't see anyone this morning. He said a few people walk by and stop to chat about the work most days.'

'OK, when he's had time to get over the shock, have another chat with him. He may remember something.'

St Tyfi's Church came into view with its twin bell tower sitting under the branches of the surrounding trees. Meadows stopped at the entrance to the churchyard where a West Highland terrier was tethered to a post. He crouched down to stroke the dog's head. The dog wagged its tail feebly and kept his muzzle resting on its muddy paws. There was blood on the tufts of fur between his toes, and parts of his white coat was stained red. Big soulful eyes looked up.

'Who is this fella?' Meadows asked.

'We think he belonged to the victim,' Hanes said. 'He was found like that. You can see where he's clawed at the ground trying to break free.'

Meadows pointed at two breakfast bowls. 'And the water?'

'Left there, and possibly food in the other bowl.'

'So, the killer made sure the dog was safe and had food and water,' Meadows said. 'Interesting.'

'An animal-loving murderer,' Edris commented.

'I'm working on identifying the next of kin,' Hanes said. 'I thought it best for the animal to be taken home rather than call the dog warden.'

Meadows nodded his agreement. 'Get some photographs taken of him, then see if you can get him cleaned up a bit. If only you could talk.' He stroked the dog's head again then stood up. 'OK, let's take look.'

'I'll leave you to it,' Hanes said.

They walked through the entrance and saw a white tent had been erected in between gravestones. White-clad figures were dotted around, scouring the ground for evidence. Metal stepping plates led to the tent and then through the graveyard.

Meadows put on protective overalls and shoe covers before placing a mask over his face. Edris did the same. As they walked towards the tent, one of the forensic officers approached them. Despite the mask, Meadows recognised Mike Fielding, head of the team.

'Hi, Mike,' Meadows said.

'Morning. This one's not pretty.' He shook his head. 'Nasty business.'

'Hanes said the same,' Edris commented.

'He was looking a bit green when we turned up,' Mike said.

Meadows' stomach tightened. For Mike to look so grim then it had to be bad. He just hoped it wouldn't be worse than what he was imagining.

'Ready?' Mike asked.

'Yeah,' Edris said and pulled up his mask.

Meadows braced himself before stepping into the tent. He heard Edris gasp behind him. He took a moment to digest what he saw before him.

The victim, Huw Jones, was lying on his back. His top half was draped over an old grave. His legs were bent at the knees and twisted to the left. Blood covered the grave and the surrounding area. Metal darts with black rubber fletching were sticking out of his body. One was lodged in his cheek, another in his throat.

'Crossbow?' Edris asked.

Meadows nodded. 'It wouldn't have taken this many bolts to kill him.'

'There must be over twenty,' Edris said.

'More than that, I'd say. Look at his arm. One has gone straight through.' Meadows crouched down. 'Looks like some have gone in his back. Difficult to see how many from this position. Do you smell that?'

'What?'

'Smells like ammonia.'

'Sorry, I don't want to get that close. I think I'm going to step outside for a moment,' Edris said and left the tent.

Meadows didn't blame him. He felt queasy himself. 'You poor guy. Someone wanted to make you suffer.' He looked again at the bolts. This was no toy, he thought. The shafts looked to be aluminium. Light enough to fly but strong.

He stood up and took a moment to study Huw. He was of a solid build with a large protruding stomach. He had thin silver hair and was clean-shaven. Underneath his coat, Meadows could see he wore a blazer and grey trousers. Black leather gloves covered his hands.

He stepped outside the tent, where Mike was talking to Edris.

'You OK, Edris?' Meadows asked.

'Yeah, I don't think I've ever seen anything quite like that.'

'No,' Meadows agreed. 'This is a ruthless killer. I'm wondering why a crossbow. It's as though they didn't want to get too close. Maybe someone who couldn't overpower him physically.'

'It's the first one I've come across,' Mike said. 'Plenty of stabbings and gunshot wounds, but not a crossbow.'

'Is the pathologist on their way?' Meadows asked.

Mike rolled his eyes. 'Daisy's stand-in likes to take his sweet time. You're not the only one who will be missing your fiancée this week. This guy is more miserable than Blackwell.'

'Is that even possible?' Edris asked.

'Wait till you meet him,' Mike said.

Meadows cast a glance around the graveyard. It was dark under the cover of the trees. The graves were mostly old stone and the writing was so worn you couldn't decipher it. There were larger plots surrounded by rusty railings and some with elaborate masonry work.

'What was he doing in the graveyard?' Edris asked.

'Some people like to wander around,' Meadows said. 'They find it peaceful.'

'There's a back entrance to the park. It's used by locals. It would have brought him up past here,' Mike said.

Meadows looked at the tent then trailed his eyes in a straight line from the body's position to an old yew tree. Halfway down the trunk, he could see a branch sticking out at an odd angle. It didn't look like it was part of the tree.

'Judging from the position of the body, it looks like our shooter hid among the trees,' Meadows said.

'That's our theory,' Mike said. 'There's something else you need to see.'

Mike led the way over the stepping plates. When they reached the great yew tree, Meadows could see that it was hollowed out. There was enough space for a person to stand inside.

'What the hell?' Edris said.

Inside the hollow, a five-foot stick figure was propped up. One of its arms was sticking out. Meadows stepped closer. It was made from a thick vertical branch that forked halfway down to form the legs. At the end of the legs, twigs, resembling toes, sprouted. Another branch had been tied horizontally with blue wool to form the arms. Twigs, like gnarly fingers, stretched out on each end. Holes had been burned into the top of the vertical branch to make the eyes. Resting at the feet was a crossbow.

An ominous feeling spread over Meadows.

'That's freaky,' Edris said.

Meadows nodded his agreement. There was something sinister about the stick figure. 'Question is, what is it doing here?'

Chapter Three

Meadows drove the short distance to Huw Jones' house. They had been informed that Huw's next of kin was his wife, Lesley. Edris was sitting in the back with the window down and the dog on his lap. Hanes had done his best to clean the dog, but blood was still visible on his coat.

'I'm guessing Huw must have walked to the park,' Meadows said as he pulled up outside the house.

The dog jumped up at the window and Edris groaned. 'I've got muddy paw prints all over my trousers and I smell of damp dog.'

Meadows turned around in the seat. 'If it's any consolation, I don't think anyone is going to notice.'

Edris gave a sigh of resignation. 'No, I guess not.'

'There's no car in the driveway. Wait here and I'll go and see if anyone is in. I don't want to let the dog think he's going home then put him back in the car.'

Meadows got out of the car, took his coat off, smoothed down his suit, and walked up the driveway. The detached house was built from red brick. It had two bay windows and an arched porch. There was a lawn with neat borders and a hydrangea planted in the middle. Everything about the house looked well cared for: clean pathways, gleaming windows, and not a weed in sight. He knocked the door and waited. He knocked again, then after a few moments returned to the car.

'What now?' Edris asked.

'We wait. It could be that she's gone out to look for her husband.'

Meadows hoped that wasn't the case. News travelled faster than broadband in the villages and towns of Wales. He wouldn't want her to hear the news in such a way, especially if she was alone.

'OK, but you can switch seats with me and sit with the dog,' Edris said.

Meadows smiled. 'I think he's quite comfortable with you.'

They didn't have to wait long. A silver BMW pulled into the driveway. A petite woman with ash-blonde hair got out and went into the house.

'OK, let's go,' Meadows said. He got out of the car and felt his stomach knot. He was about to devastate this woman's life. How do you tell someone that their loved one has been killed with a crossbow? he thought. There would be no way of softening that information. What started out as a normal day for this woman would turn into a nightmare.

He knocked the door and, moments later, it was opened.

'Lesley Jones?' Meadows asked.

He could see up close that she was an older woman. She had deep lines around her eyes and on top of her lips. Now she had taken off her coat, he could see how thin she was.

She looked at him with wary eyes. 'Yes.'

Meadows introduced himself and Edris.

The dog jumped up at her and she looked down. Recognition dawned on her face.

'Sidney. What have you been up to?' She stroked the dog's head. 'He must have got lost. My husband, Huw, must be out looking for him. I wondered why he wasn't home. I better call him. Thank you so much for bringing him home.'

She spoke quietly and Meadows got the impression that she was a timid woman. 'I'm afraid there was an incident involving your husband this morning,' Meadows said. 'May we come in for a moment?'

'Yes, of course.'

Lesley took the lead from Edris and led Sidney into the hallway. She took a towel from a rack and dried his paws. The dog lifted each paw in turn, obviously used to the routine.

'Oh, have you hurt yourself?' she said as she rubbed at a spot of blood.

'We've checked him over and he doesn't appear to have any injuries,' Meadows said.

'Where did you find him?' Lesley asked.

'Dinefwr Park,' Meadows said. 'Perhaps it would be better if we all sat down.'

Lesley nodded. 'Would you mind taking your shoes off?'

'No problem,' Meadows said. As he crouched down to take off his shoes, he noted that Lesley was already in slippers.

Lesley picked up Meadows' shoes. 'I'll just put them here for you.' She placed them on a shoe rack and then did the same with Edris' shoes. 'Come through.' She led them into the sitting room. Sidney followed, then disappeared through another door.

Lesley took a seat on a cream leather sofa and crossed her legs at the ankles. Meadows and Edris took the armchairs. Lesley looked at where Edris was sitting. She opened her mouth as if to say something, then appeared to change her mind.

Meadows spoke softly. 'I'm so sorry to have to tell you that a body, which we believe to be that of your husband, was found in Dinefwr Park this morning.'

Lesley stared at Meadows. He could see the worry in her pale blue eyes.

'Oh. I better get to the hospital.' She stood up. 'Which hospital? He's going to need a bag packed. He'll want his things. He must've been trying to call me. Where did I put my phone?'

Meadows could see the rising panic. He stood up, took Lesley gently by the arm and guided her back to the sofa.

'Mrs Jones, Lesley, please sit down for a moment.'

She sank down onto the sofa and her hand fluttered nervously at her throat. Meadows crouched down in front of her.

'I'm so sorry, Lesley. Huw was found dead.'

'Dead? Huw?' She shook her head. 'Are you sure?'

'We are fairly certain. His wallet was found with him. There will need to be a formal identification, but you don't need to worry about that for the moment.'

'Is there someone we can call for you?' Edris asked.

Lesley twisted her hands. 'I better tell the kids.'

'We can do that for you,' Edris said.

Lesley shook her head. 'I better call. I need my phone.'

'OK,' Edris said. 'I'll fetch it for you. Best you stay seated for now. You've had a shock.'

'It's in my coat pocket I think… no, I took it out. I was in the kitchen when you knocked the door.' She bit her bottom lip. 'I'm sorry I can't think straight.'

'It's OK. I'm sure I can find it,' Edris said and left the room. He returned shortly with a mobile phone and handed it to Lesley.

'Are you sure you don't want us to make the call for you?' Meadows asked.

'No,' she said, 'I can do it.'

Meadows returned to the chair while Lesley made the call.

'Sarah, can you come over? The police are here. They are saying your father is dead … yes … take your time. See you soon.' Lesley ended the call. 'My daughter is on her way.'

'How about I make you a cup of tea?' Edris said.

Lesley nodded.

Edris left the room and Lesley looked at Meadows. There were no tears, yet.

'What do I do now?' she asked.

'There is nothing you need to do right now,' Meadows said. 'If it's alright, I'd like to ask you a few questions.'

Lesley fiddled with her necklace. 'I'm not good at this sort of thing. Huw handles everything, you see.'

Meadows nodded. 'We're going to take things slowly; just answer what you can for now. We understand that Huw was a community councillor.'

'Yes, that's right.'

'For how long?'

'About six years. Maybe more. It was after he retired.'

'What work did he do before retirement?'

'He worked for the council. Planning department mostly.'

'Did he continue with that area of expertise in his role as councillor?'

'I don't understand,' Lesley said.

'I'm just wondering if Huw had specific responsibilities or interests as community councillor. Education, planning, that sort of thing.'

'Oh, well, he was involved in all sorts of things. He's the leader of the council... I mean he was... oh.' She shook her head.

Edris came back into the room and held out a mug to Lesley. She looked at it then up at Edris. 'That's Huw's mug. I can't use that. He's very particular about things like that.'

'No worries. I'll go and change it.'

'I better come with you,' Lesley said. 'There's other ones you shouldn't use.'

Lesley left the room with Edris and Meadows wondering how many other things Huw was particular about. Meadows looked around. The room didn't look lived in. Pale blue cushions were placed on the sofa and matched the colour on the walls. The carpet was almost the same creamy colour as the furniture. There were no ornaments or family pictures. Old maps had been framed and hung on the walls. There was an oak cabinet with large doors that he suspected housed the television. The room didn't have a homely feel. It was not the sort of room that Meadows would describe as relaxing. Even the dog chooses to stay in the kitchen, he thought.

Lesley came back carrying a flowery mug and set it on a coaster on the coffee table. Edris handed a mug to Meadows then settled in the armchair. He took a sip of his tea then put his mug down on a side table. He took out his notebook and pen. An old clock ticked on the mantle filling the silence.

Meadows sat forward in the chair. 'You were telling me about Huw's work as a councillor. Did it keep him very busy?'

'Yes,' Lesley said, 'he liked to keep busy. He also attended chapel regularly. He was a lay preacher.'

'Which chapel?' Edris asked.

'He moved around the chapels. He was always in demand. Mostly he was at Ebenezer.'

'When was the last time you saw Huw?' Meadows asked.

'This morning. I made him a cup of tea then he took Sidney for his walk.'

'What time did he leave?' Edris asked.

'Around seven.'

'Does he always walk the dog at that time?'

'Yes,' Lesley said.

'Did he often go to Dinefwr Park?' Meadows asked.

'Yes, every morning. It was his routine.'

'Does that include St Tyfi's Church?'

Lesley nodded. 'He goes in the back way, walks around the church, then goes to the car park. He stops at the refreshment van for a coffee. He often sees people he knows and stops for a chat.'

'How long is he usually out with the dog?' Meadows asked.

'He comes back around half eight, then he has his breakfast. He likes a cooked breakfast.'

Meadows picked up the mug of tea and took a sip. 'You weren't concerned when he didn't come back this morning?'

'Oh.' Lesley bit her lip. 'I should've been, shouldn't I? It's just I don't like to call him and disturb him. I thought someone might have stopped him on the way back for a chat. I kept his breakfast warm but then I had to go out.'

'Where did you go?' Meadows asked.

'Shopping and a WI meeting.'

'Was that in Llandeilo?' Edris asked.

Lesley nodded. 'It's what I do on a Tuesday. I'm always back to make his lunch. Unless he has council business to attend to.'

'Did he have any council business today?'

'I don't know.'

'Did he keep a diary?' Meadows asked.

'Erm, I expect he did. It would be in his study.'

'Is it OK if I take a look?' Edris asked.

'Huw has the key to that room.'

Interesting, Meadows thought. What sort of man keeps his wife locked out of a room? A man with secrets. He looked at Lesley. Her shoulders were hunched as if she was making herself as small as possible. She hadn't asked how her husband had died.

'Had Huw been worried about anything recently?' Meadows asked.

'No, he was his usual self when he went out this morning.'

'Money worries?'

'I don't think so. As I said, Huw takes care of things, the bills, insurance, that sort of thing. We have a joint account for things like shopping. There's always money in the account. I'm sure he would have said if there was a problem.'

'What about with his council work? Any disagreements?'

Lesley shook her head. 'Not that he said. Huw helped a lot of people. He said he was the bridge between the community and the government. He was a spokesperson. The one who stood up for people who couldn't fight for themselves.'

Meadows thought it sounded like she was repeating a phrase that Huw used.

'Would you say that Huw was generally well liked?'

'Oh yes,' Lesley said.

'What about family? Have there been any recent arguments?'

Lesley shrank back into the sofa. 'No.' She twisted her hands. 'Huw was a family man.'

'Is it just you, Huw, and your daughter?' Meadows asked.

'We have a son, Luke. Huw has a brother in North Wales. We see him and his family a few times a year. Then there's my sister and her husband. We all get along.'

Meadows heard the front door open.

'Mum?'

Lesley called over her shoulder. 'I'm in here, love.'

A woman rushed into the room followed by a man.

Meadows finished his tea while they settled.

'What's going on, Mum?' the man asked.

'These policemen – sorry I forgot your names,' Lesley said. 'They say your father is dead.'

Edris introduced himself and Meadows. 'And you are?'

The man looked from Edris to Meadows. He had brown cropped hair, hooded eyes, and hollowed-out cheeks. Meadows noticed he had a tooth missing and a tremor in his hands.

'Luke Jones,' he said.

'Sarah Jones,' the woman said and sat down on the sofa next to Lesley. 'Are you OK, Mum?'

Lesley nodded. 'This is my fault.'

Sarah looked at Luke, who moved to sit next to his mother. 'Of course this isn't your fault,' he said. He took her hand in his.

'Why do you think it's your fault, Lesley?' Meadows asked.

'She's just had a shock,' Luke said.

'Shouldn't she have a solicitor or something if you're going to question her?' Sarah asked.

Meadows shook his head. 'At the moment we are just gathering information.'

'It's just that I went shopping this morning even though he was late coming back. I should have tried to call him.'

'You weren't to know,' Sarah said.

Luke's legs jiggled. 'What happened?'

'Your father was found in the grounds of St Tyfi's Church this morning,' Meadows said. 'We are treating his death as suspicious.'

'Someone killed him?' Sarah asked.

Meadows saw the resemblance between mother and daughter. Both were petite with the same light blue eyes.

'I'm afraid so,' he said.

'How?' Luke asked.

Lesley put her hands up to her ears. 'I don't want to know.'

Meadows held up his hand. 'You don't need to hear the details, if you don't want to, Lesley. We're not yet certain of the exact circumstances. All we know at present is Huw was attacked when taking the dog for a walk.'

Sarah gasped. 'Oh no, Sidney. Is he…?'

'He's fine,' Lesley said. 'He's sleeping in the kitchen.'

It was then that Meadows realised that the dog didn't bark when Luke and Sarah arrived. Most dogs would, or at least come out to greet family members, he thought. The dog had obviously been trained or was traumatised by what had happened to his owner.

'Is Sidney good with strangers?' Meadows asked.

'He doesn't bark at people. If that's what you mean,' Lesley said. 'Huw said there was nothing worse than a dog that barked when a blade of grass moved.'

'Sidney had been secured to a post when we found him. I'm just wondering if he would go willingly with a stranger,' Meadows said.

'I guess,' Lesley said. 'He is very friendly.'

'This is fucked up,' Luke said.

'Luke!' Lesley scolded.

'Well, it is. It doesn't seem real. It's like some weird trip.'

Sarah gave her brother a warning look.

Lesley twisted her wedding ring. 'It's hard to take in. I don't know what I'm going to do.' Her bottom lip trembled.

'You're going to be fine, Mum,' Sarah said. 'We'll look after you. Won't we, Luke?'

'Yeah,' Luke said. He looked at Meadows. 'I think you should go now. Give Mum some time.'

Meadows nodded. 'Just a couple of things before we go. Can you think of anyone who would wish to harm your father?'

The three of them exchanged a look. It was only fleeting but enough for Meadows to notice their discomfort.

'It is really important that you don't withhold information from us at this stage. The more we know now, the better chance we have of catching the person responsible.' He looked at each in turn.

'There's no one I can think of,' Lesley said.

Luke and Sarah shook their heads.

Meadows looked at Edris and gave him a nod.

'If you could tell us where you were this morning, it would be really helpful,' Edris said.

Luke's eyes narrowed. 'Why?'

'It's standard procedure in these circumstances. Lesley has already given us an account of her whereabouts this morning. The same will be asked of all friends, family, and contacts.'

'What time?'

'If you could just give me a rough timeline of your movement this morning,' Meadows said.

'Fine,' Luke said. 'Got up this morning. Went round to Sarah's for a cuppa, then went to hang out with the boys at the garage.'

'What time did you arrive at your sister's house?' asked Edris.

'Before the kids went off to school.' He looked at Sarah.

Sarah shifted in the chair. 'Erm yeah, about eight.'

'You work at a garage?' Edris asked.

'No,' Luke said, 'I got no work at the mo. I was at a mate's house. He's fixing up an old car.'

'Name and address?' Edris asked.

Luke gave him the details.

'Sarah?'

'I got the kids up for school. They went off and I just caught up with some housework. I only work Mondays, Wednesdays, and Fridays. Travis and Co.'

'Thank you,' Edris said.

Meadows stood up. 'A family liaison officer will be in touch shortly. They will be able to answer any questions you may have and keep you updated on the investigation. I am very sorry for your loss. We'll see ourselves out.'

Meadows put on his shoes and stepped outside. Usually, he felt the weight of the family's grief on him. Not this time.

'Well, that was weird,' Edris said when they were back in the car.

'I suppose people deal differently with shock,' Meadows said. 'Although I would have expected to see more emotion from the three of them. Lesley looked more afraid than upset.'

'I think they would have been more upset if the dog had died. That's a family with skeletons to hide.'

'Yeah,' Meadows said. 'Or stick figures.'

Chapter Four

'They've gone,' Luke said. He moved away from the window and sat in the armchair.

Lesley suddenly felt cold. She wrapped her arms around her body and watched Luke make himself comfortable.

'Why do you have to sit there?' she asked.

'He's not here to complain, so what's the problem?'

'Just shift to another chair,' Sarah snapped. 'It's upsetting Mum.'

'Fine.' Luke moved to the other armchair and took a pouch of tobacco from his pocket.

'Don't think you're going to light up in here,' Sarah said.

'I need a cig,' Luke said. 'I'll make sure I don't get ash on the carpet. I'll use this mug.' He picked one up off the table.

'If you need to smoke then you can go outside,' Sarah said.

Lesley thought there was worse her son could be doing at that moment.

'Oh, for heaven's sake,' she said. 'Just let him smoke.'

'Oh, Mum, what happened?' Sarah asked.

'I don't know. He was fine when he left this morning.' Lesley looked at her two children. She would have to be strong for them now. 'It will be OK.'

'Will it?' Sarah asked. 'Luke has already lied to the police.' She glared at her brother. 'Where were you this morning?'

'With you, like I said. Just remember that. You don't want to go saying anything to the po-po. They're going to be asking all sorts of questions. They twist your answers and confuse you. We should just keep our gobs shut. Right, Mum?'

'You think I want everyone to know our business?' Lesley's throat constricted, and she felt tears sting her eyes. She fought to keep them back, but they spilt over and ran down her cheeks. 'It's going to be in the news. Everyone will be talking about us. I don't want anyone to find out. What will they think?'

'No one knows shit,' Luke said. He took a drag of his cigarette and let out a plume of smoke. 'If you need an alibi then I'll sort one for you. A couple of the boys owe me a favour. You can say you took the car for them to have a look at. Just say it was making a noise.'

'But your father always took the car to the garage.'

Luke sighed. 'The po-po don't know that.'

Lesley looked at Sarah who nodded. She loved her children so much. After everything that had happened, they were willing to lie for her.

Sarah put her arm around Lesley's shoulder and pulled her in close.

Lesley felt the warmth spread though her body. 'It's OK. I was out shopping. I already told the police.'

'Have you got receipts?' Luke asked. 'They'll ask for them.'

Lesley's stomach twisted. 'Erm… I didn't buy anything.' She saw a look pass between her children. 'You don't think that I—'

'Don't,' Luke said.

'But—'

Luke held up his hand. 'The less we know, the better.'

Lesley looked at Sarah.

'Of course we know you didn't do anything,' Sarah said.

Lesley didn't believe her but didn't push the matter. She'd have to tell them the truth, and she wasn't ready to do that. She'd learned that sometimes it was better to leave things unsaid. 'What will I tell the police if they ask for receipts?'

'I told you. I'll sort it,' Luke said. 'It doesn't matter what you've already told them. You can say you were in shock and confused. That you were going to go shopping after you'd sorted the car, but you didn't have time.'

'I don't know,' Lesley said. 'I don't think it's a good idea to involve anyone else. I did go to a WI meeting after.'

'There you go,' Sarah said. 'It'll be fine. Try not to worry.'

Luke dropped the butt of his cigarette into the mug and stood up. 'Right, I'm gonna take a look in the old git's study.'

'It's locked,' Lesley said.

'That's not going to be a problem,' Luke said.

'I don't think you should be going in there. Please,' Lesley said. 'I can't deal with this just now.'

'There's plenty of time to sort through things later,' Sarah said. 'Let me make you something to eat then perhaps you should have a lie-down.' She looked at Luke. 'I'll stay with Mum for now. You can come back later so I can get home before the kids get back from school.'

'There's no need for either of you to stay,' Lesley said. 'I'm alright. I just want to be on my own for a bit.'

'OK,' Luke said. 'Just make sure you hide that bank account. As far as the po-po are concerned, you just have the one joint account.'

'I'm sure that's what I told them.'

'Good. I've had years of dealing with their shit. I know their tricks. Just do what I say, and it'll be OK.'

'She doesn't need to be told what to do. Not anymore,' Sarah said. 'You can make your own decisions now, Mum.'

Lesley nodded.

'We'll leave you alone for a little while, but how about I come back with the kids later and we can have dinner together? You can come too, Luke,' Sarah said.

Lesley couldn't remember the last time they had been together as a family. 'That would be lovely. Right, off you go. I'll see you later.'

After they left, she locked the door then grabbed her phone. Her fingers shook as she sent a text. She paced the room until the phone rang, and when she answered her words came tumbling out.

'It's alright, Lesley,' the person on the other end said. 'I'm here for you. Remember, you are strong. You need to draw on that strength now. You will get through it.'

'I don't want anyone to find out about us.'

There was a pause before they answered. 'There is no reason why anyone should. Come and see me when you are ready.'

'Thank you,' she said. She ended the call.

She felt calmer now. She sat down and nodded her head. No one did have to find out. Not even her children.

Chapter Five

Meadows parked outside Edris' house and turned down the music. Flakes of snow fluttered onto the windscreen and melted. He hoped it wasn't going to stick to the road.

The car door opened, and Edris got in along with a blast of cold air. He wore a black padded coat, a beanie hat, and scarf. All you could see of him were his eyes.

Meadows laughed. 'Bit cold, are you?' He put the car into gear and pulled off.

'Yeah. Didn't want to get out of my warm bed this morning. I hope Blackwell got his boiler fixed. Imagine the mood he's going to be in if it isn't.'

'Don't think I want to,' Meadows said.

'Where are we going first?'

'Council offices. Someone from HR will meet us there along with a representative from the community council. Let's see if Huw had anything in his past employment or his role as community councillor that could have got him killed.'

'Yeah, or it's the wife or one of the kids,' Edris said.

'Motive?'

'Big fat insurance policy?'

'The family was acting strangely but we have nothing to suggest that any one of them is guilty. Paskin is looking into all the family members' backgrounds. Blackwell and Valentine are going to speak to the parishioners. For now, we have to cast the net wide and see what we catch.'

Edris laughed. 'A bloody cold in this weather. Any news from the pathologist?'

Meadows shook his head. 'I've asked Blackwell to see if he can hurry him along.'

It didn't take them long to arrive at the council offices where they were shown into a meeting room. Two people were inside: a tall, stern-looking woman who introduced herself as Councillor Shan Phillips, and an older man whose name was Brian Cobb.

'Thank you for meeting with us,' Meadows said as he took a seat.

'Shocking news,' Shan said. 'Do you have any leads on a suspect?'

'We are still at the early stages of the investigation,' Meadows said. 'Right now, we need background information. I understand that Huw Jones worked as a planning officer before retiring.'

'Yeah,' Brian said. 'I've known Huw for years. From when he worked here and in his role as a community councillor. I still can't take it in.'

'So, you knew him very well?'

'Yes. We would socialise outside of work.'

'How did Huw get on with his other colleagues when he worked here?' Meadows asked.

'He got on with everyone. He was the type of man who would buy chocolates and wine for his team to thank them for a good job.'

'Any disagreements?'

'None that I remember. It has been a few years since he retired. I know some could find him a bit opinionated at times. Maybe a little too straight-talking.'

'Did he keep in contact with his old colleagues?'

'Yeah. He'd often pop in. He liked to keep on top of things. He also had meetings as part of his work as community councillor.'

'Did you ever get the impression that he put pressure on people? Used his contacts here unfairly to get what he wanted?'

Brian looked uncomfortable. 'I wouldn't say he put pressure on people. Let's just say he could be persuasive.'

'Huw's previous employment here was an advantage to both sides,' Shan said. 'He knew how things worked and what could be achieved.'

Brian nodded.

'Were there any disciplinary actions in his work history?' Meadows asked.

'No, I've looked through the file this morning. No complaints,' Brian said.

'Were there any rumours about other women?'

'If there were, I never heard them,' Brian said.

Meadows turned to Shan.

'No,' she said. 'Huw was a family man. There was nothing like that going on.'

'How well do the two of you know Lesley?'

'Not very well,' Brian said. 'She would come to work parties.'

'She's supportive of his work,' Shan said. 'I've met her on a few occasions. She a bit erm... reserved. Shy, perhaps.'

'Is there anyone either of you can think of who would wish to harm Huw?' Meadows asked.

'No,' Shan said.

Brian shook his head.

'What about the committee? I know things can get heated sometimes in meetings. Does anything stand out?'

'No, absolutely not. We all get on. We have a common goal. Work together for the benefit of the community,' said Shan.

Meadows got the feeling that Shan wouldn't tell him, even if they were all at each other's throats. 'What sort of local issues was Huw involved in?' he asked.

'He was instrumental in turning the old supermarket into a community centre,' Shan said. 'The project was very successful. He listened to what the community wanted. Made sure that all the needs were catered for. Then there was the bowling pavilion where the park used to be at Three Crosses. There had been a lot of problems there with young people hanging around at night. The residents were concerned about anti-social behaviour and drugs. The park was dismantled and a bowls green and pavilion were put in its place. The issues went away. Everyone was happy.'

'I don't suppose the young people were happy,' Edris said.

'You can't please everyone,' Shan said. 'Anyway, Huw helped get funding for a youth club in the church hall.'

'I'm not sure how successful that was,' Brian said. 'It was reported that only a few younger children attended. There was nowhere for the older ones to go.'

'Hanging around a park at night wasn't the answer,' Shan said.

'No, but from what I understand, the bowling green is hardly used. The building is now used for a mother and toddler group.'

'It's because of the weather,' Shan said. 'Huw was trying to secure funding for an indoor bowls green.'

Meadows could easily imagine how these projects could cause arguments and get out of hand.

'Was there anything recent that Huw was involved in that was controversial? Something where perhaps opinions differed?' he asked.

'Well, there's Chloe Watcyn's farm,' Brian said.

Shan pursed her lips.

'What was going on with the farm?' Meadows asked.

'Chloe Watcyn owns Ynysforgan farm. It's just outside Gwynfe, not far from Garn Goch. She lives there with her husband Jac and two children. It's the largest farm in the area. Chloe put in an application to turn part of the farm into a holiday park. Some sort of glamping thing with two old barns converted to holiday accommodation.'

'Was anyone against it?'

'Yes,' Shan said. 'All the local farmers in the area. They don't want extra traffic on the road. Then a lot of them have old public right of way access and bridle paths. They haven't been used in years. There would be tourists traipsing over their land. They're afraid that gates would be left open, and livestock could escape. Then there's the littering.'

'Yes, but it would bring in money for the local community as well as the tourist industry,' Brian said. 'There are arguments for both sides.'

'I'm guessing there are a few farmers that were not too happy with Huw,' Meadows said.

Shan shook her head. 'Huw was opposed to the holiday park. The only one upset about it was Chloe.'

'What about her husband, Jac?' Edris asked.

'I think Jac does what he's told,' Shan said. 'It's Chloe that was vocal about the opposition. She turned up at a council meeting and threatened Huw.'

'Threatened? In what way?' Meadows asked.

'I'm not sure I can repeat it,' Shan said. 'Chloe Watcyn can be very crude. The language she used in the last meeting.' Shan tutted.

'When was this meeting?'

'Two weeks ago. Huw had been in contact with the highways agency. They had agreed that it would be dangerous to allow access to the holiday park. Chloe's argument was that the road is already in use. She had another plan for access but accused Huw of interfering.'

'Do you know what she meant?'

'No. You need to look at the application.'

Meadows looked at Brian. 'Would you be able to send us a copy, and any other paperwork to do with the farm?'

'Yes, of course,' Brian said.

'We'd also like a copy of the minutes for the committee meetings. The last three months would be useful.'

'I'll see what I can do,' Shan said.

'Thank you both for your time.' Meadows stood up. 'If there's anything else you remember, please let us know.'

They left the office and returned to the car which was misted from the cold. Meadows started the engine and turned up the heater.

'Do you think we should dig deeper into the community council?' Edris asked. 'I've heard of money going missing and back-handers being taken by some of them.'

'You're thinking he knew about something so was killed to keep quiet.'

Edris nodded. 'Shan in there wasn't telling all, I think.'

'No, I didn't buy her line about common goals and all working together. See what you can find out. Meanwhile, I think we should pay Chloe Watcyn a visit.'

* * *

Ynysforgan farm was reached by a series of single-track roads. Thick hedges lined the side of the road with very few passing places. Mist covered the Black Mountain range in the distance, giving it an ominous look.

'I can't see that people would want to come for a holiday here,' Edris commented. 'It's in the middle of nowhere.'

'That's exactly the reason why people would come,' Meadows said. 'To get away from their busy lives. Fresh air and no distractions. I can see why there would be concerns about traffic on the road though. It could lead to accidents. I guess it all depends on how many people the farm would cater for at once. Then there's the public footpaths and bridleways. It would be a shock for the farmers to have to accommodate ramblers. They would be responsible for keeping the path clear. Any vegetation would need to be cut back to half a metre from the pathway. It's a lot of additional work.'

'You seem to know a lot about it,' Edris said.

'Yeah. There's a public right of way through one of the fields of the commune. No one ever uses it. These rights of way are old and mostly forgotten.'

'I'm guessing you are on the side of the farmers.'

'You know me better than that. I'm not on anyone's side. I can see both points of view. Everyone should be able to enjoy the countryside. If Chloe Watcyn wants to use her land for a holiday park, then good for her. For all we know, she could be struggling to make the farm work.'

Meadows stopped the car and waited for Edris to open the gate to the farm before driving through.

'I'll drive back, and you can get the gates,' Edris said.

'OK.' Meadows parked in the farmyard and pulled up his hood before getting out of the car. The bitter cold air seeped through his trousers, reminding him of the many harsh winters he'd spent living on the commune. While open fields gave a sense of freedom, they also offered no protection from the elements.

'Let's hope Chloe is feeling hospitable. A nice cup of tea and some cake in a warm kitchen would be welcome just now,' Edris said.

The farmhouse looked to Meadows to have recently been renovated. The stonework had been pointed, and a large glass conservatory added to the side. The front garden was walled and there was a wooden play set in the middle of the lawn. To the rear of the garden, a hot tub sat on a raised decking area.

'Nice,' Edris commented. 'Apart from the smell of manure.'

Meadows knocked the door, and it was opened by a girl of about ten years old.

'Are your mum and dad home?' Meadows asked.

'Dad is with the cows and Mum is with the horses.' The girl pointed to a block of stables on the right.

'Thank you,' Meadows said.

They followed the gravelled drive to the stables. On the left was a large paddock with jump sets of various sizes. A Land Rover was parked next to one of the stalls, and four horses poked their heads out of hatches. A woman emerged from one of the doors. She was dressed in jeans, a brown wool jumper, and a green gilet. A brightly coloured bobble hat covered her head, and her blonde hair was pulled back in a ponytail. She didn't appear to notice Meadows and Edris approaching. She grabbed a bale of hay from the back of the Land Rover and carried it with ease into the stable.

'Chloe Watcyn?' Meadows asked when she came back out.

She looked them up and down. 'Yeah.'

Meadows introduced himself and Edris.

'Right,' Chloe said. 'I thought you might turn up here.'

'Why is that?' Meadows asked.

'I heard that interfering prick got done in. Doesn't surprise me. I expect the rest of those wankers are pointing the finger at me.' Chloe grabbed another bale of hay.

'We understand that you and Councillor Jones had a disagreement,' Meadows said.

'If you mean I called him a twat at a meeting, then yeah.' She disappeared into the stable.

Meadows saw Edris' lips twitch as he wrote in his notebook. He felt like smiling himself. Chloe wasn't trying to deny or play down her dislike for Huw Jones. Her honesty was refreshing, and she had a likability about her. He waited for her to reappear.

'The local farmers have objected to your plans to build a holiday park here, and Huw Jones was their spokesperson. Is that about right?' Meadows asked.

Chloe leaned against the building. 'Yeah, but don't think he did it out of his love for farming. He liked to be popular. Why would he back me when he could get a group of farmers in his pocket? He would have called in a favour at a later date. That's how he was.'

'Are all the surrounding farms against the planning?' Edris asked.

'They are now. Those who weren't bothered got persuaded by Huw. He was wrong. The holiday accommodation won't have a negative impact. I suggested the farmers could sell their produce to the holidaymakers. There are even activities they could have offered on their own land – archery, go-carts, feeding the lambs, that sort of thing. We're all struggling.'

'It seems the main concern was over the footpaths and bridleways,' Meadows said.

'I offered to help, said I'd pay for spring-loaded gates and clear some of the pathways. To be honest, I don't think anyone would be interested in walking through fields. Most of them would drive to the more well-known beauty spots. I'm not taking anything from the farmers. It was OK until Huw got involved. There were only one or two objections, then he stirred things up. The planning for the barn conversions went ahead. It's only the access. Because of his interference, I had to work out an alternative route into the park. It's going to happen. Now that Huw is out of the way, things will be a little easier. If you want to know if I killed him, then the answer is no. Although I can't say I'm sorry he's gone.'

'You'll need to tell me where you were yesterday morning,' Edris said.

'What time?'

'Between 7.30 a.m. and 9.30 a.m.'

'Tuesdays are my turn to sort out the kids. So, I was here. I got the kids up, gave them breakfast, and drove them to school.'

'Anyone else in the house other than the children?' Edris asked.

'No. My husband, Jac, would have been with the cows. Plenty of other workers around. I'm sure someone would've seen me.'

'When was the last time you saw Huw?' Meadows asked.

'Erm… couple of weeks ago. It was at that meeting.'

'The one where you reportedly made threats against him?' Meadows asked.

Chloe raised her eyebrows. 'Is that what they said? I told him to back off. He was the one who tried to threaten me.'

'Was this in the meeting?'

'No. He came up here about a week before. He made himself out to be a family man. Pretended to be interested in the welfare of the people of the community. Bollocks. He was a bully. He told me that I should withdraw the planning application if I knew what was good for me.'

'What do you think he meant by that?' asked Edris.

'He made it perfectly clear. He said he would hate for me to get hurt or my property damaged. Then he just gave me a nasty little smirk. I told him I wasn't going be intimidated by a little prick like him.'

'How did he react to that?' Meadows asked.

'Honestly? I thought he was going to hit me. He shoved me against the wall. Got right up in my face. Told me to watch myself. He seemed to be struggling to control himself. He kicked the tyre of my car before he left.'

'Did you tell your husband?' Meadows asked.

'Yeah, he said he'd smash his face in if he came near me or the farm again. Before you ask, Jac didn't kill him. Like I said, he was out with the cows yesterday morning. He wasn't alone. Jac is not a violent man. I doubt he would have hit Huw if he'd have turned up here. Now if there's nothing else, I need to get on.'

'Thank you for your time,' Meadows said.

'Sounds like Jac had good reason to kill Huw,' Edris said as they walked back to the car. 'Chloe would cover for him.'

Meadows dug his hands in his pockets. 'Yeah, and I'm thinking Huw was not the nice guy everyone is making him out to be. If he tried to intimidate Chloe, then chances are she is not the only one.'

Chapter Six

Meadows gathered the team around the incident board. All of them were wearing daffodils or leeks for St David's Day. They were joined by Sergeant Folland and a group of uniformed officers.

'Three days since the murder of Huw Jones and we have no viable suspects. Every line of enquiry has reached a dead end. Persons of interest are Chloe Watcyn, owner of Ynysforgan farm; Huw's wife, Lesley, and his children, Sarah and Luke. We don't have any physical evidence tying any of them to the murder, and no witnesses. Everyone we've spoken to so far, apart from Chloe Watcyn, only have good things to say about Huw.'

'No debt and no big insurance policy,' Paskin added.

'Despite what everyone says, I don't think we are seeing the whole picture. Chloe Watcyn can't be the only person he upset,' Meadows said. 'Witnesses have come forward who saw Huw on Tuesday morning as they were leaving for work between 7 a.m. and 7.20 a.m. He was walking alone with the dog. No one was seen following him. We estimate he reached St Tyfi's churchyard at around seven-thirty, depending on how fast he was walking. Paskin, were there any sightings in the park?'

'Not of Huw. A couple entering the park just after eight say they saw what they think was a woman hurry past them. Described as wearing a purple or dark pink jumper and a bobble hat. They couldn't be sure of hair colour, height, or any other details. Not a good enough description to tie to one of our suspects,' Paskin said.

'Interesting,' Meadows said. 'The initial report in from forensics this morning mentions fibres caught in one of the bolts. Wool mix and purple in colour.'

'So, we're looking for a woman,' Blackwell said.

'Not necessarily,' Paskin said. 'The witnesses' description was vague. Added to that, the person they saw was moving quickly. Easy to make a mistake.'

'On the other hand, the person leaving the park might not have had anything to do with the murder,' Meadows said. 'There were a lot of shoeprints at the scene. The ones identified closest to where the weapon was found were a size eight. It's not a lot to go on. No prints on the crossbow. Valentine, how did you get on with tracing the supplier?'

'You can get a crossbow easily online,' Valentine said. 'I'm still going through retailers to see which ones they stock and if any have been purchased from this area. It's slow-going. Surprisingly, you don't need a licence or even have to register a crossbow. The only requirement is that you have to be over eighteen. This particular crossbow is self-cocking with an eighty-pound draw. Not the most powerful, but at close range… well, we all saw the damage it can do.'

The team looked at the pictures on the board.

'The killer used a lot of arrows, darts, or whatever you want to call them,' Blackwell said.

'They're called bolts,' Valentine said.

'Huw must have really pissed someone off,' Blackwell said.

'Chloe Watcyn,' Edris said. 'She has a lot to gain by Huw's death. He threatened her and caused a lot of problems with her planning application.'

'What have we got on Chloe?' Meadows asked.

'Not much,' Paskin said. 'No record. Married to Jac Watcyn. Two children, a girl aged ten and a boy aged six. She owns Ynysforgan farm. The mortgage is in her name only. Her husband, Jac, put a lot of money into the farm to renovate the house and purchase livestock. The farming business is in his name. Again, Jac has no previous.

'Chloe is active on social media. Mainly pictures of the family and farm. There's a page set up for the holiday park with updates about the building progress. No negative comments on the page.'

'She also has an alibi,' Meadows said. 'Unless she killed Huw around seven-thirty, then drove back to get the children up for school. Bit of a stretch.'

'She could have made the drive in fifteen minutes, according to Google,' Edris said.

Meadows nodded. 'OK, we need to see if we can place her in Llandeilo on the morning of the murder. Other than in the shops, there is no CCTV, but someone might have a doorbell camera.'

'Uniform have canvassed the area leading to the park,' Folland said. 'Nothing so far, but there is still a chance someone will come forward. We'll speak to the farmers on the route to Llandeilo. Most are up early and would have seen Chloe's Land Rover early on Tuesday morning, if she did go to Dinefwr Park. They are single-track roads with very little traffic.'

'My feeling is that the killer carefully planned this. They would have avoided being seen. If they are local, they wouldn't have driven on the main road. They could also have parked up and walked, or they might live close enough to the park to be on foot,' Meadows said.

'Like Lesley,' Edris said.

Meadows nodded.

'We have checked all the footage from the shops in Llandeilo. There were no sightings of Lesley on Tuesday morning,' Hanes said.

'Interesting,' Meadows said. 'She wasn't carrying any shopping when she returned home Tuesday morning. We'll need to press her on that. I spoke to a representative of the WI who confirmed Lesley attended the meeting that morning. The representative wasn't present herself, but they keep a register recording the dates and those attending. We are meeting with a group of ladies who were at the meeting later this afternoon. I want to get their impression of Lesley. I can't see that she killed her husband then calmly met with the group. She has a nervous disposition. Then again, it could be an act.'

'She would have had enough time to kill Huw and get to the meeting,' Valentine said.

'Motive?' Blackwell asked.

'I didn't get the impression they were a happy family,' Edris said. 'Neither one of the children appeared devastated by the news of their father's death.'

'Yeah, but shock can do that,' Paskin said. 'The brain protects itself from reality in those situations.'

'I agree,' Meadows said. 'Although there was something off about the family.'

'Just bring her in,' Blackwell said.

Meadows shook his head. 'On what grounds? We're going to need more than we've got before we drag in a grieving widow. We'll push her for details of her shopping trip. Paskin, anything on Lesley or the children?'

'No record for Lesley or Sarah but Luke has previous. Possession and ABH,' Paskin said. 'Fined on both accounts. I'm going through their social media accounts. Lesley rarely posts. Only photos to do with fundraising and reposts from the WI. Sarah is more active, and Luke's accounts appear to be dormant.'

'Luke said he was with his sister on Tuesday morning,' Meadows said. 'She agreed, although she looked uncomfortable. We need to check it out. We also need to go through everything Huw has worked on in the past few years. See if we can identify cases where he caused upset. We know the bowling green wasn't very popular. Especially with the local teenagers.'

'Brian Cobb from the council sent details of the planning application for Chloe's farm. There was nothing in it that we didn't already know. The only thing holding up the holiday park is the objection to access.'

Meadows nodded. 'Huw's laptop is still with Chris Harley from tech. His phone has been unlocked and we need to check out all the contacts on it. Meanwhile, we keep looking into Huw's family and Chloe Watcyn.

'Oh, one more thing. This fella.' Meadows pointed to the picture of the stick figure. 'Made from hazel. No prints found on it. It was tied with blue wool. Forensics say that the wool was kinked. Likely to have been repurposed from a garment. Any theories?'

'We asked the park rangers. They didn't know anything about it,' Valentine said.

'Kids could have made it for fun and left it there,' Paskin said.

Edris laughed. 'Yeah, if it was Halloween. It's freaky.'

'OK,' Meadows said, 'for now we will treat it as if the killer left it there. Given the crossbow was next to it, it seems likely. We'll see where we are at this afternoon. Thanks, everyone.'

Meadows returned to his desk and zoned out the noise of the office as he set to work. He didn't look up from his desk until Edris interrupted him.

'Pathologist is ready to see us.'

'About time,' Meadows said. 'Let's go.'

* * *

It felt strange to be going to the morgue and seeing another pathologist in Daisy Moore's place.

Edris appeared to be thinking along the same lines. 'Mike was right when he said this one likes to take his sweet time,' he said. 'Three days for a post-mortem. Daisy never keeps us waiting this long. She always prioritises murder victims.'

Meadows smiled. 'You gonna tell him that, are you?'

'I'll leave that to you,' Edris said and pushed open the door.

A tall, thin man was sitting in Daisy's chair. He had small dark eyes and a long, pointed noise.

'Ah, DI Meadows and DS Edris. Right on time, which is what I like.' He stood up and held out a hand. 'Edward Channing.'

Meadows shook his hand and offered a smile, but it wasn't returned.

'Let's go in and I'll talk you through my findings,' Edward said.

Meadows followed him through a set of double doors and the temperature dropped a few degrees. Despite the overhead fans, there was the unmistakable smell of death that mingled with the chemicals. Metal wall and base units ran the length of one wall. The other wall was made up of rows of numbered square plates. Behind them, the deceased rested. Meadows felt a shiver run down his spine. No matter how many times he visited the morgue, he always felt uncomfortable.

Edward walked up to the metal gurney that was in the centre of the room and tore back the sheet. Huw Jones' naked body lay underneath. His skin was pale and clammy. Around the wounds, the flesh had turned a bluish green.

The pathologist swept his hand over the cadaver. 'As you would have seen at the crime scene, the victim died of multiple wounds. There is extensive damage to the tissue as well as internal organs and bones.' Edward pointed at Huw's cheek. 'Here the cheekbone was fractured. I had quite the job getting all the arrows out.'

Meadows was tempted to correct him on the terminology but let it go. What he noticed was that Edward talked without a hint of compassion. His tone was flat and monotonous. He guessed that in this line of work, it was necessary for some to disconnect themselves from the victim. In this case, it made Edwards appear cold and unfeeling.

'Were all the injuries sustained ante-mortem?' Meadows asked.

Edward considered the question for a moment. 'It's difficult to be certain. I would say most were sustained before death. Perhaps a few very shortly after. As you can see, the body is in quite a state. The injury to the throat would have been fatal. As would the one that pierced the heart. As to what order, your guess is as good as mine. There were also a number of arrows in his back. All together forty-one.'

'Bolts,' Edris said.

Edward raised his eyebrows but didn't comment. He moved to the steel counter and picked up an evidence bag. 'One for you to examine.' He handed it to Meadows.

Meadows lifted up the bag and looked at the bolt. 'Aluminium?'

'Steel alloy,' Edward said. 'Stronger and less likely to bend. If you look at the head, it's two-bladed and very sharp. You wouldn't have needed that many to kill him. Obviously, your shooter was a bad shot. Just kept firing until they were sure he was dead. You're looking for a novice. Probably never used the weapon before.'

'Crossbowman,' Edris said.

Edward turned his gaze on Edris. 'Pardon me?'

'A person using a crossbow would be a crossbowman, arbalist, or even an archer. Not a shooter.'

Meadows' lips twitched as he tried to suppress a smile. 'Can you tell us if Huw was in good health before he was killed?' he asked.

'Yes,' Edward said, 'no sign of cancer, sclerosis, or damage to the heart. He was taking blood-pressure medication.'

'Time of death?' Edris asked.

'I would estimate between 7 a.m. and 9 a.m.'

'Is there anything else you noticed?' Meadows asked.

'Everything is in my report,' Edward said.

'When Huw was discovered, there was a smell like ammonia near the body.'

Edward nodded. 'Oh yes, that was interesting. Traces of ammonia solution were found on his clothing, wounds, and on the arrows. Possibly, the killer scrubbed the equipment to clear any prints. Then again, it could have been used to cause more pain.'

'More pain than having forty-one bolts piercing your body?' Edris asked.

'It would sting somewhat, I imagine.' Edward moved to the door. 'If that's all, I have a busy morning.'

'Thank you,' Meadows said.

Edris waited until they were halfway up the hospital corridor before speaking. 'Mike was right. That one *is* more miserable than Blackwell.'

Meadows laughed. 'I don't think you helped his mood by correcting him about the bowman.'

'Yeah, I couldn't help myself. I didn't like his attitude.'

'Who knows what makes him that way? Maybe he has problems at home,' Meadows said. 'Still, I disagree with the bowman having a bad aim. I think the number of bolts is significant. The number forty-one means something to the killer.'

Chapter Seven

Meadows and Edris walked into the church hall and were met by three older women.

'You must be the detectives. I'm Elsie,' a plump, jolly-faced woman said. 'This is Joan and Mair.'

'Come and sit down,' Mair said. She looked to be the oldest of the three. Her face was a map of wrinkles and one of her eyes was cloudy.

'Thank you for meeting us,' Meadows said and joined them at the table.

'Would you like a cup of tea?' Joan asked.

'And a slice of cake,' Elsie added.

'I never say no to cake,' Edris said.

Elsie poured the tea from a large metal flask and sliced up a generous helping of cake.

'Oh, lovely,' Edris said. He picked up the cake and took a bite.

'Terrible news about Huw,' Mair said.

'Shocking,' Joan added. 'We heard he'd been chopped up.'

Meadows could well imagine how details had been passed around and exaggerated. 'No, nothing that gruesome. Although it was a vicious attack.'

'Poor Lesley,' Elsie said. 'We should go and see her.'

The other two nodded.

'Did you know Huw well?' Meadows asked.

'From chapel,' Mair said. 'He also held surgery here. He was good like that. You could pop in and talk to him about your concerns.'

'He was a good listener,' Elsie added.

'Yes, he did do a lot of good,' Joan said. 'But you never really know people. We can all put on a good show. It's only our closest that really know us.'

'Do you think Huw had a different side?' Meadows asked. He took a bite of cake.

'I've lived next door to them for years,' Joan said. 'I sometimes hear shouting coming from their house. Especially in the summer, when the windows are open.'

'So, they argued a lot,' Meadows said.

'I wouldn't say a lot. I've never heard Lesley shouting, only Huw. Then again, Lesley is very quiet.'

'Always has been,' Mair said.

'Has Lesley ever talked to any of you about Huw? Perhaps intimated that there were problems at home?'

Mair shook her head. 'She's not one to share her personal life.'

'She didn't say anything to me,' Joan said. 'I asked her a few times if everything was OK. She'd always say, "Fine". She knew she could come to me anytime.'

'I wouldn't think too much of it,' Elsie said. 'All married couples argue. It would be odd if they didn't.'

'What about the children, Luke and Sarah. Do they visit often?'

'I rarely see them,' Joan said.

'They had a lot of trouble with the boy,' Elsie said. 'Drinking and fighting.'

'And drugs,' Mair added.

'I think Huw was embarrassed by his behaviour,' Joan said. 'If I recall correctly, Luke got expelled from school.'

'What about Sarah?' Edris asked. 'Were there any problems with her?'

'Lovely girl,' Elsie said. 'Quiet like her mother. She settled down with Adam. Nice boy. They have two young children. I know Lesley goes to visit them.'

'What about Huw?' Edris asked. 'Did he visit them?'

'No,' Elsie said. 'He was a busy man. Out most nights.'

'Would it be fair to say that Huw didn't have a good relationship with his children?' Edris asked.

'Well, not with Luke,' Mair said. 'Fathers and sons don't always get on.'

Edris wrote in his notebook and finished his cake.

'Would you like another slice?' Elsie asked.

'Yes, please,' Edris said.

'What about Huw and other women?' Meadows asked. 'Were there ever any rumours?'

Elsie laughed. 'Huw having an affair? No.'

'He had strong views on family life,' Joan said. 'I think his reputation was too important to him.'

'What about Lesley?' Meadows asked. 'Could she have been seeing someone?'

'At our age?' Joan laughed. 'Lesley's whole life revolved around Huw and the children. She was too busy keeping him happy to have any time for herself.'

'We understand that Lesley attended a meeting here on Tuesday morning.'

'It was a craft session,' Mair said. 'She was late.'

'She's always late,' Elsie said.

'Well, later than usual,' Mair said.

'How late?' Edris asked.

'Half an hour, at least,' Elsie said. 'It was hardly worth her coming.'

'She was always on time when she came in with me,' Joan said. 'I don't know why she decided to start driving herself when we're both coming the same way.'

'When did she stop having a lift with you?' Meadows asked.

Joan thought for a moment as she refilled Meadows' cup. 'About six months ago. Something like that. Lesley was never a confident driver. It happens when the husband insists on driving everywhere. Before you know it, you haven't driven for years. When my husband died, I had to take a few lessons to get back on the road.'

'So, Lesley didn't drive much,' Meadows said.

'No. That big flash car was Huw's. He took her shopping once a week and she would get a lift with me for the meeting or any activities we had. Then, she got Luke to take her out a few times and started driving herself. She said she wanted some independence. She always hurried out of here to make sure she was back in time to give Huw his lunch, and for him to have the car.'

'Do you usually get a lift here with Lesley?'

'No,' Joan said. 'After all the times I drove her around, I thought she might have offered. It would have made sense for us to take it in turns.'

'Have there been any other changes in Lesley in the last few months?' Meadows asked.

The three women thought for a moment and Meadows took the opportunity to finish his tea and cake.

'There was the trip,' Mair said.

'Oh yes,' Elsie said. 'That was out of the blue. Every year, we take a trip. We alternate between somewhere in the UK and a bigger one abroad. This year we plan to go to Rome in October. A visit to the Vatican and some of the other attractions. Lesley decided she was going to come. Even paid the deposit. She's never been before.'

'Do you think she'll still come?' Joan asked.

'I don't see why not. There are still quite a few months to go. It'll be good for her.'

'You said she had never gone on a trip before. Do you know why that is?' Meadows asked.

'I think it's because she didn't want to leave Huw alone,' Joan said.

'But this time was different?'

'Maybe she really wanted to go to Rome,' Mair said.

'When you've been married as long as they have, I guess you need a break,' Elsie said.

'How long have they been married?' Meadows asked.

'Erm… I'm not sure,' Elsie said. 'I remember they had a big celebration for their anniversary. Was it thirty or thirty-five years?'

'That was years ago,' Joan said. 'I'm sure they've had a big anniversary since. They just didn't make a big fuss. Got to be over forty years that they've been married.'

'How old is Luke?' Elsie asked.

'Not sure,' Joan said.

'We all know Lesley had to get married. She was pregnant with Luke at the time; couldn't hide it. She was a lot younger than Huw. Ten years or more,' Elsie said.

'I remember the gossip at the time,' Mair said. 'Huw dating someone so much younger. I suppose it wouldn't have looked good if he didn't marry her after getting her in trouble.'

Elsie shook her head. 'For all we know, they could have been madly in love. They stayed together all these years.'

Meadows glanced at Edris. He knew he would be thinking the same thing. It was possible that Lesley had been married for forty-one years.

'Well, thank you for the tea and cakes,' Meadows said. 'You've all been very helpful.'

'Take some cake with you,' Elsie said. She wrapped a slice up in a napkin and handed it to Edris.

'Thank you, ladies,' Edris said.

'Such nice boys,' Meadows heard them say as they walked out of the door.

'Interesting,' Meadows said. 'Lesley is always late for the meetings and even later this Tuesday. So, what does she get up to? Let's get back to the station and see if the others have had any luck.'

* * *

Meadows waited for Blackwell to arrive back at the office before he called the team around.

'What have you got?'

'Luke Jones didn't go to see his sister on Tuesday morning as he claims,' Blackwell said. 'His vehicle was picked up on the camera on the A40 driving towards Carmarthen just after eight. It's a bit tight. If he killed Huw before seven-thirty, ran to his car, and put his foot down, he could have made it to the location of the camera.'

'Speeding?'

'No, he was in the limit.'

'Valentine, what have you got?' Meadows asked.

'Nothing of interest on Huw's computer; no recovered deleted files, no threatening messages received or sent,' Valentine said. 'Nothing in his work over the last few years stands out as being controversial. I'm still checking out the bowling green.'

'Paskin?'

'Nothing more on Chloe,' Paskin said. 'Uniform drew a blank with doorbell cameras but they have spoken to the farm owners on the way to Llandeilo. No one saw Chloe or heard a vehicle before eight. Most of them were occupied on the land, so it doesn't rule her out.'

Meadows filled them in on what they had learned from the woman in the WI.

'Sounds like Lesley was making some big changes,' Paskin said. 'The driving, a trip to Rome, and possibly meeting someone on Tuesdays. I don't get her being late because she was shopping. Once or twice, but not all the time.'

Valentine nodded. 'There were no sightings of her in the shops. She has got to have been up to something dodgy on Tuesday. Why else lie about it?'

'Perhaps she wanted permanent independence,' Blackwell said. 'Why settle for half a house in a divorce settlement when you can have the whole lot?'

Edris interrupted the discussion. 'Got it. Marriage certificate for Huw and Lesley Jones. It confirms they have been married exactly forty-one years.'

'A bolt for each year of marriage bliss,' Blackwell said.

'Or one for each year of Luke's life,' Edris added.

'Would Lesley or one of the children make it so obvious?' Meadows asked. 'Easy to find out how long they've been married. Then there's the stick figure. Where does it fit into this?'

'We're not certain it does,' Paskin said.

'Motive?'

'It sounds like he was a dick,' Blackwell said. 'Maybe she just snapped and killed him.'

'If she snapped then she would have stabbed him or hit him over the head. This was planned,' Meadows said.

'Maybe she didn't want the mess in her house. You saw the carpet. Imagine trying to get blood out of a cream deep pile,' Edris said. 'It was so clean it didn't look walked on.'

'Luke or Sarah,' Paskin said. 'Doesn't sound like either of them got on with Huw. Perhaps they decided to free their mother.'

'Other than the neighbour hearing shouting, we have no evidence that it was a bad marriage,' Meadows said.

'We can't ignore the fact that the number of bolts matches the number of years they were married,' Blackwell said.

'I agree,' Meadows said. 'But a charge is not going to stick with what we've got.'

'Then we bring all three in. They could be in it together,' Blackwell said. 'One of them might crack. We let them think that forensics has found something.'

'It does sound like Lesley was already planning a life without Huw,' Valentine said.

Meadows considered the idea. 'Edris?' he said.

'Yeah, I agree,' Edris said.

Paskin nodded.

'OK, bring them in for a formal interview in the morning,' Meadows said. 'It's Saturday tomorrow, so we should catch them all in. I want phone records, bank statements, and a search of all three properties.'

The team is right, he thought. Everything points to the family. He turned to look at the board. The problem was it didn't feel like a domestic case to him. Huw Jones was executed. It was cold and calculated. He hoped they were not making a mistake.

Chapter Eight

I feel like I am losing control. My thoughts are no longer my own. It's like a hundred televisions on full volume playing around me. I can't still my mind. People talk to me, and I can't take in what they are saying. I nod my head and hope they don't notice.

The news is full of Huw Jones. Everywhere I go, people are talking about it. Not the other one, though. He still hasn't been found. Just goes to show what an awful creature he was. It's been weeks and no one has missed him. I went back to the house a few days after I killed him. I don't know how I found the strength to do it. The smell made me feel sick and I had to go out several times. Moving him wasn't easy. I had to do it in the dark. I couldn't risk being seen. Not yet. I cleaned the house after I disposed of him.

Scrubbed so hard my arms ached. The cleaning was good. I felt I washed away the memories. Removed the stain of shame. It only lasted for a little while, but it was good to get some release from this torment.

The nightmares came back worse than before. I woke one night because the wind was moving the door knocker. That constant banging drove fear through my body. I thought the stick dolls were outside. I crept down the stairs. Part of me knew all I had to do was tie up the knocker, but I couldn't open the door. I could visualise them waiting for me, standing with their accusing eyes.

I can't rid myself of them. They are a feeling, a memory. It's like pine needles; the scent reminds you of Christmas and it brings on the feeling of childhood excitement. The stick-dolls feeling isn't pleasant. It's fear. It's something so horrendous you want to curl up into a ball because you can't face it. It's your worst nightmare.

When the gun went off and I saw the blood, I had those feelings, but I couldn't grasp the memory. I realised the only way to rid myself of these demons was to remember.

I followed Huw. He had the same routine every morning so it wasn't difficult. The hardest part was going into the grounds of Dinefwr. I avoided looking at the castle.

Huw always walked with his shoulders back and head held high. Strutting. He had a way of nodding at people like he was bestowing a greeting on someone who should be grateful for his attention. He thought he was better than everyone, that he was important and deserved respect.

I knew what he really was. The real Huw. I stood by the grave in the churchyard and waited for him. He called out so I moved and hid in the hollow of the yew tree. Huw came into the graveyard and looked around. Then he looked at the grave I had been standing on. I fired the first bolt and it hit him in the shoulder. He spun around and I fired another one into his back. It was comical to watch. He was trying to reach the bolt and didn't seem to know what was happening. I moved around and kept firing. All forty-one bolts. A suitable payback. Forty-one bolts for forty-one miserable years.

It was the blood I wanted to see more than anything. I knew it would bring back the memory that I had been searching for. When it happened, it was like every bolt had been fired into my own body. The pain was so intense I fell to my knees. I couldn't move. Punch after punch came with each memory. I saw clearly. It was something that could never be unseen again.

I don't know how I managed to get myself up. I ran then. I didn't care who saw me. Now I know everything, and I know what I have to do. I don't know if I've got the strength, but I have to try. I have to make things right, then I can end this pain. There is no other way.

I wind the wool around the stick doll and try not to let my tears fall on it. I place it next to the other six. They all have to pay for what they did. A small part of me wants someone to stop me but that little voice is drowned out by the rage. I hope in some way this helps all of you that are suffering. Gives you courage. Removes the invisible gag.

* * *

I hit send and another post goes live. I wonder, how many people will read it? How many will know how I feel? Know the same pain? I can see I've picked up new followers since the last post. Then there are those who have been here since the start of the journey. They have been so supportive and given advice. Without them, it would have ended long ago.

I check the social media posts where the last blog link had been posted. It's been shared a number of times and there are a lot of comments. I don't have long before I have to leave, but reading the responses is comforting. Most of the time I feel so alone and the battle with the darkness is constant. I scroll down and read a few.

> *Pip: Thank you for sharing. This must have been so difficult for you to write.*

> *Rob: Very intense rescue scene. I hope this helps you to move on.*

Kim3: You're so brave. Going back to those memories must've been so hard. You have inspired me to keep trying.

Taz: Now it's time to let the inner child free to live their life.

No, no, no. They don't think it's real. I did try writing letters to the inner child to see what surfaced. It worked initially. Helped me remember, but I couldn't trick my mind. I had to act out the rescue scene. I need to make them understand. There is a way. It's risky, but it needs to be done.

Chapter Nine

Meadows felt uneasy as he entered the interview room with Valentine. If Lesley wasn't involved in her husband's murder, then he would be adding to her trauma by bringing her in.

Lesley was sitting next to her solicitor – a stern-looking woman with purple-rimmed glasses. She introduced herself as Ruth Emery. While Valentine made the introductions for the tape, Meadows studied Lesley. She looked pale with dark circles under her eyes. Thin arms were wrapped around her body in a hug. Meadows knew he was going to have to get her to relax and trust him if he was to get any information from her.

'Thank you for coming in to talk to us, Lesley,' he said. 'I appreciate this is a difficult time for you but there are a few questions we need to ask you.'

Lesley nodded.

'We've had a chance now to speak to some of Huw's old work colleagues as well as the council committee members. They gave us some details of his work. Did Huw talk about the planning application on Ynysforgan farm?'

'No, he didn't talk to me about council business.'

'What about Chloe Watcyn? Did he mention her?'

'No. I don't think so.'

Meadows saw the colour creep up Lesley's neck. It was clear that she was lying but he couldn't think of a reason why. It would be in her interest to throw suspicion on Chloe.

'Are you sure?'

'Yes,' Lesley said.

Meadows continued to talk about Huw's work until he saw Lesley relax a little, then he changed the line of questioning.

'We also spoke to your neighbours. They reported occasions when they heard shouting coming from your house. Is it fair to say that you and Huw argued a lot?'

Lesley shrank back in her chair and shook her head. 'Huw could be loud when he was on the phone. That's probably what they heard.'

'Did Huw often get agitated with people on the phone?' Valentine asked. She leaned forward. 'He had an important role in the community. He must have had to be firm with people.'

'Oh yes,' Lesley said. 'That's right. He was firm.'

'I expect there were occasions when he lost his temper,' Valentine continued.

'Sometimes he got annoyed,' Lesley said. 'You know what men are like.'

Valentine nodded. 'I can tell my boyfriend is in a mood as soon as he walks through the door. You can see the steam coming off him. One wrong word and he's off on one. I think the whole street can hear when we have an argument.'

'I didn't argue with Huw,' Lesley said.

'Sometimes it's best to keep quiet,' Valentine said. 'It makes life easier, doesn't it?'

Meadows noticed that Lesley was looking uncomfortable. She was twisting her hands and her eyes looked watery.

'I just meant that we didn't argue,' Lesley said.

'Not at all? You must have had some disagreements,' Valentine said.

'Well, yes, but not big arguments.'

'Did Huw shout at you?' she asked.

Lesley shook her head.

'We've heard that Huw had a temper. Did that ever turn physical?'

'No,' Lesley said.

'Were you frightened of him when he lost his temper?'

'No.' Lesley looked at her solicitor. 'I don't want to talk about it anymore. I just want to go home.'

'I think my client has answered your questions on the state of her marriage,' the solicitor said.

'How did Huw get on with Luke and Sarah?' Meadows asked.

'Fine,' Lesley said.

'There were some issues with Luke, though. We understand your son has some problems with alcohol and drug abuse.'

Lesley's eyes widened in alarm. 'Luke doesn't have anything to do with this. He wouldn't hurt anyone.'

'He has a record for ABH and possession,' Meadows said.

'That was a long time ago,' Lesley said. 'He had a few problems when he was a teenager. He started hanging out with a group of boys who were always in trouble. He's good now. He works, sometimes. He has his own place. He's not involved with drugs.'

'How did Huw react when Luke got into trouble?' Meadows asked.

'Like any father. He tried to help him. He was tough on him, but it was for his own good.'

'Tough in what way?' he asked.

'He just stopped him going out. Made sure he didn't have money to buy alcohol.'

'What about physical punishment?'

'No. Nothing like that. There was some shouting between them. All teenagers try to push the boundaries. They got past that. Luke grew up and they got on OK.'

'Would you say they were close?' Meadows asked.

'They had different interests so they didn't spend a lot of time together. They were just like any father and son.'

'What about Sarah?' Valentine asked. 'Fathers always have a fondness for their daughters.'

Lesley's expression softened but her eyes remained fixed on her hands. 'Yes. Girls are a little easier.'

'Did Sarah see a lot of her father?'

'Erm… She's busy with work and the children, but she comes over when she can.'

It was clear to Meadows that Lesley wasn't going to give them an honest picture of their family life. She would protect her children, no matter what she thought they had done.

'I'd like to go over your movements on Tuesday morning,' Meadows said.

'I already told you what I did on Tuesday morning,' Lesley said.

Meadows smiled. 'We just need to clarify a few things. You said you cooked breakfast for Huw, but he didn't come home at the usual time. You didn't want to be late so you left the house at around quarter to nine. Is that correct?'

'Yes.'

'Are you sure of the time?'

'Yes.'

'Where did you go?'

'I went shopping.'

'You didn't carry shopping into the house when we saw you arrive on Tuesday morning,' Meadows said.

'I didn't buy anything. I just like to wonder around the shops.'

'We checked the CCTV in all the shops in Llandeilo,' Valentine said. 'You didn't go into any of the shops there.'

'I was shopping in Ammanford.'

'You told us you were in Llandeilo,' Meadows said.

Lesley shook her head. 'I don't remember. Tuesday is a blur.'

'My client had just heard of her husband's death,' the solicitor said. 'I'm sure you can appreciate she was in shock at the time.'

'Of course,' Meadows said. 'Would you by chance have kept a parking ticket?'

'No, I don't think so.'

'That's OK. We can check,' Valentine said. 'You have to put your registration into the machine so there will be a record.'

Lesley looked flustered for a moment. 'Oh, I don't park in the car park.'

'Where did you park?' Meadows asked.

'I don't remember exactly. I park on the roadside and walk in.'

'What shops did you visit?' Valentine asked.

Lesley shrugged.

'We will be checking the CCTV in all the shops. It would be helpful if you could remember the ones you went in,' Valentine said.

'I mostly just walk around,' Lesley said.

'OK, so after you went shopping, you went to a WI meeting, is that correct?' Meadows asked.

'Yes.'

'You were late arriving at the meeting,' Meadows said.

'Only a little,' Lesley said.

'Half an hour,' Meadows said. 'Why were you late?'

'I forgot the time.'

Meadows nodded at Valentine. 'Lesley, it's really important that we know where you were on Tuesday morning. There is no judgement here. If you were seeing someone else, then we can be discreet. Sarah and Luke don't need to know.'

'Someone else? You mean an affair? No… No… I have never been unfaithful.'

'Where do you go on a Tuesday morning?' Meadows asked. 'You are frequently late for the WI meetings. There is over an hour on the morning Huw was murdered that you can't account for.'

'I told you I went shopping. I do the same thing every Tuesday. I go to the shops then I go to the WI meeting. It's the only morning I have the car.'

Meadows nodded. 'I heard you have a holiday planned.'

'Yes, I'm going to Rome.'

'Was Huw OK with that?'

Colour crept up Lesley's neck. 'Yes, he thought it would do me good to get away.'

'You've been married a long time.'

'Yes.'

'How many years?'

'Forty-one,' Lesley said.

Meadows paused. He knew he'd have to talk about the number of bolts found in Huw's body. If Lesley wasn't the one to kill Huw, then it would be a traumatic thing for her to hear. He leaned forward and lowered his voice.

'Lesley, has the family liaison officer discussed the results of the post-mortem with you?'

Lesley nodded.

'So, you are aware of how Huw died.'

'A crossbow.' Lesley covered her mouth and her eyes brimmed with tears.

'Is this necessary?' the solicitor asked.

Meadows held up his hand. 'I'm sorry, Lesley, but I have to tell you that the number of… erm… injuries to Huw was forty-one.'

Lesley gasped. 'No… it can't be.'

There was a knock at the door. It opened and Sergeant Folland poked his head through. 'Sorry,' he said. 'I need a word.'

Meadows left the interview room; he could tell by Folland's face that it was serious. 'What's up?'

'Another body has been discovered.'

Chapter Ten

Meadows drove through the villages with Edris sitting in the passenger seat. He was quieter than usual. People walking on the pavements were wrapped up in coats and hats. Some had dogs in tow while others had stopped for a chat. Heavy dark clouds lurked above and threatened to empty. Meadows knew that soon the gossip would start. Another body in such a short space of time was likely to send shockwaves and fear through the community.

'You OK?' Meadows asked.

'Yeah. It doesn't sound good.'

'No,' Meadows agreed. 'In Folland's words, it was a grim discovery.'

'It may not be related,' Edris said.

'Two murders in a week, just over eight miles apart and both pensioners. I don't like the odds.'

The house was easy to spot. Outside, there were two police cars, an ambulance, and the familiar SOCO vehicle. On the pavement opposite, a small crowd had gathered.

Meadows got out of the car and looked around. The back door to the ambulance was open. Inside, a man was sitting with a blanket around his shoulders and an oxygen mask covering his mouth. Two white-clad figures were walking up the path to the house. PC Hanes was standing outside the door.

The house was a semi-detached council property and part of an estate. The houses were uniform and sat in pairs, each sharing a pathway. There was a small patch of overgrown grass in front of the house which grew up against the wall. Back access was between the properties. Meadows imagined it wouldn't be easy to get in and out of the house without being seen by the neighbours.

He turned to Edris. 'Let's suit up and take a look.'

They stepped behind the van to put on protective clothing, then made their way up the pathway to where Hanes was standing.

'Not my week,' Hanes said. 'I thought I'd seen the worse I could see on Tuesday.'

'That bad?' Edris asked.

Hanes nodded. 'Victim is Bryn Thomas. Sixty-nine years old. He was found in the bedroom by his son, Teilo.'

'I take it the son is the one with the paramedics,' Meadows said.

'Yeah. They are treating him for shock. I didn't get much out of him when I arrived. He was in a hell of a state. Said something about bringing his father lunch. I had a word with the ambulance crew; they want to take him in. They are concerned about his heart rate and blood pressure.'

'Tell them they can get on their way, and see what information you can get from that lot.' Meadows glanced towards the crowd. 'Then send them on their way. Thanks.'

Meadows stepped through the front door. Directly in front of him was a staircase covered in a worn carpet.

'We'll take a look down here first,' Meadows said.

'I'm in no hurry to go up,' Edris said.

The door to the sitting room was open. Meadows walked in and looked around. The walls were magnolia and bare. The air was heavy with stale cigarette smoke.

Against one wall was a grey cloth sofa with sagging cushions. A matching armchair with a small side table was placed near the fireplace. The only other furniture in the room was a coffee table. It was piled up with electrical components and charging cables. Forensics had placed a marker next to two mugs. Meadows stepped closer and peered at the rim of one of them.

'Bryn Thomas had company. Looks like lipstick.'

Edris nodded his agreement.

There wasn't anything more to see in the sitting room, so they followed the metal footplates into the kitchen. A forensic officer was dusting the back-door handle. She gave Meadows a nod and carried on working.

'A break-in then,' Edris said.

'Looks that way,' Meadows said.

The kitchen window behind the sink had been smashed and glass covered the draining board. The sink was filled with dirty dishes. Meadows scanned the rest of the kitchen. Various items were on the worktops but nothing stood out as odd. A small table with two chairs was pushed up against the wall. It had a plastic tablecloth which was covered with crumbs. Two sets of keys, a wallet, and an ashtray sat near the edge along with a foil-covered plate.

They left the kitchen and walked up the stairs. Meadows could feel apprehension fluttering in his stomach. Every time he encountered a body at a crime scene, he couldn't help imagining that person's last moments. The fear they must have felt. He'd seen so much pain and suffering, yet he couldn't turn off the emotion and allow himself to become desensitised. At the top of the stairs were three open doors. On the left was the bathroom where two forensic officers were checking the sink and shower. The room on the right looked to be used as a workroom. There was a desk with various wires and tools. The room directly ahead was where the activity was focused.

Two forensic officers were on their knees taking samples from the carpet. Another was taking photographs.

High-intensity LED lights illuminated the room. Mike Fielding was controlling the scene.

'OK for us to come in?' Meadows asked.

'Yeah,' Mike said. 'We'll give you some space. Another nasty one.'

Meadows waited until the forensic officers had left the room then stepped inside. Bryn Thomas was lying on the bed. His legs and arms were bare. Eight sacks were piled on his torso. They were placed two abreast and came up under his chin and down to his groin.

'What the hell?' Edris said.

'Sand and cement,' Meadows said. He stepped closer and saw that the top two bags had a hole torn into them. 'It looks like water has been tipped over the top.'

Bryn's eyes were open and his mouth gaping. A lump had formed on his right temple. It was indented in the middle and blueish in colour. Long scraggly hair lay limply on the pillow. Meadows leaned in, to look at Bryn's arm. Age had taken muscle mass and left thin sagging skin. Five livid lines ran from the elbow to the wrist. The initial puncture wound could be seen, then the weapon had been dragged to tear the flesh. Blood had run from the wounds and seeped into the mattress.

'It's exactly the same marks on each limb,' Meadows said. 'Too symmetrical to be made by a single instrument. Looks like some sort of rake.'

The wounds on Bryn's thighs made Meadows stomach squirm. He didn't like to think about whether the wounds had been inflicted post- or ante-mortem. His feeling was it was the latter.

'The killer would have had to carry all these bags upstairs,' Edris said. 'Why? If they wanted to pin him down, they could have just tied him up.'

'Good point,' Meadows said. 'He's not a big man. Looks like he took a nasty blow to the head. Perhaps enough to knock him out. Maybe to give the killer time to bring up the sacks. It looks like the purpose was to crush him to death.'

'This is weird,' Edris said. 'The killer would have to purchase the sand and cement, then drive it here. How many bags can you carry at once? They would have had to make a few trips from the car and between the houses. Risky.'

'Unless the bags were already here,' Meadows said. 'The thing is, this looks like a statement to me. It's not something that has been used for convenience.'

'Those wounds don't look made by something that you'd have lying around the house either,' Edris said.

Meadows nodded and stepped away from the body to look at the rest of the room. There was an old oak wardrobe which was so large it blocked half the window. Against the opposite wall stood a matching chest of drawers. On the top, he could see another marker. He moved closer to get a better look. He felt a cold shiver run down his back.

'It's the same killer.'

Edris came to stand next to him and they both looked down on the two stick figures that were lying side by side. One had a pink triangle piece of cloth tied to make a skirt. White wool had been wound around the body and arms. The second figure was wound with blue wool.

'A man and a woman or a boy and a girl,' Meadows said.

'Whatever they are, they are giving me the creeps,' Edris said.

'I know what you mean,' Meadows said. 'Come on, I think we've seen enough.'

They left the house and Meadows was grateful for the sharp, cold air that filled his lungs. It felt like the smell of death had followed them and clung to their clothes. Edris quickly removed his protective clothing which he put into the marked bin. Meadows did the same. As they walked down the path, they saw Hanes talking to an older man.

He was bald with liver spots covering his scalp and face. Meadows guessed him to be in his late seventies, possibly older.

'This is Jim,' Hanes said. 'He lives next door.'

'I'm not sure I want to go back in,' Jim said. 'To think there's only a thin wall between us. I can't believe it. Poor Bryn.'

Meadows noticed that Jim's eyes were heavy with tears. 'Were you and Jim good friends?'

'We've been neighbours for years. Two old men on our own,' Jim said. 'We'd chat most days.'

'Do you know Bryn's son?'

'Teilo, yeah. Nice lad. During the pandemic he always called to check on me. He's going to be devastated.'

'Was Bryn divorced?'

'No, widowed. His wife died a long time ago. Cancer or some illness. He really didn't talk about it and it's not the sort of thing you ask.'

'When was the last time you saw Bryn?'

'Last night. We went for a pint.'

'How was he?'

'Fine, well, maybe a bit quieter than usual. We had a chat then got back about nine.'

'Do you think he had something on his mind? Perhaps he was upset or worried.'

'I suppose he wasn't his usual self. He cheered up a bit later.'

'Did you see anyone hanging around or hear anything during the night?' Meadows asked.

Jim shook his head. 'I watched some TV and had a glass of whisky; it helps with my chest. Then I went off to bed. Once my head hits the pillow, that's me for the night.'

'Did you notice if Bryn had any visitors yesterday or over the last few days?'

'Teilo was here yesterday morning. Not for long. I thought I heard Bryn shouting.'

'Do you think they were arguing?'

Jim thought for a moment. 'No, not really. I only heard Bryn. He could be a bit loud sometimes. It was more like he was telling Teilo off for something. Bryn was alright but he could be a miserable bugger. Had a temper on him so it wasn't unusual to hear him raise his voice. He'd have a go at anyone. No one would dare park in his space. Someone tried telling him the road belonged to the highway and not him.' Jim laughed but it was tinged with sadness. 'It was a youngster. He tried to give Bryn lip. Bryn was waving his fists and shouting. The kid soon jumped in his car and moved it. Anyway, Teilo seemed OK when he left. He gave me a wave.'

'Did you see Bryn after Teilo left?' Meadows asked.

'Yeah, he went out in the afternoon. You must think I spend all day at my window. It's just that I have a clear view from where I sit to watch TV. Bryn always had a habit of slamming the door when he left.'

'Other than Teilo, did Bryn have any visitors?'

'People come to bring computers for him to fix, so you often see strangers wandering up the path.'

'Anyone acting suspiciously? Meadows asked.

Jim shook his head.

'Do you know if Bryn was having any building work done?'

'There was a delivery of stuff. They dumped it out the front. It's gone now so I guess Teilo must have moved it round the back.'

'What was he having done?'

'I don't know. It only came a couple of days ago. Maybe Thursday. I was going to ask Bryn about it, but I forgot. Is it important?'

'We just need to know about any unusual activity or visitors. You've been very helpful, thank you,' Meadows said.

'That's the second one now,' Jim said.

Meadows turned back. 'Sorry?'

'The second one to be killed. I saw the other one on the news. Do you think I'll be safe? What if they come back? I'm on my own.'

Meadows could understand Jim's worry. 'PC Hanes here will take a look around your property. He'll be able to assess if it's secure. If not, he can arrange for someone to visit. They can do things to help, like a chain on your door and window locks. Also, if you are worried at all, no matter what time, you dial 999 and we'll get someone out to you.'

'Thank you.'

'Come on then, Jim, let's take a look,' Hanes said and they walked off.

'Do you think the old man is in danger?' Edris asked.

Meadows shrugged. 'The killer may think he saw or heard something. Best get uniform to drive by over the next few nights. At the very least, it will reassure him.'

Edris nodded. 'A lot of the senior members in the community are going to be worried.'

Meadows thought of his own mother who lived alone only a couple of miles away. He tried to shake off the dark thoughts. 'We need to catch this killer and quickly so they can sleep easy.'

Chapter Eleven

Meadows could feel Daisy's body against his. It was warm and cosy in the bed and he didn't want to get up. Dawn was breaking and through the bedroom window he could see the tops of the trees swaying. A few seconds later, the alarm went off.

'Five minutes,' Daisy said.

Meadows swung his legs out of bed. 'I'll make you a coffee.'

In the kitchen, he gazed out of the window, waiting for the kettle to boil. His thoughts turned to the stick figures. Was the killer making the next one? He looked again at the trees that surrounded his cottage. He imagined the killer picking twigs, looking for ones that most resembled a figure. There was something childlike about them. He took a mug of coffee up to Daisy, then showered and dressed before leaving the cottage.

He was the first one in the office so he had a chance to study the crime scene photos and the video walk-through before the team arrived.

'Sorry about your Sunday morning lie-in,' he said to a miserable-looking Blackwell. 'I am aware that you are supposed to be off.'

'Yeah, well, I didn't want to take a rest day when we have some nutter on the loose.'

Meadows nodded then gathered the team around. 'Our second victim, Bryn Thomas.' He pointed to the photo on the board. 'How is he connected to our first victim?'

'Nothing so far,' Paskin said. 'I've checked all Huw Jones' contact numbers. No mutual friend on social media. The only slim connection is that Bryn lived in a council house and Huw used to work for the council. Bryn Thomas moved into the house over twenty-five years ago.'

'It's a bit of a stretch,' Edris said.

Paskin nodded.

'I've taken a look through the crime scene photographs,' Meadows said. 'There were no laptops or other devices in Bryn's home. Given that he repaired computers, we would expect to see a few of them. At the very least, his personal computer. But there were just lots of charging cables.'

'Maybe the killer was after something on his laptop,' Valentine said. 'The killer breaks in, kills Bryn, and is not sure which laptop is his so takes them all.'

'Yeah, but it looks like Bryn was tortured,' Blackwell said. 'I'd say it was more personal than a simple break-in.'

'Perhaps the killer wanted to know what information he had and if he had told anyone,' Valentine suggested.

'We need to find out if Bryn ever fixed a computer for the Joneses or Chloe Watcyn,' Meadows said.

'Why Chloe Watcyn?' Paskin asked. 'Given the number of bolts match Luke Jones' age, and the number of years Lesley was married to Huw, it seems unlikely that Chloe is involved.'

'I don't think we can rule her out completely,' Meadows said. 'She still has motive for killing Huw. We need to see if she had any connection to Bryn Thomas.'

'I'll get onto it,' Paskin said.

'Blackwell, did you get anything more out of Luke Jones yesterday?'

'Nothing useful,' he said. 'He's still saying he went to his sister's house. I told him his vehicle had been picked up on the A40. He said he went to see a mate in Carmarthen. I'll check it out but no doubt he knows a few people who would lie for him.'

'Paskin, what about Sarah Jones?'

'She didn't have anything negative to say about her father. Then again,' Paskin said, 'she didn't give a picture of a wonderful relationship with him. She was... erm... indifferent – yeah, that's how I would describe her emotions. Again, we have nothing to tie her to the murder of her father and no real motive. Not everyone gets along with their parents.'

'Well, you saw for yourself what Lesley was like yesterday,' Valentine said. 'Still insisting that she went shopping. She appears fragile, if that's the right word. I don't get the grieving-widow vibe. There's something not right. I just can't put my finger on it.'

'I know what you mean,' Meadows said. 'Request her medical files. I want to see if she has a history of depression or anxiety. If so, what medication she takes. That could have a bearing on her emotional state. It will be interesting to see if she's had any unexplained or frequent accidents over the years.'

'Domestic abuse?' Valentine asked.

'Chloe Watcyn said that Huw had a temper and was threatening towards her,' said Edris.

'If we can believe her,' Blackwell said. 'There are no reports of violence from anyone else we've spoken to.'

'No, but these things are often hidden. The only people to know are the wife and children,' Meadows said.

'Where does Bryn Thomas come into it?' Edris asked.

'Good question,' Meadows said.

'Maybe Lesley was seeing Bryn. We don't know where she spends her Tuesday mornings. Or any other morning for that matter,' Valentine said.

'If he was her lover then why kill him?' Blackwell asked. 'It doesn't fit.'

'Until we can rule them out, we have to keep digging. Then we have these.' Meadows pointed to the stick figures on the board and told them his theories. 'It's possible that the only connection between Bryn and Huw is the killer and it's not someone on our radar. I want to find out everything we can about Bryn Thomas. We know he liked to frequent the pub. Speak to everyone who knew him. There has to be a common interest, person, or incident between the two victims. They were targeted for a reason. We'll be interviewing Bryn's son, Teilo, this afternoon. I'd like a full background check on him. Also, we need to track down the delivery of the sand and cement. See who ordered it and when the delivery took place. Thanks, everyone.'

* * *

Meadows parked the car outside Teilo Thomas' brown-stone cottage.

'Only six minutes to drive from here to Dinefwr Park,' Edris said. 'Do you think he could have done that to his own father? He was in a state yesterday.'

'Who knows,' Meadows said. 'People are capable of anything when pushed. We still have to rule him out and get information. I don't relish having to get him to recount his experience. He was given sedatives at the hospital. Hopefully he's still got enough in his system to keep him calm.'

The door was opened by a woman with red curly hair, blue eyes and a smattering of freckles over her face. Her eyes had the telltale signs that she had been crying. She introduced herself as Nerys, Teilo's wife.

'Teilo's in the sitting room,' Nerys said. She lowered her voice. 'He's still a little groggy.'

Teilo stood up to greet them when they entered the room. Meadows dwarfed him as he shook the offered hand and surveyed him. Teilo was slim with dark brown hair and soft brown eyes. He wore a pair of light denim jeans and a loud-coloured T-shirt.

'I'm sorry to intrude at this difficult time but it's important that we ask you some questions,' Meadows said.

'I understand,' Teilo said. 'Please, have a seat.'

'Would you like something to drink?' Nerys asked.

'Tea would be lovely, thank you,' Edris said. 'White with no sugar for both of us.'

Meadows and Edris took a seat in the armchairs and Teilo returned to the sofa.

'I am aware that you experienced a terrible shock yesterday,' Meadows said. 'We'll take things slowly and anytime you feel it's too much, we can stop.'

Teilo nodded. 'I help people to deal with trauma but when it happens to you, it's different. I fell apart yesterday.'

'That's understandable,' Meadows said. 'What is it that you do?'

'I'm a therapist.'

Meadows imagined that he had a way with people. He had a soothing voice and a gentleness about him.

'What sort of therapy?' Edris asked.

'Bereavement mainly, but I also help people with depression, anxiety, and trauma.'

'Do you work out of a clinic?' Edris asked.

'Sometimes I work at the drop-in centre in Llanelli as well as other clinics, but mainly from home. This is my consulting room.'

Meadows looked around. The walls were pale green with large seascape prints. On the coffee table were various objects, including a snow globe. A small desk and bookcase were stood against the back wall.

'I can see it now,' Meadows said. 'Everything is set up to make you feel relaxed.'

Teilo smiled. 'I don't have people laying on the sofa, but the décor seems to work.'

Teilo talked a little bit more about work then Nerys came in with the tea and settled herself beside him.

Teilo took a sip of tea and set the cup down. 'I guess we need to talk about Dad now.'

Meadows nodded. 'We understand your father lived alone.'

'Yes. My mother died when I was eight years old. Dad never remarried.'

'I'm sorry to hear that,' Meadows said. 'Do you mind telling us what happened to your mother?'

'She had breast cancer,' Teilo said.

'So, it was just you and your father.'

'For a little while. Then I went to live with my aunt and uncle. I guess it was difficult for him to cope with me and his grief. I didn't see it that way at the time. I suppose he just wanted to do what he thought was best for the two of us.'

Meadows could imagine how that would cause resentment. 'It appears that you managed to keep a good relationship. From what your father's neighbour says, you were a regular visitor.'

'If I'm honest, that wasn't always the case. It's only over the past four years that we started to get to know each other.' Teilo glanced at Nerys. 'During the pandemic, Nerys persuaded me to make regular checks on him. I guess we all realised how fragile life was at the time. We spent a lot of time talking on the doorstep. When isolation was over, I kept up the visits. Our relationship grew from there.'

'Your father was retired?'

'Yeah, well mostly. He used to work for OA Electricals. He loved fixing things. He started working on computers. After he retired, he kept doing repairs from home. He said it topped up his pension and stopped him from getting bored.'

'We did notice a lot of components and charging cables laying around but no laptops.'

Teilo's brows furrowed. 'Oh, they're probably in the spare bedroom. That's where he worked, but his own laptop should be in the sitting room. He was always on it.'

'There were no laptops, or any other devices found in the house. All the rooms would have been checked.'

'How many devices should have been in the house?' Edris asked.

'I don't know,' Teilo said. 'He had his main laptop. Then at least two others he kept. Mine should have been there. He was waiting for a replacement screen. It kept flickering. He had a few old ones he kept for spares. Then there would have been the ones he had in to fix for clients. He kept the details in a book, one of those duplicate receipt books. He gave out a receipt and put a label on the device. Is that what happened? Someone broke in to steal computers?'

'We are still at the early stages of our investigation. It is possible that he saw some sensitive information on one of the computers he was working on. Did he mention anything to you about something he'd seen?' Meadows asked. 'Maybe just a general comment.'

Teilo shook his head.

'He didn't really talk about his works,' Nerys said.

'Did your father know Councillor Huw Jones?' asked Meadows.

'The man that was murdered in Dinefwr Park?' Teilo asked.

'Yes,' Meadows said.

Teilo stiffened. 'Oh God, do you think the same person killed my dad?'

'It's a possibility,' Meadows said. 'Did your father know Huw Jones?'

'No, I don't think so. We talked about him a little bit. Just what had been on the news.'

'When was the last time you saw or spoke to your father?'

'Friday morning. He asked me to get some boxes down from the attic. I had a break between clients, so I went up to help him.'

'How big were the boxes?'

'They were small. Shoebox size.'

'What was in them?'

'Old photos in one and paperwork in the other, I think.'

'Did he say why he wanted them?' Meadows asked.

'He said he was having a clear-out.'

'The neighbour thought he heard shouting on Friday morning. Did you have an argument?'

Teilo looked perplexed. 'No. Dad was shouting to me from the landing while I was up the attic. I didn't see the boxes straight away as there were only two and they were tucked under the eaves.'

'Bryn wasn't a patient man,' Nerys added. 'He did tend to raise his voice to get a point across.'

Teilo nodded. 'He was insisting the boxes were there. He was right, of course.'

'Would you say that your father was upset that morning?' Meadows asked.

'I wouldn't say upset, agitated maybe. I didn't stay long. He seemed to be in a hurry for me to leave. He said he had work to do.'

'Was it usual behaviour for him?'

Teilo shrugged. 'He could be grumpy at times.'

'Was your father planning building work in the house?' Meadows asked.

'He wanted a garden shed. The spare room was getting crowded with all his bits. He was going to start laying the base when the weather got better. I was going to help him, although I'm not any good at manual work.'

'We know he had a delivery of sand and cement. Did you move the bags?'

'Yeah, I did that on Friday morning.'

'Was your father expecting you yesterday?'

Teilo nodded. 'Nerys had made lasagna. I told him I'd drop a plate over for him. I sent a text to say I was on my way.'

'Was the door open when you arrived?'

'No, but I have a spare key. I though it odd because he usually leaves the door unlocked during the day. His car was parked outside. I opened the door and called out to him. When I didn't see him downstairs, I thought he might have popped out somewhere. Sometimes he'd walk to the shop. I was going to leave the food in the kitchen. It's when I went through that I saw the broken window. I was worried, so I went upstairs and that's… that's when I found him.' Teilo's voice broke, and he put his hand to his mouth momentarily.

Meadows could see the tears in Nerys' eyes. He gave them both a moment before continuing. 'Had there been any changes in your father's behaviour over the past few weeks? Did he seem worried? Quieter than usual?'

'No, not that I noticed. Even if there was something troubling him, I doubt he'd speak to me about it. He wasn't one for talking about feelings. He didn't think much of my work. He had an old-fashioned view that people just had to suck it up and get on with it.'

'I think he was proud of you in his own way,' Nerys said.

Teilo shook his head and sadness filled his eyes. Nerys took hold of his hand and gave it a gentle squeeze.

'What about relationships? Was your father seeing anyone?' Meadows asked.

'No, not that I knew about. I'm sure there had been a few over the years. He mainly had his computers and went for a few pints in the evenings.'

'There was a mug found at the house with traces of lipstick. Did he mention a friend that might be visiting?'

'No. There were people who dropped off and picked up laptops and tablets, but I don't think he would have invited anyone to stay for a cup of tea.'

Meadows gave Edris a nod.

'It's standard procedure to ask everyone who knew your father where they were on Friday evening and the early hours of Saturday morning,' Edris said.

Teilo nodded. 'After I saw Dad on Friday, I had a few appointments with clients. Nerys and I had dinner together at around six then I watched some TV and read for a while. I went up to bed at about eleven.'

'So, you were both in all evening?' Edris asked.

'I was here until half seven,' Nerys said. 'I went off to work. I'm a nurse at Glangwili Hospital. I was on shift until eight, Saturday morning. I came home and had a couple of hours' sleep, then made lunch. I try to stay up when I have a break in shifts.'

Edris nodded, made some notes, then looked at Teilo. 'Did you have any phone calls or go online during the evening?'

'Erm... no... oh,' he said, 'I sent Nerys a goodnight text before I went to bed.'

'What did you watch on the TV?'

'A documentary on the NXIVM organisation.'

'Thank you,' Edris said.

'I think that will be all for now,' Meadows said. 'A family liaison officer will contact you and they will keep you up to date on the investigation.'

Teilo nodded. 'I would like to see him. It's just… well I'm not sure I can. I know it's important for my last memory of him not to be…' Teilo shook his head.

'There is no rush to make a decision,' Meadows said. 'There will be a post-mortem. After that, a visit can be arranged but only if you want to. It's not for everyone. Take your time to think it over.'

'Thank you,' Teilo said.

'We'll see ourselves out,' Meadows said.

* * *

They were in the car when Edris' phone rang. Meadows heard the excitement in his voice.

'We're needed back at the station,' Edris said. 'Paskin has found something.'

Meadows turned the car around and headed back to the station. His mind whirred as he drove the winding roads back to the station. They were the last to arrive back and the air was crackling with tension when they entered the office. Valentine, Paskin, and Blackwell were gathered around Paskin's computer.

'You better take a look,' Blackwell said. He moved to allow Meadows a clear view of the screen.

Meadows sat down and read the words on the screen with increasing disbelief.

'They are describing Huw Jones' murder,' Edris said, reading over Meadows' shoulder. 'Is this for real?'

'There are details here that only the killer would know. Knowledge of the stick figure has been kept strictly within the investigation. Even the families haven't been informed. How did you find this?' Meadows asked.

'It came through in the comments of the appeal post we put out on social media,' Paskin said. 'There was a link posted with a suggestion to check it out.'

'Have you contacted the person who posted the link?'

'I tried responding to the comment but there's been no reply. The account is new, with no profile pictures or other posts. Maybe they wanted to remain anonymous and not get involved. I've asked Chris Harley from tech to take a look but to prioritise the origin of the blog.'

'The link could have been sent by the killer,' Blackwell said. 'It's out there for anyone to see. They probably wanted to make sure we read it.'

'What's worse is they mention making more stick figures, or dolls as they call them,' Valentine said. '"I place it next to the other six dolls," they wrote. This was after Huw, and there were two for Bryn, which leaves another five.'

'They are writing about another killing here' – Meadows pointed at the screen – '"He still hasn't been found" and "When the gun went off and I saw the blood".'

'Maybe something from their past,' Blackwell said.

Paskin shook her head. 'There's another posting before this one.' She minimized the document and called up a second one.

'This is dated three weeks ago,' Meadows said. He read through the blog post with the others crowded beside him.

'This can't be a true account,' Edris said. 'The body would have been found by now.'

'Not necessarily,' Meadows said. He opened the blog post relating to Huw Jones. 'The killer talks about going back and moving the body a few days after the murder. They could have buried him anywhere.'

'So, we've got three murder victims,' Valentine said.

'What we've got is a serial killer,' Blackwell said.

Chapter Twelve

It was another cold, early morning as the team gathered around the incident board. The tension in the air was palpable. No morning banter and no mugs of coffee, just a sense of urgency.

'You've all had a chance to read through the two blog posts,' Meadows said.

The team nodded.

'The comments were interesting,' Valentine said. 'A few of them mentioned a rescue scene and the inner child. What do think it means?'

'I don't know,' Meadows said. 'It is concerning that people talk about being inspired. Tech is looking into tracing anyone that commented on the blog. I think our priority now is to find the first victim. What do we know?'

'"Beyond the house and tree is inky darkness." It sounds like somewhere remote,' Valentine said.

'Then there is the use of a shotgun which was under the victim's bed,' Blackwell said.

'Most farmers have a firearm. I think we're looking for a farm,' Paskin added.

'We're not short of those around here,' Blackwell said. 'Added to that, the murder could have taken place anywhere.'

'We need to start somewhere,' Meadows said. 'Start by canvassing farms. Welfare checks on as many as we can. This is someone who lived alone and has not been missed.' He glanced at the incident board where the blog posts had been pinned.

'This murder was different from the other two, unplanned. It sounds like the gun went off accidentally. The killer is familiar with the house. They mention memories of the kitchen and they knew the gun was kept under the bed. They were close to the victim. We find the victim and we have a chance of finding the killer.'

'Are we ruling out the Jones family and Chloe Watcyn?' Blackwell asked.

'I don't see how we can,' Paskin said. 'The killer mentioned the number of bolts relating to years.'

'We'll keep the lines of enquiry open for both the Joneses and Chloe Watcyn. We also need to look closely at Teilo Thomas,' Meadows said. 'Enquiries haven't turned up any new leads but there must be a link between the victims. We just have to keep digging.

'The killer is also telling us something about their victims. In the first blog post, they talk about the victim not showing signs of shame. In the second, they say, "I knew what he really was," when referring to Huw. What did these men do?'

Valentine looked at her notes. '"I put the gun to his mouth then trail it over his chest to his groin." This sounds sexual. A rape, perhaps.'

Paskin nodded. 'Huw and Bryn could have been involved.'

'What about the freaky stick dolls?' Edris asked.

'The stick dolls have some meaning to the killer. They have nightmares about them,' Meadows said. 'The blog writer also talks about the sight of blood bringing back memories. Perhaps they lived in that house as a child and witnessed something. We could be looking at an incident that happened years ago.'

Meadows pointed to a photo of Bryn Thomas' house. 'I looked through the crime scene photos and video walk-through at Bryn's house. I noticed the boxes Teilo talked about are missing. He thought there was paperwork and old photographs in them.'

'Maybe Bryn put them back up in the attic,' Edris said.

'I already asked Hanes to check; they're not there. Why? What was in those boxes that the killer needed to remove? Why did Bryn ask for Teilo to get them down hours before he was killed?'

'Maybe Bryn himself destroyed them,' Paskin said.

'That's a possibility,' Meadows said. 'OK, Blackwell and Valentine, you better warn Lesley and the family about the blog. Question them about their connection to Bryn Thomas. Show them photos of the stick dolls and see what reaction you get. We also need to get their devices examined. Edris and I will check in with tech, then see if Bryn's post-mortem turned up anything of interest. Our priority is to find victim one. We'll touch base this afternoon. Thanks, everyone.'

* * *

It was always hot in the digital forensic office no matter the weather outside. The blinds were closed to stop any glare hitting the many screens. The only source of light came from the LED bulbs that dotted the ceiling. Fans whirred, fingers clacked on keyboards, and the team's eyes were fixed to screens. No one looked up as Meadows and Edris made their way to Chris Harley's station.

'Oh, hi,' Chris said. He stood up and stretched. 'I was just working on your blogger.'

Chris was one of the few who were taller than Meadows. At six foot four, he looked down on most people, and had the habit of stooping. He had a mop of wild, long curly hair, wore thick-rimmed glasses, and spoke quietly.

'Good to see you, Chris,' Meadows said. 'Have you got anything interesting for us?'

'It's a bit slow-going,' Chris said. He plonked back down in his seat. 'As you know, the person who posted the link was using a new account. I haven't been able to trace the email used to set it up. Likely they used a burner.'

'You can have a burner email?' Edis asked.

'Yeah, they work by–'

Edris held up his hand. 'Remember it's me you're talking to. It will go over my head. I get the picture, though. Same sort of thing as a burner phone.'

Chris laughed. 'Not quite, but yeah, OK. Disposable. I haven't been able to trace the IP address. My guess is they are using a VPN, same as the blogger. I would say they are one and the same. The second blog post came from a different address. That one is traceable. I've contacted the service provider, but you know how these things go. They are reluctant to give out information. I've put in a formal request so should have something back soon.'

'Will that be able to give us the location of the killer?' Edris asked.

'I'm not promising anything,' Chris said. 'It is odd that they've gone to all this trouble to hide their identity yet let their guard down on the second blog post. The blog itself has an anonymous domain name and hosting plan. There are plenty of services that offer this option.'

'Don't you have to pay for them?' Meadows asked.

'Yeah,' Chris said. 'But getting anywhere with the host is near on impossible. We're not talking UK providers. It's not all bad news though. I've been checking out the comments on the blog, as you requested. I came across a reference to a forum.'

'The talk of a rescue made us wonder if there was something on the dark web encouraging this sort of thing. It does happen,' Meadows said.

'You're thinking some sinister group?' Chris shook his head. 'From what I've seen, the users that are commenting are not hidden. This is just a regular site. If the blogger was on a forum before branching out, then I may be able to get some info there. I'll have something for you soon.'

'Are you saying you can trace the killer that way?' Edris asked.

Chris shrugged. 'Depends on the site. Usually, you have to sign in with an email to comment. The admin might give us something. First, I have to identify the user. I'm hoping they weren't so careful when they were on the forum. At the very least, you'll get a chance to see what topics were discussed.'

'Will you be able to get the blog shut down?' Meadows asked.

'Working on it,' Chris said. 'Not sure what good it will do. The number of shares is increasing as we speak. It's too late to stop people seeing it. Some are copying and pasting. I imagine the blogger has multiple social media accounts. I've located some. All they need to do is set up another blog, same method, and the posting starts again. Half the department is working on containing it.'

'You think it could go viral?' Edris asked.

Chris nodded.

'That's what the killer wants,' Meadows said. 'They want to expose the victims for their wrongdoing and gain sympathy. In the process, they might encourage others to seek revenge. Especially if the killer isn't caught. We need to put a stop to it.'

Chapter Thirteen

It was good to see Daisy sitting at her desk instead of Edward Channing. The miserable pathologist had made the last visit all that more unpleasant.

'Great to see you back,' Edris said.

'I've heard that a lot,' Daisy said. 'Edward is not that bad when you get to know him.'

'I guess you can get used to anyone if you work with them long enough,' Edris said. 'We all put up with Blackwell.'

'Yeah, and we all put up with you,' Daisy said with a smile. 'Come on, I'll take you through.'

It had only been a few days since their last visit. Meadows felt sad to be viewing another person who'd experienced a violent death. He watched Daisy step up to the metal gurney and pull back the sheet to Bryn's neck. It was more dignified than when they had viewed Huw Jones' body. That time, the sheet had been completely removed.

'As you would have noticed at the crime scene, Bryn sustained an injury to the right temple.' She pointed to the wound. 'You can see a dent in the swelling. The skin isn't broken so you're looking at the use of a blunt object.'

'Would the blow have been enough to render him unconscious?' Meadows asked.

'My guess would be yes, although I can't say with any certainty,' Daisy said. 'What I do know is, if he was unconscious, he woke up at a later stage. There are signs of a struggle as well as sand and cement particles under his fingernails.'

Meadows had a vision of Bryn clawing at the bags as he struggled to breathe under the weight. Pity swelled in his chest. He tried to push the thoughts away and concentrate on the investigation. Daisy had moved to Bryn's arm and was holding it gently.

'If you look at the injury here, you can see the entry point. This is where the wound is deepest and there is substantial bruising. I imagine that the weapon was hit into the arm with some force then dragged. It tore through the flesh. I've looked at different implements that could have caused this sort of damage. The closest I found is a hand cultivator or claw rake. Most have three prongs, but there are ones with five prongs, which is consistent with the injuries. It's the same on the other arm and both thighs.'

'Nasty,' Edris said.

Daisy nodded. 'Poor soul. His ribs were fractured.'

'Was that caused by the weight of the sacks?' Meadows asked. 'There were eight of them. Water was poured on top, which would have made them heavier.'

'No. Blunt force trauma. The ribs were broken before the sacks were placed on top of him. The injury caused segments of the ribcage to break free and move independently. Cause of death was compression asphyxia. The weight of the sacks together with the broken ribs would have prevented effective breathing.'

'Would he have taken long to die?' Edris asked.

'It wouldn't have been quick,' Daisy said.

Edris shook his head. Disgust was evident on his face. 'So, the killer just sat there and watched.'

Meadows felt a sickness in the pit of his stomach.

Daisy pulled the sheet back over Bryn and gently smoothed it. 'Bryn showed signs of heavy drinking and smoking over a number of years. Damage to the liver and lungs. The toxicology report shows alcohol and high levels of paracetamol and promethazine.'

'What's that?' Edris asked.

'It's an antihistamine. It's found in some cold remedies. It would have made him drowsy.'

'I'm guessing even more so with the alcohol,' Meadows said.

'You guess correctly,' Daisy said.

Meadows' phone bleeped. He looked at the screen and saw a message from Mike Fielding.

'Gotta go,' Meadows said. 'Mike wants to see us.'

'See you later,' Daisy said.

* * *

The drive to the forensic lab didn't take long, and Mike was in reception waiting for them.

'I've got a couple of things to show you,' Mike said. 'Easier to explain in person but I will send a report.'

Mike led them to the lab, keyed in the code, and they stepped inside.

'We've got a good set of prints from the mug as well as DNA from saliva. Nothing on the database but you can work on sending us some prints to match.'

'Yeah, we need a suspect first,' Edris said.

'We've eliminated Teilo Thomas and his wife Nerys. We had to take samples from them to isolate any unknown prints found in the house.'

'Well, that's a start,' Meadows said.

'I wouldn't rule them out just yet,' Mike said. He moved to a computer and pulled up a picture of the broken windowpane in Bryn's kitchen. 'While the window was broken from the outside, this is not how the intruder entered the house. An effort had been made to put shoeprints onto the sill and draining board, but the shoes were not worn during the attack.'

Mike pulled up a set of photographs covering the sitting-room carpet, the stairs, and Bryn's room, as well as a series of close-ups.

'As you can see,' he continued, 'there are no traces of glass through the house. Minute fragments of glass would have been embedded into the soles and distributed as the intruder walked around.'

Mike clicked on another photo. 'This is taken near the sink and back door. There's your glass. It looks like the window was broken *after* the attack. My theory would be that the killer comes in through the back door, kills Bryn, then goes outside to break the window. They come back inside to make the prints, then leave through the back door.'

'I'm guessing they didn't want to wake Bryn when they broke the glass. The keys to Bryn's house were on the kitchen table if I remember correctly,' Meadows said.

'Both front and back door keys, yes,' Mike said.

'The killer has a key and wanted us to think it was a break-in,' Edris said. 'That's going to narrow it down a bit. Starting with Teilo Thomas.'

'Thanks, Mike,' Meadows said.

'Oh, I'm not finished yet.' Mike moved to a worktop. 'Take a look at this.' He passed Meadows an evidence bag.

'Looks like the remains of a photo,' Meadows said.

'It is. There was a log burner in Bryn's house. Looks like it was in regular use. We've managed to get a partial image from a couple of them. I won't bore you with the details. You can see it better on a screen.' Mike handed Meadows a tablet.

'It looks like a very old photograph,' Meadows said.

Edris peered at the image. 'Man and woman.'

'Could be a younger Bryn,' Meadows said.

'There's some more,' Mike said. 'Swipe across.'

The next one was of four people. Two men and two women. The men were dressed in suits. Another one was of a group of six.

'Looks like a wedding photograph,' Meadows said. 'The clothes look like they are from the seventies.'

'If it's Bryn and his wife, why burn them?' Edris asked.

'Good question,' Meadows said. 'The other question being, who are the other people in the photo? Can you send these to me, Mike?'

'Yeah, no problem,' Mike said. 'There are a few other bits from the fire we are working through. Looks like documents. We may be able to get a few words. Most of it is too badly damaged.'

'Bryn Thomas' receipt book is missing, which lists his clients. A few names among those words would be really useful.'

Mike laughed. 'Not asking much, are you?'

'If you find the name of the killer among the ashes, I'll buy you a bottle of whisky,' Edris said.

'You're on,' Mike said.

'Thanks, Mike,' Meadows said. He turned to Edris. 'I think we need to speak to Teilo again. Maybe he can tell us who the people in the photos are.'

Edris nodded. 'He can also explain how someone got into his father's house using a set of keys.'

Chapter Fourteen

Teilo tried to concentrate on what his client was saying but it wasn't sinking in. He felt like his head was underwater and everything was muffled. He tried one of the grounding techniques he often used. Take in the details, he thought. Handbag, coffee cup, snow globe, picture. He rubbed his fingers over the fabric of the chair and tried to concentrate on feeling the texture. He kept doing this until his focus returned. The client had paused.

'You're doing really well,' Teilo said.

'I feel like I'm going backwards,' the woman said.

'No, look how far you have come. You could barely leave the house when I first saw you. You struggled to tell me what had happened to your son. You would choke every time you tried to say his name.'

The woman gave him a sad smile. 'It still hurts to say his name. Every time I look at his picture, I feel like someone has punched me in the stomach.'

'It will hurt,' Teilo said. 'Just remember what we talked about. When you look at his picture, think about when and where it was taken. Think about how you felt at the time.'

'I chose one where we were on holiday. Would you like to see it?'

'Yes, please.'

The woman opened her handbag and took out a photograph. She looked fondly at it then handed it to Teilo.

Teilo looked down at the smiling six-year-old. In one hand, he held a spade; his other waved in the air. In front of him was a bucket and a partially built sandcastle. Behind him, the waves were frozen in time.

'It's a lovely photograph,' Teilo said. 'Do you remember the day well?'

'Yes. We spent all day on the beach. He didn't want to leave, except to get an ice cream.'

'He looks happy, and I bet you were smiling on the other side of the camera. It's a lovely memory to cherish. When you look at this photo, I want you to remember the warmth of the sun. The feeling of sand on your toes. Hear the waves lapping. Look at the joy on your son's face. Recapture the memory of the happy day. All those memories are there for you to keep. No one can take them away. You will always remember him and miss him. There will be pain, but don't let it overshadow this.' He pointed to the picture. 'I want you to go to this place. Allow yourself to smile at the memory.'

The woman nodded and took the picture back. She stroked it lovingly before putting it back in her bag. Teilo could feel her sadness. He wished he had the power to take her pain away. It was a tragedy he saw all too often. A little boy with his life ahead of him taken by a careless driver. Over the limit and speeding. The car had mounted the pavement two years ago.

'I thought I was doing well,' the woman said. 'Then I saw those murders on the news. Another two lives ended. Those men had families, partners, children, maybe grandchildren. I think about how they must be feeling.'

Teilo felt his mouth go dry. He leaned forward, picked up his mug, and took a sip of his coffee. He concentrated on the taste as he placed the mug down carefully.

'There will always be articles in the news that are upsetting. Sometimes they can be a trigger. Some triggers you can avoid. Others are not so easy. A sound or a smell. These can sneak up on you when you least expect it. You have the tools to deal with these now.'

'It's not that,' the woman said. 'I like to watch the news and follow the police pages on social media. It's hard to explain. I like to see a story to its conclusion. That someone is caught and punished. It also helps to know I'm not the only one suffering.'

'Have you given any more thought to joining a support group?' Teilo asked.

The woman shook her head. 'I'm not ready to talk to others face to face. I will see the pain on their faces. I don't think I'd cope. For now, I can observe from a distance. It feels safe. It was OK until someone posted a link to a blog.'

'What sort of blog?'

The woman leaned forward and dropped her voice. 'It was the killer of those two men. He wrote about it.'

Teilo felt his skin prickle. Nerys had told him it was too soon to be working and she was right, he thought. But it was what he liked doing. Helping people. He thought it would be a distraction, and besides, he didn't want to let anyone down. There had been no reason for any of his clients to know his troubles. The time he spent with them was their time. He hadn't expected this. The woman was talking about what she had read. He tried to block out the words. He needed to stop her.

'Perhaps it's not a good idea to read this sort of thing,' Teilo said. 'You need to concentrate on the positive things that are going on in the world. The news only reports the sad and horrific stories. You rarely see a good news story, but they are out there.'

'I know,' she said. 'But once I started reading, I couldn't stop. They went into all sorts of details. I was seeing inside the mind of a killer. Then I started to have flashbacks: the car coming towards us, the pain, the blood, seeing him lying there. The more I see it, the more I think I could have saved him. If I had moved quicker or thrown him clear of the car. I should have protected him.' The woman bent over and sobbed. She clutched her stomach as though in physical pain.

Teilo felt frozen. He didn't want images of the accident in his mind. He had his own horror to keep at bay. Get a grip, he told himself. If this woman could live with what she had been through, then the least he could do was put her first and not think about his own problems. He looked at the walking stick leaning against the chair. Her leg had been crushed in the accident. He knew how many operations she'd had. The months of physio, and still she would always walk with a limp. He admired her so much. The fact that she could get up in the morning and keep breathing after all she'd lost was a testimony to her strength. He suddenly felt ashamed that he had let his own grief slip in. He handed her a box of tissues.

'Sorry.' The woman took a tissue and blew her nose.

'You've nothing to be sorry for,' Teilo said. 'Crying is good. It helps let go of the emotions. Now it's time to be good to yourself. When you go home, I want you to do something nice. Take a long soak in the bath, go for a walk, or better still, start drawing again. It's something you said you love to do.'

'Maybe I will,' the woman said.

They practised some breathing techniques then the session came to an end. As Teilo let the client out, he saw Meadows and Edris approaching the house. It was the last thing he wanted. He had another hour before the next client and he wasn't prepared to talk about his father. He wanted to address those thoughts when he was alone.

'Sorry to interrupt you,' Meadows said when he reached the door. 'There are a few things we need to discuss with you.'

'I've got a little time until the next client arrives,' Teilo said. 'I thought it was best to keep working.'

Meadows nodded. 'Sometimes, a little distraction is good.'

Teilo led them into the sitting room but didn't offer them a cup of tea. He wanted to get the conversation over with as quickly as possible. He wanted to be calm and professional when the next client arrived, not worked up.

He watched the two detectives settle themselves into the armchairs then he plonked down on the sofa.

'Firstly, we need to make you aware of a blog that's been posted and shared on social media,' Meadows said. 'The writer is claiming responsibility for the murder of Huw Jones.'

'My client mentioned something about a blog. Of course, she doesn't know that it was my father that was murdered. I haven't had time to look at it. To be honest, I don't know if I want to. You said last time that there was a possibility that Huw Jones' murder was connected to my father's. Do you think that is the case now?'

'Yes, we're fairly certain we are looking for the same individual in connection to both murders,' Meadows said.

'I take it this blogger has written about my father,' Teilo said.

'Not as yet but it's possible they might. We are doing everything we can to get the site shut down but it's not a simple procedure,' Meadows said. 'We would strongly advise you not to read the blog and perhaps stay away from social media. The details of the last post were very distressing.'

Teilo shook his head. 'That poor family. Do you think it's a hoax? I know you get all sorts of disturbed individuals who claim to be responsible for murders.'

'There are certain aspects of the case we can't share with you,' Meadows said. 'What I can tell you is that at this stage we are confident that the blog is genuine. We will, of course, keep you updated on the progress. Meanwhile, it is inevitable that the blog will be picked up by the press. While we can request that they don't publish the details, we can't stop them reporting it. You may be approached by reporters.'

Teilo nodded. 'I have no intention of talking to them.'

'I'd like you to take a look at some photographs,' Edris said.

'I can't.' Teilo turned his head away. The last thing he wanted to do was lose control of his emotions in front of the other two men.

'It's OK,' Meadows said. 'They are only photos of stick dolls.'

Teilo leaned forward and peered at the screen that Edris held out to him. 'What are they?' he asked.

'Have you ever seen these or something similar?' Meadows asked.

'No. What has this got to do with Dad?'

'We don't know,' Meadows said. 'They were left at your father's house and also near where Huw Jones was found.'

Teilo sat back. He didn't want to look at them anymore.

'There were also some remnants of photographs found in the fireplace of your father's home,' Edris said. 'They are badly damaged, but we would like you to take a look to see if you can identify the people.'

Teilo nodded and took the tablet from Edris. 'This is my Mum and Dad. Taken on their wedding day. My auntie had a similar photo in her house.'

'If you swipe you can view the next one,' Edris said.

Teilo swiped the screen. 'Ah, my auntie and uncle with Mum and Dad.' He moved to the final photograph. 'I don't know these people.'

'Is there someone that might be able to identify them?' Edris asked.

'My auntie, Rhoda Williams, but she's not well at the moment. She's in hospital. She had a stroke and now the doctors have discovered an aneurysm so she'll have to have surgery. I told her that Dad has passed but I didn't go into any details. I thought it would be too much for her.'

'We understand,' Meadows said. 'We'll give her some time to recover and then perhaps we will be able to talk to her.'

'I'll let her know,' Teilo said. 'I'll be going down to see her tomorrow evening.'

'Where does she live?' Edris asked.

'Treorchy.' Teilo gave them the address.

'Thank you,' Edris said. He took the tablet from Teilo.

'Do you know if your father was taking antihistamine tablets for an allergy?' Meadows asked.

'Not that I'm aware of,' Teilo said. 'He did have a cough. It had been troubling him for a while. I tried to persuade him to go to the doctor, but he was stubborn.'

'So, it's likely he would have been taking a cough remedy.'

'I guess so. I've seen him drink cough mixture from the bottle and follow it with a glass of whisky. Why?'

'His toxicology report showed a high level of antihistamine and paracetamol.'

'Oh,' Teilo said. 'Chances are he didn't read the label. He certainly wouldn't have used a spoon.'

Meadows nodded. 'We noticed a fireplace in your father's house. Did he often light the fire?'

'Yes. Most of the time he didn't bother with the heating, he'd just light the fire. He said that was enough for him.'

'Is it likely that the fire would have been lit on Friday?'

'Yes. It was alight when I saw him Friday morning.'

'Is there any reason why your father may have burned the photographs?'

'He said he was having a clear-out, but I can't see why he would burn those ones,' Teilo said.

'Have you seen the photographs before?' Meadows asked.

'Not those,' Teilo said. 'Dad didn't keep any photos of Mum around. I guess it was too painful. To be honest, we didn't talk about it. Was there anything else? It's just I need to prepare for my next client.'

'There are a couple of things we need to go over,' Meadows said. 'Forensic officers have now completed the examination of your father's house. They have been able to establish that the kitchen window wasn't the point of access.'

'I don't understand,' Teilo said.

'Fragments of glass would have been carried through the house. The window was smashed to make it look like a break-in,' Meadows said.

'You see our problem,' Edris said. 'The door wasn't forced so that only leaves one option. The intruder had a key. Other than yourself, who else has a key to your father's house?'

Teilo's mind went blank and he felt panic snaking its way around his chest. He rubbed his hands over his face. 'Erm… I think Jim next door has one. Just in case Dad lost his.'

'Anyone else?' Meadows asked.

'I don't think so.'

'Well, that would only leave you and your father's neighbour with access to the house,' Edris said.

Teilo couldn't speak for a moment. Both Meadows and Edris were looking expectantly at him. The silence was uncomfortable.

'I don't know,' Teilo said. 'I guess he could have given a key to someone. I know he used to leave one outside under a stone. I told him he shouldn't do that. I was sure he had taken it away. Maybe he didn't.'

Edris leaned forward. 'Someone would still have to have known about a spare key.'

'Are you saying someone he knew and trusted did that to him?' Teilo shook his head.

'Are you sure the door was locked when you arrived on Saturday?' Meadows asked.

'Yes. I used my key to get in.' Teilo looked at Edris who was scribbling in his notebook.

Meadows leaned forward in his chair. 'When we spoke to you last, you said that you had taken two boxes down from the attic.'

'That's right,' Teilo said.

'There was evidence of paperwork along with the photographs being burned. It's possible that your father didn't want anyone to see what was in those boxes. Perhaps something from his past. Did he ever mention a name of someone you weren't familiar with? Talk about an old friend?'

Teilo could feel sweat gathering on his forehead. He didn't want to think about the past. It was like steam in a pressure cooker. He could only let a bit out at the time. Then he would shut the lid firmly. Meadows was still talking but his voice sounded distant. He rubbed his fingers against the arm of the chair.

'Are you OK?' Meadows asked.

'Yeah, sorry. I can't stop thinking about... my mind just wanders. I guess I'm still a little spaced out.'

Meadows nodded. 'We do appreciate how difficult this is for you, but we need to get as much information on your father's background as possible.'

Teilo nodded. 'I'm not sure how much help I can be. I didn't see that much of him when I was growing up.'

'How old were you when you went to live with your auntie and uncle?'

'About nine.' Teilo leaned forward, grabbed a mug from the table, and drank. There was only a mouthful of cold coffee left but it was enough. He concentrated on the flavour as he shook away memories of leaving his home.

'Are they your mother's or father's relatives?' Meadows asked.

'My dad's sister and her husband. It's just my auntie now. Uncle Rob died last year.'

'Was the family originally from the Rhondda?'

'I'm sure it's my uncle's family that lived there. My auntie moved there when she married him.'

'So, your father grew up in this area,' Meadows said.

Teilo set the mug down. 'I think so.'

'Are you sure he never mentioned Huw Jones?' Meadows asked.

Teilo shook his head. 'Only when he heard about the murder on the news.'

'What about Lesley, Luke, and Sarah Jones? Are those names familiar to you?'

'No. I'm guessing they are Huw Jones' family.'

Meadows didn't comment.

'What about the name Chloe Watcyn?' Edris asked.

'No. I don't think so.'

'Did your father talk about where he went to school? Or his previous employment? Places that had a special meaning to him?'

'No. Nothing like that,' Teilo said. 'My auntie would probably know. She's ten years older than Dad. Are you thinking Dad had some dark secret in his past? He was just an ordinary man. There really isn't anything else I can tell you.' He picked up his phone and checked the time. 'I'm going to have to start preparing for my next session.'

'OK,' Meadows said. 'There is just one more thing. Given that both Huw Jones and your father were targets, we have to ask you for details of your whereabouts last Tuesday morning.'

'Erm… Tuesday. I would have been here with a client. I'll just check for you.'

Teilo stood up and moved to the desk that was positioned against the wall. He opened a drawer and took out a diary. 'Ah yes,' he said as he flicked back the pages. 'First appointment was at 8 a.m.'

'Can you give us the client's name?' Edris asked.

'I can't, sorry. Confidentiality. I could ask their permission to pass on their details.'

'I see,' Edris said. 'The problem is, without their confirmation, it makes it difficult to firmly establish you were in the house.'

'I can't even show you my appointment book,' Teilo said. 'Oh, hang on.' He picked up his phone and scrolled through his text messages. 'Yes, I remember now. My client had a flat tyre that morning. I can show you the message if I block out the name with my finger.' He turned the phone for Edris to see.

Edris read aloud.

> *Client: I'm going to have to cancel this morning. I'm sorry it's short notice. I've got a flat tyre.*
>
> *Teilo: No worries. I can come to you if that helps. I have another client at 9.15 so it would be a shorter session.*
>
> *Client: No, it's OK. I'm waiting for the RAC then I'll have to get off to work. Are you available late afternoon?*
>
> *Teilo: I can fit you in at 6 p.m.*
>
> *Client: That's great. Thanks so much.*
>
> *Teilo: No problem. I'll see you later.*

'Thank you,' Edris said. 'While this is helpful, it would be beneficial to have your client confirm this.'

'The first text came at 7.45 a.m.,' Meadows said. 'Where were you at that time?'

'Here,' Teilo said. 'I was preparing.'

'Was your wife here?'

'No. She was on a night shift. She got home around eight-thirty.'

'How long does each session last?' Meadows asked.

'An hour,' Teilo said. 'I try to leave at least fifteen minutes between sessions if I'm working at home, sometimes longer.'

'Your second client was due at 9.15 a.m. last Tuesday. Did they arrive on time?'

'Yes.'

Meadows stood up. 'OK, thank you.'

Teilo felt himself relax.

'We will need to take your laptop, and any other devices that connect to the internet for examination,' Edris said.

'We will be asking the same of any family members connected to the case,' Meadows added.

'My laptop and tablet are there.' Teilo pointed to the desk. 'The laptop is one of Dad's old ones. As I told you last time you were here, he had mine for repair. Anyway, I did move some of my documents from my laptop to this one. You're welcome to look. There is nothing confidential on there. I keep the names of my clients in my appointment book. Dad was paranoid about hackers. I think some of it rubbed off on me.'

Edris put the devices into plastic bags and gave Teilo a receipt.

'We will also need to take your phone,' Meadows said.

'I can't give it to you,' Teilo said. 'It has the contact details of my clients. You are welcome to examine it here. You can look at my apps and browsing history. Even my social media account. Just not my contact list.'

Meadows nodded to Edris who took the phone. He looked at the call logs, social media accounts, and checked the browsing history before handing the phone back.

'We'll get your laptop back to you as soon as we can,' Meadows said. 'Thank you for your cooperation. We'll keep you updated.'

Teilo saw them out with a sense of relief. He knew this wouldn't be the last he saw of them. He had lied to them twice, and it was only a matter of time before they found out the truth.

Chapter Fifteen

Meadows was the first in the next morning. He grabbed a tea from the kitchen and settled at his computer. The first thing he saw was an email from Chris Harley. He noticed it was time-stamped at 11.31 p.m. He smiled to himself.

Chris could always be counted on to give his all and some more. He opened the mail and read.

> *I managed to track down the forum the killer visited before starting the blog. The username is 1magpie. Link below.*
> *Chris*

Meadows clicked the link and the forum loaded. It was a support group for people who had suffered trauma and were struggling with mental health. The link took him to the point when 1magpie had joined the group. He took a sip of his tea and started reading.

> *1magpie: Hi, I'm new here and desperately need help. I feel like I am losing my mind.*

> *Admin: Welcome to the group, 1magpie. Please read the rules pinned to the top of the page. This group is to support individuals and share experiences. It's a safe place and there is no judgement. All members of the group have been through a traumatic experience and are here to support only. We urge anyone who is having difficulty to seek professional advice. The are contact numbers of organisations on the help page.*

> *Kim3: Welcome to the group. You'll find us a friendly bunch.*

There were a few more welcomes along the same lines.

> *1magpie: Thank you all for the warm welcome. I don't know where to start. I've always suffered with my confidence and felt like I was running from something. Despite that, I have managed to live a good life. Recently, I saw a child draw a picture of a stickman. It brought up feelings of terror, the like I've never felt in my life. It was so bad I was physically sick. Since then, I've been suffering from nightmares. I wake up screaming. It's got so bad that I'm afraid to go to bed. I'm so tired now. I just want it to end.*

Kim3: I'm sorry to hear you're having these problems. Something similar happened to me. It sounds like the stickman has triggered you. Perhaps you had a traumatic experience in childhood, and it has now resurfaced. It may be an idea to seek professional help. A therapist can help you explore the feelings you are having and possibly find the root cause.

1magpie: I can't do that. I had thought of going to the doctor to get something to help me sleep but I can't have that on my medical records. I'm struggling to keep going. Sometimes I feel like I want to end it all. These intrusive thoughts are with me constantly now. Can't sleep and can't eat.

Astra: If you see a therapist, it will be confidential. If you go private, you don't need a referral. No one has to know.

1magpie: That's not possible for me. It's complicated. I'm just looking for some advice. Some tips to help me sleep and deal with the dark thoughts. I've read through the threads and know some of you have been in a similar situation. I so admire your strength and determination. Your stories made me cry and gave me hope. I guess what I'm asking is what worked for you?

Pip: If I'm honest, it's a long road but hang in there. You can get through this. I'll tell you what worked for me but it's not for everyone. My therapist used the inner-child technique. It's a way to access those painful memories that were never processed. I don't know if it will work for you because I, at least, remembered my childhood trauma. You start by writing a letter to the child – your younger self. Tell them that you are there for them. You are ready to listen to them when they feel able to tell you their concerns. The child then writes back. It might be a few letters.

1magpie: I'm willing to try anything.

Rob: I also used this method. It did work for me. I wrote about ten letters until I was able to verbalise my trauma.

Once I felt able, I wrote a rescue scene. This involves rescuing the child from the situation. It can take any form you like. It sort of tricks the mind so it feels like there was a resolution. That the trauma was dealt with. Sorry, I'm not good at explaining how it works. There are lots of articles you can read to help you. I've put in some links below. Please, don't try and do this alone. You need a professional to guide you.

There were more posts from other users offering advice and then 1magpie posted a letter to their inner child. Meadows read the letter than sat back.

'Have you been in all night?'

Meadows looked up and saw that Blackwell had entered the office.

'Not quite but it was a late night. Chris found the forum so I'm just reading through it.'

'I'll make a start,' Blackwell said. 'The others are grabbing a coffee.'

Meadows nodded and returned to the forum. His thoughts turned to Teilo and how he had protected his clients. Could the killer have taken the advice and visited a professional? If so, how far would that person go to protect them? He couldn't see that Teilo would protect someone who killed his father, but another therapist might. They may not realise that what the killer was describing is fact and not fiction.

There was another letter written to the inner child from 1magpie. Meadows had hoped he would find something that would give them an insight into their identity, but it was all about emotions and encouragement. In the background, he heard the team settle, then silence as they all started reading the postings on the forum.

1magpie wrote something on a post about starting up a blog. The idea being that they would feel like they were writing to the child. They thought it might help others. Most on the forum agreed it would be a good idea and would follow and share the blog. There was a gap of about two weeks before the next post.

1magpie: I'm in a dark place now. Memories have come back to me. Only flashes to start with. I don't know how much is real. I can't do this anymore. Now I think I know what happened and I'm drowning in shame. Everywhere I go I see people looking at me. It's like they know my dark secret. They can see what I am. It's like a stain on my skin I can never wash off. I want it to stop.

Pip: I'm so sorry to hear this. Trust your memories. This is your mind's way of trying to process what happened. It's a dark tunnel but you will come out the other side. I spent many years feeling shame that wasn't mine to carry. You won't feel like this forever. Please don't give up. We are all here to help you.

Admin: This is the number for the Samaritans. If you can't seek professional help then please talk to them. It's all confidential. Just having someone on the other end of the line to talk to can help.

Kim3: The Samaritans helped me so much. Please call them.

A couple of days later there was another post.

1magpie: I'm OK. Still fighting. I've remembered a lot more. I know what I have to do to make this go away.

There were a few more comments, then a link to the blog post. Meadows sat back and waited for the rest of the team to catch up.

'We're dealing with someone on the edge,' Blackwell said.

'I can't help feeling a little sorry for them. Something bad must've happened in their past,' Valentine said.

'Yeah, but these victims are pensioners. How long in the past are we talking? It could be fifty years or more,' Blackwell said.

'Or forty-one,' Edris said. 'Forty-one bolts for the number of miserable years.'

Blackwell shook his head. 'How the hell are we going to dig up something from that long ago?'

Edris shrugged. 'It would help if we had a clue as to what the incident was.'

'We could be looking at a paedophile ring,' Valentine said. 'The talk of shame. That's sadly what victims often feel. Then there's the photographs being burned. Bryn Thomas' laptop was taken. He could have had images.'

Meadows nodded. 'Whatever it is, it's clear the killer is dealing with a trauma that was so horrific they buried it deep in their subconscious. A part of them wants to be stopped. What else have we learned about this person?'

'They're not eating and are sleep-deprived. That's going to show in their appearance,' Paskin said.

'Teilo looks tired,' Edris said.

'So do Lesley and Luke,' Valentine added. 'Sarah doesn't look much better.'

'We haven't turned up any other viable suspects,' Blackwell said. 'It has to one of them.'

'Any one of them could be the blogger or none of them.' Meadows rubbed his hand over his chin. He could feel the team's frustration. 'All we have is DNA from the mug left in Bryn Thomas' house and fibres found with the bolt. Bryn could have had a visitor that has nothing to do with the murder. Teilo and his wife, Nerys, already gave samples for elimination. Ask the others to do the same. At the very least we can rule them out. What reaction did you get when you showed them photos of the stick dolls?' Meadows asked.

'They all claimed they hadn't seen them before,' Valentine said.

'They looked confused,' Blackwell added. 'They didn't understand why we were showing them and what they had to do with Huw's death.'

'None of them admitted to knowing Bryn Thomas,' Valentine said. 'Luke Jones was angry more than anything. He'd read the blog. There is also a lot of unpleasant comments on social media. Some pointing the finger at Lesley.'

'Did any of the family members respond to these comments?' Meadows asked.

'No,' Paskin said.

'Interesting,' Meadows said. 'If Luke was that angry, you'd think he'd try to defend his mother. I also noted that the blogger didn't respond to comments. They'd been interacting with the group on the forum.'

'The family won't be commenting now. We've taken all their devices,' Edris said.

'While the blog is still up, do you think we should try communicating with the writer?' Paskin asked.

'It might work but we're going to need professional help. Anything we write could aggravate the killer. Look into it and we will need to run it by the boss,' Meadows said.

'What will you need to run by the boss?'

They all turned to see DCI Nathaniel Lester had entered the office. Lester was responsible for the overall running of the individual teams in the county. When he turned up it was a sign that the situation was serious.

'Sorry to interrupt your briefing.' Lester looked at Meadows. 'Can I have a word?'

Blackwell raised his eyebrows but didn't comment.

Meadows followed Lester to his office at the far end of the building. He wasn't overly concerned. While it was clear by his demeanour that Lester wasn't happy, he always found his boss to be fair.

'What's the progress on the case?' Lester asked as soon as Meadows closed the door.

'We're still trying to link the victims as well as look into their pasts. We haven't been able to interview Bryn's sister, Rhoda. She's just undergone surgery. Hopefully she'll be up to answering questions soon. She just needs a little time.'

'Time you haven't got,' Lester said.

Meadows nodded. 'The sand and cement delivered to Bryn's house was ordered by Bryn himself, so that's another dead end. Priority is finding the first victim. I feel this is our best chance. The killing was accidental, not planned like the other two.'

'I talked to Folland. You've got uniform out doing welfare checks on half the farms in Wales,' Lester said.

'Not quite. We're concentrating on the Llandeilo area and circling out. It's slow-going because most of the farmers are out in the fields. It takes time to track them all down.'

'If you think this is the best way forward then I'll organise drafting in some extras from other stations.'

'Thanks.'

'Resources isn't my concern at the moment,' Lester said. 'I take it you've seen this morning's headlines.'

Meadows shook his head. He didn't bother with excuses. 'I am aware that the blog has been shared on social media and it's picked up a large number of followers.'

Lester pushed his tablet towards Meadows. 'Take a look at that.'

Meadows looked down and read.

Stick doll killer claims a third victim
The killer of Councillor Huw Jones has released a blog post on how they tracked and murdered their victim. Huw Jones was discovered in Dinefwr Park with multiple injuries early last Tuesday morning. He'd been out walking his dog. Sources tell us that a stick doll was found at the scene.

The second victim, Bryn Thomas, was discovered in his home on Saturday afternoon by his son. While no details have been released on the cause of death, unconfirmed rumours suggest that a further two stick dolls were found in his home.

An older blog post by the killer details the murder of an unidentified male, making a total of three victims. Police have been seen checking the area since the blog came to light but have yet to comment.

Fear is growing…

Meadows stopped reading. 'We tried to contain the information, even asked for the media's cooperation. I suppose you can't blame them. It's all over social media so they had to write something. At least they didn't quote from the blog.'

'The news is the least of our worries. We've got a social media frenzy on our hands. I've already had a call complaining about the number of visitors to Dinefwr Park. They can't cope with the car parking. People are traipsing down to where the body was discovered and taking videos, putting up stick dolls and posting it on bloody TikTok. Then we've got these amateur detectives coming up with their own theories.'

'They may be worth a look. We've exhausted all lines of enquiries, apart from both victims' immediate families.'

Lester glared at him. 'I hope you're not suggesting we take these people seriously.'

Meadows shrugged. 'People are guarded with the police but will gossip among themselves.'

Lester shook his head. 'All they are doing is trying to make us look incompetent. Added to that is the sheer volume of calls from the community, who are rightly terrified that they will be the next victim.'

Lester was getting red in the face and Meadows didn't have the answers. What he did know was that the public needed reassurance.

'Perhaps it would be a good idea to call a public meeting,' Meadows suggested. 'It would give the community a chance to air their concerns and ask questions. It would also keep the press happy.'

'I'm not sure about opening up questions to the public in front of the press. I think for now we'll put out a press release with a stern warning. Something like, "anyone caught interfering with the investigation or posting defamatory comments will be prosecuted". That should calm things down.'

Meadows' phone bleeped, alerting him to a text. 'Excuse me a mo.' He looked at the screen. 'It's Chris Harley from tech. He's got a location for the blogger.'

'Go,' Lester said.

Chapter Sixteen

The office crackled with tension as they all waited for the call to come through.

'Ty Gwyn farm is the farm next to Ynysforgan farm,' Paskin said.

'Chloe Watcyn,' Edris said. 'I bet that's no coincidence.'

'The owner of the property is Malcom Isaac. As far as I can tell, there is no one else living there. No firearms licence attached to the property.'

'Doesn't mean there's no firearm,' Meadows said. 'Some of these farmers have shotguns that have been passed down and were never registered.'

'Hidden under the bed, like the one the blogger wrote about,' Valentine said.

The phone rang and Meadows answered. He listened, then ended the call. 'The firearms unit is ready. They will meet us there. Paskin, find out any information you can on

Malcom Isaac, please. Valentine and Blackwell, you're with us.'

Meadows drove with Edris while Blackwell and Valentine followed. Edris appeared to be excited and confident that they were going to make an arrest. Meadows didn't feel the same. His stomach was knotted. He was leading the operation, and he was responsible for the team's safety. So many things could go wrong, he thought. With them following a single-track road, they would be easy to spot. There were open fields with borders lined with trees. It would be easy for someone to hide and take a shot.

'You're quiet,' Edris said.

'I'm just wondering if we shouldn't have waited until after dark.'

'Nah, they would see the headlights coming. Besides, it would be harder to spot the killer.'

'Yes, but it also makes it harder to spot us when we are out of the car. I guess we just have to trust the firearms unit. They wanted to go now and they know what they're doing. What's troubling me is why the killer would leave this address open to trace.'

'Maybe they got careless,' Edris said.

'No, I don't see it. I think this is a deliberate act.'

'OK, so they want to get caught. They said as much in the blog.'

'Let's hope it's that.'

'Are you thinking it's a trap?' Edris asked.

'No, I don't think so. Why would they target the police?'

'Well, I bloody well hope it's not a trap,' Edris said. 'Only one bar on my signal.'

Meadows smiled. 'It's not like we need to call anyone. We've got all the back-up we need.'

They arrived at Ty Gwyn farm and parked at the bottom of the track, behind the firearms unit's vehicles.

The team was handed bulletproof vests by the head of the unit, a man called Rikki Stansfield.

'We're going to approach the farm by foot from here,' Standfield said. 'Your team can wait until we've cleared the house and outbuildings. Stay out of sight. One of my team will stay with you.'

'OK, thanks,' Meadows said.

'We may as well get back in the car,' Edris said. 'It's too cold to be standing around.'

They all got into one car and waited. The time moved slowly, and the atmosphere was tense. Meadows watched the armed officer pace back and forth. His eyes were alert and his hand poised on his weapon.

'There're taking their time,' Blackwell complained.

'We would have heard shots if there was a problem,' Edris said.

The radio crackled to life and Standfield's voice filled the car. 'All clear. No sign of the suspect but there's something you need to see.'

'On our way,' Meadows said.

'Bloody typical,' Blackwell said. 'Well, he's going to get a shock when he gets home.'

They couldn't drive down the track because the firearms unit's vehicle was blocking the way. Instead, they were told to wait until someone came to escort them.

'I don't see why he can't walk with us.' Edris glanced at the officer who was still pacing.

'In case the suspect tries to escape in a vehicle,' Valentine said. 'They could be lurking over the brow of the hill in a Land Rover or on quad bike.'

'They'd just go around the vehicles,' Blackwell said.

'Not if Action Man shoots at them,' Valentine said.

A woman from the firearms unit joined them and they walked side by side up the track. Meadows pulled his hood up against the wind and dug his hands in his pockets. At first, the track sloped upwards and when they came to the peak, the farmhouse came into view below. Meadows stopped.

'What is it?' Blackwell asked.

'Let's walk along the bank,' Meadows said.

They moved onto the rough grass and walked above the track until they came to a spot where they were looking down at the house. They could see the firearms team moving through the fields towards the barns. Meadows looked at the broken fence surrounding the old farmhouse. Next to it was an old oak tree; its bare branches stretching out to brush at the windows.

'This is it,' Valentine said. 'It's the house the blogger wrote about.'

'Oh yeah,' Edris said.

Standfield was standing at the door of the farmhouse.

'I think I know what it is he wants us to see,' Meadows said. 'Blackwell, you better get forensics out here. I'll go in alone. We need to keep the footfall to a minimum.'

Meadows left the group and walked down the bank. He felt like he was following the killer's footsteps as he walked up the path and through the door into the farmhouse. The inside was just as the killer had described. A dingy kitchen with an airing rack hanging over an unlit stove. The clothes were creased and stiff. There was a faint aroma of bleach in the air, which did little to mask the smell of damp, and something more unpleasant.

'Through here,' Standfield said.

Meadows stepped through the door into a sitting room. The smell of stale urine and faeces churned his stomach. An armchair was positioned next to an open fireplace. It was splattered with blood. The carpet was stained brown where a pool of blood had soaked in and dried. It was mixed with other bodily fluids. A shotgun was lying on the floor. The tree outside blocked most of the light coming through the window, but even in this dim setting, Meadows could see a blood splatter pattern on the wall.

Against the far wall, there was an old oak table that held a laptop. It was plugged into the mains.

Meadows walked over to the laptop and examined it. He could see a label on the bottom right corner. It had a reference number and Bryn Thomas' name and address. He turned his attention to the bloodstains.

'Whoever was shot here didn't walk out,' Stansfield said. He trailed his torch beam across the carpet.'

Meadows nodded his agreement. 'Judging by the amount of blood, I doubt he was alive when he was moved. I think we've found the crime scene of the killer's first victim.'

Meadows stepped outside and was grateful for the cold air that cleared the lingering smell.

'Forensics are on their way,' Blackwell said. 'Is it Malcom Isaac?'

'Don't know,' Meadows said. 'There's no body.' He explained what he'd seen inside. 'Malcom Isaac's vehicle is here and no one else is supposed to be living on the property. It looks like he was the killer's first victim. I'm guessing they left the address traceable so we could discover him.'

'They could have left directions to the body,' Blackwell said.

'The killer said they came back to move the victim,' Valentine said. 'I don't recall there being mention of a location.'

'Could have moved him anywhere,' Edris said.

'It wouldn't make sense to put him in a car and dump him somewhere else,' Meadows said. 'Not when you're surrounded by all this land.'

* * *

The firearms unit left, and forensics arrived. Soon the farmhouse was a hive of activity. Sergeant Folland had sent as many uniformed officers as he could spare. They gathered in a group, rubbing their hands together. Vapour trailed out of their mouths as their breath hit the cold air.

'We have a lot of land to cover,' Meadows said. 'Cadaver dogs are on their way, but we need to make a start when we still have daylight. Forensics have identified blood on a wheelbarrow and a trailer that's attached to a quad bike.'

'So, we find the quad tracks and follow them,' Hanes said.

'Let's hope it's that simple,' Meadows said. 'As you can see, there are a number of tracks leading from the farm and going in different directions. I'm guessing those are from regular use. If the killer took the quad on a different route, it may be that the tracks won't be visible. Going by the date of the first blog post, the body was moved some weeks ago. We've had rain, snow, high wind, and frost in the last few weeks. The tracks could have been covered. The ground is hard so I doubt the killer would have been able to dig a sizeable hole. We're looking for a shallow grave. Look for disturbance in the earth. Grass wouldn't have had time to grow back.'

'There is always the possibility that he was dumped out in the open,' Edris said.

'We all better be careful where we walk then,' Blackwell said.

Edris wrinkled his nose.

They split into groups and set off. Meadows was with Hanes, Taylor, and a younger officer named George Bailey. They spread out and made their way across the first field with their eyes downcast. Up and down the field they walked until they had covered the whole area. It was slow going through the damp grass, and Meadows' toes were beginning to hurt from the cold.

'I should have put on thermals,' Hanes said.

'I wouldn't say no to a hot cup of tea,' Bailey said.

Taylor laughed. 'You're a bunch of pussies.'

'Are you telling me you're not freezing?' Hanes said.

'I've got tights on under my trousers, and I'm layered up under my jacket. I learned my lesson standing around patrolling that protest last week.'

They moved to the next field where grazing sheep bleated and scuttled away.

'At least this one is smaller,' Bailey said.

The light was starting to fade, and they all pulled out their torches to illuminate the ground.

Hanes talked into his radio but got the same response back from each team. Nothing had been discovered. They grew quiet as they continued to search. At the entrance to the next field was a large barn made of corrugated sheets. Some of the sheets were hanging by one nail, while others lay on the floor. Inside was a small stack of hay.

'The firearms unit have already checked it out,' Meadows said.

'That's good,' Taylor commented. 'It doesn't look safe.'

'This whole place is run-down,' Hanes said. 'Where are all the animals? We've only seen sheep.'

'Looks like the land is used for crops,' Meadows said. He shined his torch on what looked like plough marks.

'Doesn't look like anything has been grown here for a while,' Bailey said.

'Maybe it's been left to fallow,' Meadows said. 'Malcom Isaac is in his early seventies. I guess he was winding down.'

Tall thistles grew among the grass and caught on their clothes. When they were midway across the field, Meadows thought he caught a foul stench on the breeze. He stopped.

'Do you smell that?'

The other three shook their heads.

'Maybe you can smell sheep shit,' Hanes said.

'It doesn't smell,' Taylor said. 'We've just walked through a field full of it.'

Meadows sniffed the air and pointed to the right. 'There's definitely something. The wind is coming from that direction. Come on, let's spread out and walk across the field.'

They moved along silently. As they got further across the field, the smell became stronger.

'I smell it now,' Hanes said and covered his mouth.

'Me too,' Bailey said.

'Better give the others a shout,' Meadows said.

Hanes called it in on his radio as they continued to walk towards the source of the smell. Ahead, Meadows could see a large mass on the grass. The smell was so strong now, it was difficult not to gag. Bailey started to retch. Taylor's eyes were watering and Hanes looked pale.

Meadows stopped and looked at the three officers. He knew, like himself, they were struggling. Yet all three of them would go with him without complaint. He didn't want to put them through that ordeal. On the other hand, he didn't want to embarrass them.

'I don't think we should all proceed,' Meadows said. 'We don't want to contaminate the crime scene. Best you make a start on securing the area.'

Bailey looked relieved. 'I'll go and fetch the tape.'

Meadows tried not to smile as Bailey turned and almost ran from the scene.

'Never seen him move so fast,' Taylor said.

'Can't say I blame him,' Hanes said.

'You've had your fair share of this last week,' Meadows said. 'Go on, off you go, you two. It's going to take you some time to set the cordon.'

Meadows proceeded alone until he was standing looking down at what he guessed to be the remains of Malcom Isaac's body. The cold weather had slowed the decomposition. The body was black, bloated and almost unrecognisable as human. The flesh had started to fall away, and it appeared that wild animals had pulled away parts of the limbs. As he fought the nausea, he looked at the ground around the remains. A circle of stick dolls surrounded the body. Each one of them was a different shape and size but they all had blue wool wrapped around the arms and body. Black holes made up their eyes, which all looked inwards. Meadows counted fifteen of them.

There was nothing else to see so he walked back across the field. He breathed deeply but the smell still lingered. It clung to his clothes. All he wanted to do now was to strip off and have a hot shower, but he knew that was a long way off.

Blackwell was waiting by the barn. 'Found him then?' he said.

'Yeah, well, what's left of him,' Meadows said.

Valentine was next to arrive. Meadows described what he had seen.

'Looks like we've got a nutter on our hands,' Blackwell said.

'Still, I don't understand why no one reported him missing,' Valentine said. 'He's been dead for a few weeks.'

'He lived alone,' Meadows said. 'The sad reality is that there are many in the same situation. No one checks on them. Some people don't see another soul for weeks. I'm guessing that is the case here. According to the blog, the killer was able to come back and move him without fear of being caught. They took their time placing him and surrounding him with stick dolls.'

Edris came running towards them.

'You took your time,' Valentine called out.

Edris came to stand next to them and took a moment to catch his breath. 'I was up the top field when Hanes called it in. Paskin just phoned through the information on Malcom Isaac. His next of kin is Chloe Watcyn. She is his daughter.'

Chapter Seventeen

Chloe Watcyn's farm was next door to her father's farm. Meadows and Edris could have walked but they took the car. Edris had complained he was already freezing without walking down the track and up another. Valentine and Blackwell stayed behind to assist with the search of the property.

'Chloe has already admitted to knowing Huw Jones and arguing with him,' Edris said. 'Now her father has turned up murdered. The killer knew the house and where the gun was kept. It's got to be her.'

'If we go by the blog, then yes, she is a suspect, but she may not be the only one. According to Paskin, Malcom has another daughter, Anna. Then there's Chloe's husband and any number of other people who have worked on Malcom's farm.'

'Chloe has motive. With her father out of the way she could expand the holiday park. Without Huw Jones, it will be easier to convince the farmers to back her plans. She's a grieving daughter, so she'll get their sympathy.'

'What about Bryn Thomas?'

Edris shrugged. 'Maybe he fixed her computer and saw her plans.'

'If only it were that simple,' Meadows said. 'We still have to bear in mind the trauma suffered by the killer. The stick dolls and blood that triggered the memory.'

'Maybe all that is nonsense. Made up to throw us off the real motive.'

'There is that possibility, but it would be an elaborate ploy. We need to tread carefully for now. We treat Chloe like any other family member of a murder victim. If she has nothing to do with her father's death, then this is going to be a shock for her.'

Meadows parked in the yard and once again they were met by Chloe's daughter.

'Mum's feeding the pigs,' the little girl said. 'Go that way.' She pointed to the left.

'Great,' Edris said. 'I was hoping for a nice hot cup of tea in front of a fire, and I don't like pigs.'

Meadows laughed. 'Don't tell me you're scared.'

'Dangerous creatures,' Edris said.

They followed the path past the stables, an open barn, and a chicken coop before coming to the pigs. Chloe watched them approach with her hands on her hips.

'You bloody lot again,' Chloe said. 'This is harassment.'

'Could we go to the house to talk?' Meadows asked.

'No,' Chloe said. 'I haven't got time to sit around chatting. I've got work to do.'

'Is there someone who could do that for you?' Meadows asked. 'I'm afraid we have some bad news.'

'Well, spit it out,' Chloe said. 'If it's that bad, it's not going to make a difference if I'm standing here or in the house.'

She has a point, Meadows thought. 'I'm very sorry to say that, earlier today, we found a body, which we believe to be that of your father, at Ty Gwyn farm.'

'Oh,' Chloe said. She picked up a bucket and tipped the contents into the trough.

The pigs rushed forward, grunting and squealing, as they fought to get to the food. Edris took a few steps back. Meadows watched Chloe for a reaction, but her face gave nothing away.

'I suppose I better ring my sister,' Chloe said. 'I'll do it on the way back to the house.' She pulled a mobile phone from her jacket pocket.

Meadows heard the ringtone then a woman's voice answered. Chloe repeated what Meadows had told her then hung up.

'She's on her way. She won't be long. It's better you tell us together. I don't want to repeat it all later.'

'That's fine,' Meadows said.

They followed Chloe into the farmhouse. The warmth hit them as they stepped through the door.

'You can sit down,' Chloe said. 'I'll make some tea.'

When Chloe busied herself with preparing tea, Meadows took a seat at the large pine table and looked around. It was a sharp contrast to Malcom's house. The cream kitchen cabinets looked new, and the worktops were thick slate. A navy-blue double AGA range was at the heart of the kitchen. Copper pots and pans were hanging above.

In the bright light of the kitchen, he studied Chloe's face. She didn't wear any make-up. Her skin was clear but under her eyes were dark shadows.

Chloe placed two glasses of milk and a plate of biscuits on a tray.

'I'm taking these through to the children,' she said. 'I suppose their dinner is going to be late.'

She left the kitchen and returned a few minutes later, made the tea, and placed two mugs in front of Meadows and Edris then fetched one for herself before settling at the table.

'Where does your sister live?' Meadows asked.

'Ffairfach,' Chloe said. She picked up her mug and took a sip.

The door opened and a woman entered with a waft of cold air. She had the same dark blonde hair and blue eyes as Chloe but was a smaller build.

'My sister, Anna,' Chloe said.

Meadows introduced himself and Edris.

'What's going on?' Anna said.

'I told you. They've found a body, and they think it's Dad,' Chloe said.

'What do you mean, found a body?' Anna asked.

'Sit down,' Chloe said.

Anna took a seat next to her sister. Her face was creased with worry. 'Has he had an accident? Is he OK?'

'Found a body means dead,' Chloe said.

'No,' Anna said. Tears filled her eyes.

'I'm very sorry,' Meadows said.

'Where did you find him?' Chloe asked.

'He was in one of the fields,' Meadows said.

'Are you sure it's him?' Anna asked.

Meadows noticed the quiver in her voice. 'The house was empty, and his car is there. We understand that your father lived alone.'

'Yeah,' Chloe said.

'Is it possible that there could have been someone else at the farm?' Meadows asked.

Chloe shook her head. 'He has help in the spring but that's it. He manages himself during the winter months.'

'Would he have gone away?'

Chloe raised her eyebrows. 'He never left the farm. Once he worked out how to order online, that was it. He had everything delivered.'

Meadows nodded. 'There will need to be a formal identification, but it seems likely that it is your father we found in the field.'

'Chloe, can't you just go and look?' Anna asked.

'I'm not doing it,' Chloe said.

'I'm afraid we're going to have to use dental records or DNA to confirm identity. The body has been exposed to the elements. Possibly for a few weeks,' Meadows said.

'Oh God.' Anna covered her mouth.

'We will work on getting confirmation as quickly as possible,' Meadows said. 'In the meantime, we will need to ask you both a few questions.'

Anna nodded and Meadows noted that Chloe looked annoyed. It was as if her father's death was more of an inconvenience than anything else. He gave Edris a nod.

'How long has your father lived at Ty Gwyn farm?' Edris asked.

'I think they moved there in the early eighties,' Chloe said.

'Where did they live before?'

'Kent, I think,' Chloe said.

'How long has your father lived alone at the farm?'

'Since he and our mother divorced,' Anna said. 'So over twenty years.'

'Do you know why the marriage broke down?' Edris asked.

'Is that any of your business?' Chloe snapped.

'We just need to build up a picture of your father's life,' Meadows said.

'Fine. My father was a dick,' Chloe said.

'In what way?' Edris asked.

Meadows saw the two women exchange a glance. 'Was he violent?' he asked.

'Not particularly,' Anna said.

'They argued a lot,' Chloe said. 'Mum put up with his shit for years. She stayed with him for our sake. Shouldn't have bothered. She left when Anna turned eighteen.'

'Can you give me your mother's name and address?' Edris asked.

Chloe gave him the details.

Edris scribbled in his notebook then went through the family history and a list of friends and family. It was mainly Chloe that answered. Anna sat quietly, wiping her eyes.

'What about other relationships?' Meadows asked. 'Did you father see other women after the divorce?'

'Not that I know of,' Chloe said.

Anna shook her head.

'Is it possible that he could have been having an affair?' Meadows asked.

'I don't think he would find anyone who'd put up with him,' Chloe said.

'When was the last time you saw or spoke to your father?' Meadows asked.

'Dunno,' Chloe said. 'I've been busy with the farm and the park. A month ago. Maybe more.'

Meadows looked at Anna.

'Probably about the same. Maybe longer. I haven't seen him for a while.'

'What about the grandchildren? Would they have visited him?'

Another look passed between the sisters. There was a flicker of something in Chloe's eyes. Meadows wasn't sure what emotion he had witnessed, fear or anger. Chloe took a sip of her tea, then appeared to compose herself.

'He wasn't good with the children. There's so much old machinery laying around,' Chloe said. 'Even the outbuildings are crumbling. It's not a safe place for them. I don't let them go wandering around on their own.'

'He didn't take much interest in my boys,' Anna said. 'He wasn't the grandpa type.'

'When you saw him last, did you notice any changes in his behaviour?' Meadows asked. 'Did he seem upset or worried about something?'

Anna shook her head.

'Same old miserable bastard,' Chloe said. 'He came to moan about the holiday park.'

'Was he against it?'

'He wasn't particularly supportive. He thought I could make better use of the land.'

'Did he actively oppose the planning application?'

'The new access would be going through his land, so no.'

'Who benefits from your father's death?' Meadows asked.

'Me,' Anna said.

'Ty Gwyn was the largest farm in the area,' Chloe said. 'Then Dad bought this place. He only wanted the land. The house was derelict when I bought it from him. He gave me the land as part of my inheritance. Then he sold me pieces of his land, acre by acre. He wasn't happy about it. He'd loved lording it over the area. He was the first one to buy a combine harvester and he did all sorts of deals with the farmers. He got them to plant their fields then he'd cut the crop and take a percentage of the profit. Foot-and-mouth then bovine disease had left most of the farms struggling so he took advantage. He overstretched, buying this place, but he was greedy. Eventually, the farms recovered, and they no longer needed Dad to survive. In the end, he couldn't manage the land. He could barely keep his head above water. So yeah, I had my inheritance, but I worked hard to purchase the rest of the land and Anna will get Ty Gwyn.'

Interesting, Meadows thought. He imagined Malcom Isaac had upset a lot of farmers in the community over the years.

'We found a shotgun in your father's house. Were you aware he kept a firearm on the property?'

'Yeah,' Chloe said.

'Do you know where he kept it?'

'Under the bed,' Anna said.

Chloe shot her a look.

'Who else knew about the shotgun and where it was kept?' Meadows asked.

Chloe shrugged. 'Who knows? He could have told anyone.'

'Why are you asking about the shotgun?' Anna asked. 'Did someone shoot him?'

'We won't know until the post-mortem, but it does look like the gun was fired and someone was injured in the house.'

Anna paled. 'I think I'm going to be sick.' She jumped up from her chair and moved to the sink.

Chloe followed her. 'Just take a few deep breaths,' she said.

Anna did as instructed, then started to sob. Chloe fetched a glass, filled it from the tap, and handed it to her sister. Anna sipped the water. Meadows could see her hands shaking.

'Sorry,' Anna said between sobs.

'It's OK,' Meadows said. 'Take your time.' He watched the two sisters for a moment. Could one of them be the killer? Chloe came across as tough, straight-talking, and focused. There was a possibility that she was hiding an inner turmoil. Anna, on the other hand, was struggling. It could just be grief and shock for her father, even though it appeared that they didn't have a good relationship.

While these thoughts went around in Meadows' mind, Chloe had managed to calm Anna. Both women were now sitting at the table.

It was time to move the questions to more uncomfortable territory. There was no way of avoiding the subject of the blog, but he knew that the mention of it would inevitably lead to one or both of them reading it. They may resist for a while, but curiosity would get the better of them. If they were innocent, to inflict that on them was cruel and went against his nature. He took a sip of tea and gave Edris a nod.

'Did your father know Councillor Huw Jones?' Edris asked.

'Yeah,' Chloe said. 'Everyone around here knew him.'

'Did your father get on with him?'

'Yeah. Back when things were going well for Dad, their friendship was of mutual benefit. Huw was involved in planning. Dad needed to widen access to the farm to move his machinery. With Huw's help, he got mirrors put up on the roads, opposite the entrance of other farms. In return, Dad helped raise Huw's standing in the community. He had no problem getting voted in as local councillor.'

'How long would you say they've been friends?'

'Over twenty years.'

'Did your father know Bryn Thomas?'

'No,' Chloe answered quickly.

'That was the man that was found murdered in his house last Saturday,' Anna said.

'That's right,' Edris said. 'Did you ever hear your father mention him?'

'I don't think so,' said Anna slowly. 'Do you think the same person killed Dad?'

'It looks like all three are connected,' Meadows said. 'I don't know if you are aware, but there has been a lot of speculation on social media over Huw Jones' death.'

'I saw something on Facebook,' Anna said.

'I haven't got time to piss about on social media,' Chloe said. 'I've got my web page that I update but that's about it.'

'Apparently, the killer wrote a blog on how they murdered Huw,' Anna said.

Meadows was glad he didn't have to be the one to make them aware of the posts. 'Did you read it?' he asked.

'Of course not,' Anna said. 'There's supposed to be details on how they killed him. I could never read something like that.'

'The thing is there was another blog post written before that. It describes your father's house and the gun under the bed.'

'You mean some sick bastard has written about killing my father?' Chloe said. 'That's disgusting.'

'The writer of the blog knew the house well, knew about the gun, and that your father would be alone. It would have to be someone close to him.'

'Are you accusing one of us?' Chloe asked. 'Then go ahead and arrest us or leave.'

'What? No,' Anna said. 'You can't think we would kill our own father.'

'No one is accusing you,' Meadows said. 'We need to ask these questions. Is there anyone you can think of that would want to harm your father?'

'Plenty of people,' Chloe said. 'I told you he cashed in when other farmers were struggling. It's how he extended his land. He bought from his neighbours at a cheap price when they were desperate.'

'Would these neighbours have been frequent visitors to the house? Known about the shotgun?' Meadows asked.

'I don't bloody know,' Chloe said. 'You're going to have to speak to them.'

'Did your husband get along with your father?'

'Jac has nothing to do with this,' Chloe said. 'They were civil to each other but that's about as far as it goes. They didn't argue, and Jac gains nothing from my father's death.'

'We will need to talk to him.'

Chloe folded her arms across her chest. 'I'll let him know.'

'What about your husband, Anna?'

'Rhys didn't have much to do with him,' Anna said. 'My father didn't approve of my choice of husband. He thought I should marry someone interested in farming.'

'Is that it?' Chloe asked. 'I've got to cook dinner for the kids.'

'We won't keep you much longer,' Meadows said. 'There has been mention of an incident that took place a number of years ago. It may have involved your father, Huw Jones, and Bryn Thomas.'

Chloe's eyes widened. 'What incident?'

'It's unclear at present. Can either of you remember something that occurred at Ty Gwyn? Perhaps when you were younger.'

'Nothing I can think of,' Chloe said.

'Anna?'

Anna looked at Chloe. 'Erm... I don't think so.'

'OK. Perhaps you could think about it. It may be a memory of someone being there that was upset. Something you saw or heard that didn't feel right.'

'There's nothing,' Chloe said.

Meadows gave Edris a nod.

'We will need both of you to give us you whereabouts on the morning of Huw Jones' murder and the evening of the murder of Bryn Thomas,' Edris said. 'It's so that we can eliminate you from our enquiries.' He gave them the dates and times.

Chloe huffed. 'This is ridiculous. I've already told you where I was last Tuesday morning. As for the Saturday, I would have been here in bed. It's a working farm so we all go to bed early.'

'Anna?'

'Tuesday morning, I would have been getting the boys ready for school. Erm… Saturday night, I was home, with my family.'

'We will also need to take any of your devices that connect to the internet,' Edris said. 'It's just for examination. We won't keep them long.'

'I hope you don't want the kids' tablets,' Chloe said.

'I'm sorry. All devices need to be examined.'

'And if I say no?' Chloe asked.

'It would be the quickest and easiest way to eliminate you both,' Meadows said. 'I appreciate it's an inconvenience, but us having a search warrant would be a lot more intrusive and disruptive.'

Chloe's eyes narrowed. 'You're treating us like suspects.'

'We've had to examine the devices from the families of the other victims,' Meadows said. 'I assure you that you haven't been singled out.'

'Just give them what they need,' Anna said. 'They have a job to do.'

'Fine,' Chloe said.

'Anna,' Meadows said, 'could you go with Detective Edris to collect the devices from your home, please?'

'Now?'

Meadows nodded.

'I'll be back as soon as I can,' Anna said.

Meadows went with them to the car to collect evidence bags. When he returned to the house, he could hear protests from the children. He stepped into the sitting room. A boy of around six years old was holding tightly to his tablet and crying. His sister was sitting on the sofa with her hands behind her back.

'Gracie, give me the phone,' Chloe said.

'No!'

'I'm sorry but we have to take them,' Meadows said. 'I'll get them back to you as soon as I can.'

The children eyed Meadows warily

'Fine.' Gracie handed her phone to Chloe.

Chloe took the tablet from her son then stomped back into the kitchen. Meadows followed.

'Are you happy now?' Chloe asked.

There was nothing Meadows could say. He opened an evidence bag and Chloe dropped the phone in. He labelled the bag then repeated the procedure until all the devices were accounted for.

'We are going to need your husband's phone.'

'Good luck with that,' Chloe said. 'I can't ring him as you've taken mine and he could be anywhere on the farm.'

'No problem,' Meadows said. 'I'll send someone to collect it.'

Chloe opened a cupboard door and took out a saucepan. 'I need to start making food.'

'That's fine. As soon as Detective Edris gets back, I'll be on my way. Is there anything else you can tell me about your father while we wait?'

'No,' Chloe said. She took a knife from the block.

The smell of onions filled the kitchen as Chloe chopped. She forced the knife down, so it banged against the board.

'Did your father socialise with Huw Jones?'

'Dunno,' Chloe said. She kept her back turned.

'It sounds like he'd known him for a number of years. Did you ever see Huw around the farm when you lived at home?'

'Not that I remember.'

'What about people your father employed? I imagine there would be quite a few given the original size of the farm.'

'Yeah, they came and went.'

'Anyone in particular that you remember working there for a long time?'

'No.'

It was clear to Meadows that Chloe wasn't going to give him any information. He sat quietly until he heard a car pull up.

'Looks like they are back,' he said.

'You can see yourself out,' Chloe said.

Meadows stood up. 'I'll get the devices back to you as soon as I can.'

Meadows stepped out of the house and felt the cold air sting his face. The yard was lit up by outdoor lights, and Anna and Edris were walking towards him. Even under the artificial light, he could see Anna's paleness. Her arms were wrapped around her body, and it looked like every step was an effort.

'Thank you for your cooperation,' Meadows said.

Anna nodded. 'You'll have to excuse Chloe. She tells it how it is, always has.'

'She seems angry,' Meadows said.

Anna gave him a weak smile. 'Anger is her default mode.' She walked past him and into the house.

* * *

'Chloe didn't seem bothered about her father's murder,' Edris said as soon as they were back in the car. 'Probably been expecting the news.'

'You think she killed him?' Meadows asked.

'Yeah. She knew where the gun was kept. With her father and Huw out of the way, she'll have no problems getting her holiday park up and running.'

'You could be right, then again, the blogger strikes me as someone who is struggling to control their emotions. I didn't see any signs of anxiety. Anna was the one struggling to hold it together.'

'Yeah, but that's probably from shock,' said Edris. 'Chloe would've had time to prepare for our visit.'

'If we're going to go by reaction, then Lesley, Luke, and Sarah acted in a similar way to Chloe when we gave them news of Huw's death.'

'Yeah, I guess, but Malcom's death was unplanned. It was the start of it. It has to be one of the sisters,' Edris said.

Meadows nodded. 'They're involved somehow. Something went on in that house. Did you see Chloe's face when I asked about an incident at the house?'

'Yeah. She definitely knows something.'

'Question is,' said Meadows, 'was it something so traumatic she killed her own father? If not, then who is she protecting?'

Chapter Eighteen

Chloe was furious. She could feel the adrenalin running through her body but, with no outlet, it turned on itself. Her stomach cramped and her skin tingled. She wanted to break something. She gripped the saucepan handle, and it took all her control not to hurl it across the room. She heard Anna come in and the chair scraping back as she sat down. She could sense her sister staring at her. When she could stand it no longer, she turned around.

'Chloe, what have you done?' Anna shook her head.

'Really? You are going to sit there and accuse me? You think I blew our father's brains out?'

Anna's eyes narrowed in suspicion. 'The police didn't say he had been shot in the head.'

'Think what the fuck you like,' Chloe said. 'Just go home.'

'No. We have to talk about it. Don't you even care?'

'Why should I? The old bastard is dead and he's still causing trouble.'

'Well, at least try and act like you care. Maybe we should go to the house.'

'Are you out of your mind? It's going to be crawling with police. I doubt they will let us near the place.'

'Maybe not, but they might tell us something. It might not even be him,' Anna said.

Chloe couldn't believe how stupid her sister could be. 'Well, it's not going to be anyone else. No one goes there. We just need to let them get on with it. There's nothing else for us to do.'

'We can't just sit here and pretend everything is normal.'

'I'm not going to pretend. I don't know why you're getting so upset.'

'He was our father.'

'Yeah, and that should mean something, but it doesn't. What did he ever do for us, except cause misery? At least, you'll get the house. I suppose that's something.'

'I don't want the bloody house,' Anna said.

'Then sell it.'

'Nobody is going to buy a house that someone was murdered in.'

'Fine. I'll have it.'

'You've already got your half of the land. You bullied him into giving to you.'

'Bullied him!' Chloe screeched. 'That man made my life hell. No amount of money could make up for what he did.'

Anna jumped up from the chair. 'What you said he did.'

Chloe clenched her fists. She could feel her nails digging into the palms of her hands. She wanted to grab Anna and shake some sense into her. Her chest was heaving, and her breath came out in short burst. 'You were too young to remember, or maybe you've just chosen to forget.'

'Mum, what's going on? Why are you shouting?'

Chloe looked away from Anna and saw her daughter standing at the kitchen door.

'Nothing is wrong. I'm just talking to Auntie Anna. Go and watch some TV or something. Dinner won't be long.'

'I'll come in and see you before I go,' Anna said.

Gracie huffed and left the kitchen.

A loud hissing came from the cooker behind her. Chloe turned to see that water had boiled over the top of the saucepan. She cursed and grabbed the handle to move it.

'I need to get on,' Chloe said.

'I'll give you a hand.'

Chloe wished her sister would just leave. She didn't want to talk anymore. It would only lead them to the past, and she was afraid of what she would say. What if Anna didn't remember? She didn't really want to put that on her. Then there was the other thing. Anna had nightmares for months after.

'What are you going to tell the kids?' Anna asked. She opened a cupboard and pulled out some plates.

'I've told them their grandfather has been hurt. They didn't ask for details.'

'Maybe I should bring the boys up. We can sit them down together to tell them he's dead.'

'What for? I doubt they'd even notice he's gone.'

Anna set the plates down with a clatter. 'It's their grandfather.'

'You can put on a show if you want, but I'm not going to upset the kids. When was the last time you took the boys to see him?'

Anna looked away.

'You didn't bother because you know that...'

'What do I know? Just because Luke—'

'Don't you dare. You know nothing about it,' Chloe hissed. She could feel the shame returning. It burned her face and made her stomach feel like it was filled with worms. 'You can't go mentioning his name. As far as the police are concerned, we don't know him.'

'What about his mother; Lesley, isn't it? You said you saw her at the farm. That I do remember.'

'Lesley won't say anything. She'll protect Luke.'

Chloe's mind slipped back to that day. Her father and Lesley were in the kitchen. They didn't know she was at the door listening. She suddenly felt sick. She grabbed a glass of water and drank it slowly.

'Chloe?' Anna stepped closer.

Chloe snapped out of her memory. 'What?'

'I said, what are we going to do now?'

'Nothing. We just carry on as normal until the police have confirmed his identity.'

'People will already be talking. They will want to come and pay their respects. You are going to have to appear upset.'

Chloe huffed and leaned against the worktop. 'Yeah, you're right. If we don't say anything, they are going to wonder why. Then they will start talking and we don't want that. Keep them focused on the murder itself, that will give them plenty to talk about. We will need to listen out for gossip. You can keep an eye on Facebook; I haven't time for that. I suppose we're going to have to give him a decent send-off. I'd rather put him on the compost heap but we better act like grieving daughters. Put on a generous spread after. That way, we can control things; listen to what's being said.'

Anna shook her head. 'We should keep things simple. Family only or we could say he wanted one of those cremation-only things. They are popular now. I don't think I can face a lot of people. Especially if you're going to…'

Chloe's anger ignited. 'If I'm going to what?'

'Mouth off like you usually do. I don't want to be worrying about what you'll say if you have a few drinks.'

Chloe laughed bitterly. 'Afraid I'm going to incriminate myself?'

'It's not funny.'

'Isn't it? You think I killed him.'

'I didn't say that.'

'You didn't have to. Look, as much as I like the idea of sending him off on his own in a box, it's not going to look good on me.'

'Is that all you care about?' Anna asked.

'Yes. I could lose everything. I need the support of the community. Actually, this could work in my favour. No one is going to block the access application after this. They would look like right dicks. The holiday park will be buzzing. You know how people like all that true-crime stuff. Morbid curiosity. They will be staying next door to where a murder took place.'

'You're sick,' Anna said.

'Yeah, and ask yourself why.'

'You need help. Maybe you should get some therapy.'

Chloe shook her head. 'I'm not having everyone talking about me.'

'That's not how it works. It's confidential. I've been.'

Chloe felt a mixture of surprise and hurt. She didn't like the idea that Anna would choose to confide in a complete stranger over her own sister. Then, another thought struck her: what had she told the therapist?

'You never told me.' Chloe heard the edge in her own voice.

'That's the point. It's confidential. A safe place for you to talk without any judgment.'

'I don't want to talk about it,' Chloe said. She didn't add that she was too ashamed. 'I think we should find that blog. People leave comments on those things. I want to see what's being said.'

Anna looked horrified. 'I'm not going to look. I don't want to read the details. It makes me sick just thinking about it.'

'We have to look,' Chloe said. 'So far, the police haven't linked Dad to Bryn Thomas.'

She watched Anna to see her reaction to the name. There was nothing. She knew she'd have to be careful what she said next.

Anna opened a drawer and started plucking out knives and forks. 'I don't know who Bryn Thomas is. What has he got to do with Dad?'

Chloe felt her stomach twist. She was going to have to jog her memory. She had no choice. It would bring it all back. 'He's Teilo's father. You remember Teilo?'

Anna's hands stopped moving and she looked confused for a moment. Then her faced paled. 'Teilo… Aneria. Oh, God. What if he… you said that Dad…'

'Now you get it,' Chloe said. 'Teilo might talk.'

Chapter Nineteen

The police have finally found him. I guess I should feel some sense of relief, but I don't. There's still a long way to go before I can rest. There is plenty of talk and speculation, yet no one has come forward to tell the police what he did. It says something about a person when they are left to rot in a field, and no one notices they're missing. If I hadn't led the police there, he would have laid in that field until he was reduced to bones. Even they would have been carried away and eaten by wild animals. Wiped from the face of the earth without a trace. If only it was that simple.

I so wish I could do that to my memories; wash them away so nothing remains. The problem with that is you take away the good memories. Even if they are only few, it's all I have. When I no longer exist, other people's memories will still be out there. They'll live with them daily, sneaking up when they least expect it, creeping in to contaminate their lives. It's like a permanent stain you can't remove.

The stain of shame that you think others can see. Now is the time to speak up.

I've read so many of your stories. It's soul-destroying. I can never understand the pain people inflict on those who cannot fight back. I was never brave enough to speak up. I buried all the horrors so deep, it damaged me from within. A rot I didn't know was there. It ate away slowly at me. Now the lid has been opened, I can't shut it. My only consolation is that I can do for others what they can't do for themselves. Tip the balance and show those monsters that, no matter how much time has passed, the debt has to be paid.

I hope the police's latest news will bring peace to some of you. Yes, it will stir up traumatic memories, but you can be free now. The stain was never on you. It was his shame! You can speak up, shout, and scream. Let it out and let it go.

It's too late for me. Now the only thing that keeps me going is to see the end. I'm so close. Any one of them could have stopped it. The abandoner, the abuser, the one who stayed silent, the one who turned their back, and the child killer. Their cowardly actions I can never forgive.

The little stick dolls stare accusingly at me. The memories play on loop. All the while, I nod and smile. I pretend I'm OK. That's what we all do, put on a show, a face for the outside world. It's only a thin veil that keeps the animal in us from lashing out. I hate what I have become, what I've needed to do to try and numb the pain. I am shrouded in a darkness so thick, I can't see a way out. I just have to hold on a little longer. Everything is set.

Chapter Twenty

Meadows finished reading the latest blog post and sat back in his chair. The office was silent as all eyes were on screens reading the same thing. He knew time was running out for the next victim. The team were working flat out, running on adrenalin and a desperate need to catch the killer. He read over the words again, looking for any clues as to the identity of the killer. There was nothing. He moved out of his chair and stood by the incident board. The rest of the team moved their chairs and gathered around.

'Thoughts?' Meadows asked.

'Other than put out a warning to anyone involved with the victims, I don't see what we can do to prevent another killing,' Valentine said.

'Problem is, they are not going to make themselves known,' Blackwell said.

'I thought Chris was getting the blog taken down,' Edris said.

'He did,' Paskin said. 'It's a new blog which has spread through social media. The followers appear to be taking the killer's side. I'm keeping a watch on the comments. The killer doesn't respond to any. Not even the ones our phycologist adviser wrote.'

'It was worth a try,' Meadows said. 'At least, one good thing has come from the latest blog post. We now know the motive. The abandoner, the abuser, the one who stayed silent, the one who turned their back, and the child killer.'

'Do you think they apply to the victims in order?' Edris asked.

'That would make Malcom the abandoner,' Blackwell said. 'Huw the abuser, and Bryn the one that stayed silent.'

'Isn't staying silent and turning their back the same thing?' Paskin asked.

'Depends,' Valentine said. 'Maybe the silent one only knew about it. Whereas the one that turned their back was present but didn't take part or step in to help.'

'Yeah, but what is the "it" they are staying quiet about?' Blackwell asked.

'It's obvious: a child has died,' Edris said.

'None of the victims had a record,' Paskin said.

'Then we look at unsolved cases,' Meadows said. 'Start local and expand the search.'

'What about a cover-up?' Valentine suggested. 'Could look like an accident or even illness when it wasn't.'

'And how are we supposed to find a child that supposedly died by accident and didn't?' Blackwell asked.

'Well, the child would have a connection to the victims,' Valentine said.

'What about if someone was pregnant, hid it, then got rid of the baby when they were born?' Paskin asked. 'That would be abandonment, silence, a killer, and probably an abuser. The killer talks about how speaking up "brings peace for some of you" and the fact that "it was his shame."'

Meadows shook his head. 'Look at the language used by the blogger. Child killer implies an older child, not a baby. Then there's the trigger for the memory. Being pregnant and losing that child is not something the mother is likely to have forgotten. There were a lot of stick dolls surrounding Malcom Isaac. They all had blue wool. It could well be that he was abusing young boys.'

'So Malcom is the abuser,' Edris said.

Meadows nodded. 'Perhaps along with Huw and Bryn.'

They were all silent for a few moments as they digested the idea.

'That would mean they killed a boy and somehow covered it up,' Edris said.

'Not impossible,' Meadows said. 'Perhaps he threatened to tell. I think our best option is to concentrate on the death of minors in the area. In the second blog post, the killer mentioned avoiding Dinefwr Castle. See if there were any accidental deaths in that location. I still think it's worth bearing in mind the concealed pregnancy theory. It could be that the killer witnessed something like that.' He turned to look at the board. 'Where are we with Malcom's family and acquaintances?'

'His ex-wife has been on holiday for the past twelve days so we can rule her out,' Blackwell said. 'She's still travelling around so I haven't been able to make contact with her. I'll keep trying.'

'Still tracing anyone that worked on the farm,' Paskin said. 'Nothing found on the devices taken from the family members. Even Chloe's husband, Jac, handed over his phone. Nothing found on the Teilo's or the Joneses' devices either.'

'A few people came forward to say they had left laptops with Bryn or had picked them up,' Blackwell said. 'We know of three devices that are missing but there could be more.'

'We've got the one found in Malcom's house,' Meadows said. 'It appears our killer is using the laptops to write the blogs and upload them. Using different devices from various locations makes it all difficult to trace. They also needed a spare to lead us to Malcom.'

Blackwell nodded. 'One woman did say that she had gone into Bryn's house and had a cup of tea with him while waiting for software to download. It was the Thursday before Bryn's murder. She agreed to give fingerprints to compare to the ones found on the mug.'

'So, he did entertain clients,' Edris said. 'That lipstick could have come from anyone.'

Blackwell huffed. 'All we're left with is the purple wool found on the bolt.'

'And the sighting of someone running from the park,' Paskin said. 'Which may or may not have been a woman.'

'We still have Rhoda Williams, Bryn's sister, to interview,' Edris said.

'Yeah when the doctor says she's fit enough,' Blackwell said.

'Teilo's client came forward,' Valentine said. 'They confirmed that they had an appointment at 8 a.m. the morning of Huw Jones' murder. They cancelled because of a flat tyre.'

'Teilo wouldn't have been able to predict that,' Edris said. 'There wouldn't have been enough time for him to murder Huw and get home for a client.'

Meadows nodded. 'It would be tight. We know Malcom and Huw knew each other. We need to establish a connection to Bryn. All three men didn't have a good relationship with their children. Why?'

'Teilo got on OK with his father,' Edris said. 'He was in a state.'

'Yes, but he only formed a relationship with Bryn later in life. His father sent him to live with his auntie.'

'There's the abandoner,' Blackwell said.

Meadows nodded. 'Now we have to work out what the other two are guilty of and who else is in the picture. This started with Malcom. We need to concentrate our efforts there. Every relative, every contact. I'm also interested to see where his money came from and how he managed to acquire so much land. Check out the neighbours. I want to know the background of every family.' He glanced at the board again and a thought struck him.

'Chloe's farm.' He pointed. 'She said the house was derelict when her father gave her the land. Paskin, see if you can find out who owned the property before Malcom. These farms are usually passed down. Why was this place abandoned?

'We also have the old photographs found in Bryn's fire. We still need to identify two of the people. What if the other victims had photographs? These would be old. The type that would be put up in the attic. Once forensics have finished in Malcom's house, we need to go there and search it. We'll go and see Lesley at the same time, see if Huw had any photos stashed away. I'll give forensics a couple of hours then chase them up. Meanwhile let's see what we can turn up on Malcom.

'I know how tired you all are, and I appreciate the work you've put in. I've got the sub team coming in the morning so you can all take a well-deserved break.'

'What about you?' Edris asked.

'I'm fine. OK. Let's get to it.'

They all moved back to their desks and the office became a hive of activity. Phone calls were made, old records checked, statements cross-referenced, and forensic reports re-read. Meadows had just got off the phone when DCI Lester walked in.

'I've organised a meeting with the local community and press on Saturday afternoon. Do we have anything promising to give them?'

Meadows wished he did. He filled Lester in on their progress.

'I'll just go with the usual "We are following several lines of enquiry" then,' Lester said. 'Now, all of you, go home and get some rest. That includes you.' He looked at Meadows.

'As soon as I've spoken with Mike Fielding,' Meadows said. He grabbed his jacket and left the office with Edris. He didn't want to take time off. Not when there was a threat of more victims.

* * *

Meadows could see the exhaustion on the forensic team's faces as he followed Mike Fielding through the office. The sheer volume of evidence from three crime scenes and the rising panic in their local community was taking its toll.

'I do appreciate all the extra time you and the team are putting in,' Meadows said.

'If it can help catch this lunatic then it'll be worth it.' Mike stopped outside a door and scanned his card. The door bleeped and they all stepped inside.

Meadows looked around. There were people working at various stations. Most of them were dressed in protective clothing, with some wearing gloves and goggles as they handled vials. There was an underlying hum from the machinery and the lights were bright. They entered through another door, which led into Mike's office.

'OK, let's start with the gun.' Mike hit the keyboard and the screen came to life. 'This is the shotgun recovered from the scene. We've tested it and it was the weapon used to shoot Malcom Isaac. We're working on tracing the origin of the weapon. It's old, not valuable. We know Malcom kept a shotgun on the property. No other weapon was found, and it matches the description given by his daughter. I think it is safe to assume it was Malcom Isaac's shotgun. It's been wiped so there's no prints.'

'I expected as much,' Meadows said.

Mike tapped the keyboard again and a picture of a wheelbarrow appeared. There were also close-up shots of blood and other matter. 'This was used to transport him from the house into the trailer.'

'It would have taken some strength to get him into a wheelbarrow alone,' Meadows said. He tried to picture the scenario, but nothing worked in his mind. 'You wouldn't be able to lean over the front of the wheelbarrow and drag him in. If you tried from the side, it would tip over. That only leaves the option of lifting him up and dumping him.'

'I think I may have the answer for you,' Mike said. 'From close analysis of the carpet and chair, it appears the killer dragged him into the chair then tipped him in. It's one of those chairs with a mechanism that lifts, to make it easier to get to a standing position. It would still take a huge effort but it's doable for one determined person. If you look at the photos of the trailer, you can see he was dragged in.'

Meadows looked at a series of photos. They all backed up Mike's theory. 'I did notice a smell of bleach when I was at the scene. I take it the house was cleaned.'

'Yes. All the door handles, kitchen tops, and sink were thoroughly cleaned. The sitting-room carpet, and upstairs bedroom have been hoovered. I imagine this was done by the killer as the other rooms don't look like they have been cleaned in years.'

'What about under the bed? The blogger describes crawling to retrieve the gun.'

'There as well. They did a thorough job. Don't give up hope just yet. It's a large, carpeted area so a lot of testing still needs to be done. You'd be surprised what lurks among the pile of carpet.'

'Did you come across any old photographs while you were there?'

'Can't say I saw any personally, but we were only sweeping the place for devices and anything we could extract DNA from.'

'I want to take Malcom's daughters to the house and go through any paperwork and photographs he might have stashed away. See their reactions.'

'Give us another day.'

'That's fine,' Meadows said. 'I was thinking of waiting until after the meeting Lester has arranged.'

'I heard about that. I wouldn't like to be the one facing the community and press.'

'No, I don't envy him. Can you give us a heads-up when you've finished in Malcom's house? I need to make sure Chloe, Anna, or anyone else don't have the opportunity to go in and remove any evidence.'

'No problem,' Mike said.

Meadows' phone trilled and he took it from his pocket. He saw Paskin's name on the screen. He hit accept and put it on speakerphone.

'I thought you'd gone home,' Meadows said.

'Yeah, I was about to,' Paskin said. 'I've just got off the phone with the Land Registry. Chloe's farm was originally owned by Bryn Thomas until 1992. Before that, it was owned by his father. It was sold to Malcom Isaac with the stipulation that the land could only be used for farming. Apparently, such clauses are not unusual.'

'That gives Chloe motive for all three killings,' Edris said.

Meadows frowned. 'If it wasn't for the blog, she'd be our prime suspect. What I'd like to know is how Malcom persuaded Bryn to give up the family farm.'

* * *

Meadows felt relieved to be walking through the door of his cottage. The heating was on, and he could smell something cooking in the oven. Even better was the fact that Daisy's car had been parked outside.

'You look as tired as I feel,' Daisy said when he entered the kitchen.

Meadows kissed her and pulled her close. It was a nice feeling to have someone to come home to. 'Lester has insisted I have the day off tomorrow.'

'Good,' Daisy said. 'You need to rest and clear your mind.'

'Shame you've got to work,' he said.

'I've just come back from a break. You hungry?' she asked.

'Not really.'

'There's a vegetable casserole in the oven. I picked it up from your mum's on the way home. She spoils us.'

'She enjoys cooking. I guess you couldn't persuade her to come and stay with us.'

'No. To stop you worrying, she's going to stay at the commune for a few days with Rain. She said she can help him out with the wedding preparations. It sounds like your brother is in his element.'

'Yeah, he would be. I'm glad she's gone to stay with him. It's not that I think she's in any danger, it's just…'

'I know. You'll catch them soon. I have every faith in you.' She kissed him again before pulling away.

Meadows smiled. 'I'm glad you do because so far we have nothing.'

'I'm afraid I can't help you there. I got nothing helpful from the post-mortem. Cause of death was a gunshot wound. It wouldn't have taken him long to die. You know he was moved after death. As for time, we're looking at around three weeks, plus or minus a few days. I printed the report for you.'

'The killer wrote about the murder on the 15th of February. It could have been the same day or a few days after. It's not going to help us place the killer at the scene.'

'As you don't have work tomorrow, I think you should go to the shed for a special smoke. Take the report with you. I'm going to have a couple of glasses of wine and put my feet up. With a bit of luck, you'll get your appetite back. You need to eat.' Daisy took a corkscrew from the drawer. 'Maybe we can have an early night.'

'I like the sound of that,' Meadows said. 'I'll go and get changed.'

After a quick shower, he put on some comfortable clothing and went outside to the shed. Daisy had already been out and turned on the gas fire.

He took a seat in the old armchair and slid his hand down the side of the cushion to retrieve a tin. He plucked off the lid and inhaled the aroma of cannabis. It was on rare occasions that he indulged but tonight he felt like he needed it. He rolled a joint, lit it, and inhaled. It took a few moments before it took effect. He felt his shoulders relax. The tension in his neck evaporated and his arms and legs became heavy. He picked up the post-mortem report and started reading. Daisy was right, there wasn't anything useful.

He took the last drag of the joint and put it out in the ashtray. His eyes were heavy now, so he closed them and thought about the case. This all started with a drawing of a stick figure. A child's drawing. He thought about the children of the victims. Chloe was angry but she wasn't stupid. Why write a blog that could implicate herself and her sister in the murders? Luke was another angry one, a troubled teenager and drug addict. All of which pointed to a childhood trauma. Sarah and Anna, the younger siblings and the quieter ones. Then there was Teilo, traumatised by finding his father. Was there a previous tragedy in his life?

Five stick dolls left. The next victims already chosen. These were the people that could stop the killer, but they were unlikely to come forward. He was drifting into sleep. He was in a field surrounded by stick dolls, some with skirts and others with blue wool. Blood ran from their eyes. All had faces, except one, which was covered.

A hand on his shoulder made him jump.

'Are you going to come in and have something to eat?' Daisy asked.

'Yeah.' Meadows stood up and stretched. There was something about the dream that felt important. He tried to grasp it, but the details were dispersing like wisps of smoke. It's the children, he thought.

'I need to speak to Lester.'

'You need to eat and sleep,' Daisy said. 'It can wait until the morning.'

It felt like he had only just shut his eyes when the alarm went off. Daisy got up and he tried to fall back asleep, but his mind was already whirring. He got up, showered, dressed and headed downstairs.

'What are you doing up?' Daisy asked.

'I'm going to see Lester.'

Daisy raised her eyebrows. 'It's supposed to be your day off.'

'I won't be long. I think it might be the children of the victims that are connected. I want to get them in a room together and see how they react. Then I'll pop into the office. The sub team are going to Chloe's with a search warrant. They need to check there are no devices hidden on the farm and I need to make sure they cover Malcom's property. That's it, I promise.' He grabbed his car keys and headed out.

It was another chilly morning and daybreak hadn't yet chased away the dark. As he neared his car, he could see something on the windscreen. At first, he thought it was a fallen branch. Then a coldness crept over him as he realised it was a stick doll held in place by the windscreen wiper. A piece of cloth was wrapped around the middle to make a skirt.

Meadows ran back into the house.

'What's wrong?' Daisy asked, seeing his shocked expression.

'You need to pack a case and go and stay with your father for a few days. There was a gift left on my car. Either it's a prank or the killer has chosen their next victim.'

Chapter Twenty-one

Dawn Gibson stepped through her front door and set down her suitcase. It had been a shock coming back to the Welsh winter weather after spending ten days, all-inclusive, in Sharm El Sheikh. She wished she had packed a warmer coat to wear when she had come out of the airport. Her husband, Simon, came in behind her and shut the door.

'Put the kettle on, love,' Simon said. 'I'm gasping for a cuppa. I'll take the cases up.'

Dawn switched the lights on in the sitting room before walking into the kitchen. She didn't take off her coat. The heating had been set to come on low to stop the pipes from freezing and it only just took the chill out of the air. She turned up the temperature and filled the kettle.

It was quiet in the house and after spending the holiday in the company of friends, the silence felt odd. She grabbed the remote control from the kitchen counter and hit the on button. The wall-mounted television sprung to life. She wasn't bothered about the channel, she just wanted background noise. While she waited for the kettle to boil, she rooted around in the freezer for something quick to make for dinner. It was approaching six, almost an hour past their usual dinner time. She found a lasagna and put it in the microwave to defrost.

Simon came into the kitchen, and she handed him a mug of tea.

'Nice to be home,' he said, and plonked himself down in the chair by the table.

'Yeah, but it was a lovely holiday.' Dawn picked up her own mug just as the evening news came on.

'Police have named the latest victim of the so-called "Stickman Killer" as Malcom Isaac,' the newsreader announced.

The mug slipped from Dawn's hand and crashed to the floor. Hot liquid splashed her legs, but she didn't move. Her eyes swivelled to the screen where a picture of Malcom was being shown.

'What's wrong?' Simon asked as he jumped out of the chair.

Dawn turned to look at her husband. His face was creased with concern. She quickly pulled herself together.

'Oh, I don't know. It just slipped from my hand. I guess I must be tired from the travelling.'

'It's only a cup, love,' Simon said. 'Don't look so worried.'

Dawn wanted to turn back to the television and listen to the rest of the news, but she didn't dare with Simon in the room. She grabbed a wad of kitchen towel, mopped up the tea, and swept up the broken mug. She then busied herself making food before settling at the table. Simon opened a bottle of wine and poured her a large glass. She tried not to gulp it down. The shock of hearing Malcom's name hadn't worn off. She tried to keep up a normal conversation but inside she was counting down the time until she would be able to google the news.

Simon put down his knife and fork. 'That was lovely, thanks.'

'Why don't you go chill for a while,' Dawn said. 'I'll clear up.'

'Nah, come on, we'll do it together.'

Once the washing-up was finished, Simon carried the bottle of wine through to the sitting room and settled on the sofa.

'I think I'll go up, unpack then have a bath,' she said.

Simon nodded and switched on the television. Upstairs, Dawn quickly unpacked and went into the bathroom, where she knew she wouldn't be disturbed. As the bath filled, she scrolled through the articles online. There wasn't much more about Malcom other than naming him as another victim. As she read further down, she saw a name that made her blood freeze. She became dizzy and clung on to the bathroom sink. Panic snaked around her body and squeezed until she felt like there was no oxygen in the room. She wanted to shout out to Simon, but she was paralysed. The phone fell to the floor with a thud. With a shaking hand, she turned on the cold-water tap. She splashed the water over her face then stared at the running water, willing herself to breathe. Cupping a handful of water, she splashed it over her head. Gradually, her breathing returned to normal.

After a few moments, she picked the phone up then turned off the bath taps. She sprinkled a few drops of lavender into the warm water and inhaled. It always worked and she felt calm enough to look at the phone again.

The other two victims were named as Bryn Thomas and Huw Jones. She had a vague memory of Huw but it was Bryn's name that had caused the panic. The name that drove fear into her heart like shards of glass. She'd never wanted to hear that name again. She read the rest of the article and looked for more information. There wasn't a lot. Only that the murders had been gruesome, and the killer had written about them. She didn't want to search for the blog. What she needed was someone with information.

She jumped into the bath and quickly washed herself. There was no way she could relax now but she needed Simon to think that everything was alright. She had to look like she had been soaking in the water. She dipped her head under to wet her hair then got out. She tried to block out the images that flashed through her mind: the farmhouse, the taste of blood in her mouth, and the shouting. She shook her head. She couldn't go there now. There was only one person she could call, and it was the last person she wanted to talk to. It had been years. She didn't even know if the phone number would work.

Dawn left the bathroom and crept to the top of the stairs. She could hear the television. Simon would have finished the bottle of wine and would likely have fallen asleep. She moved into the bedroom and closed the door gently before sitting on the bed. She scrolled through her contacts and found the one she was looking for. She'd only kept it for one reason. She pressed call and waited. With each ring of the phone, her legs jiggled up and down with nerves. She was about to change her mind and hang up when the call was answered.

'I wondered when you would call.'

'Hello, Pat,' Dawn said. 'It's been a while.'

Pat laughed. 'A while?'

'Time has just gone. The years have flown by.'

'Yeah, it must be fifteen years or more since you last needed my help.'

Dawn felt a stab of anger. 'You could have called me.'

As soon as the words were out of her mouth, she regretted it. She needed information and Pat was the type of person that would withhold it for spite.

She softened her tone. 'How have you been?'

'Good,' Pat said.

'I expect you are retired now.'

'For a few years now. I took early retirement. Never been happier.'

'That's good to hear,' Dawn said.

'I thought I'd be bored after working all my life but it's quite the opposite. People always calling around. Going on outings. I seem to be in constant demand. I'm even being interviewed.'

'Interviewed?' Dawn didn't like the sound of that.

'Yes. I'm being featured in an article about the old school and the community.'

Relief washed over Dawn. She had assumed it was about the murders. 'Oh, that sounds interesting.'

'It is. The article will centre around my life and the changes I've seen over the years. The journalist said that being a prominent figure in the community...'

Dawn zoned out. Pat liked to boast, and she really wasn't interested. She waited for a gap, then jumped in. 'I'm so pleased for you.'

'So how are things with you? Still on your own?' Pat asked.

'Yes.'

'Well, you always wanted a quiet life,' Pat said.

Dawn was done with the small talk. She needed to move the conversation on. She didn't care what Pat thought about her life. She would never let her know about Simon and the life she had built. That life could so easily be taken away. She needed to be strong now, to find out what Pat knew.

'I've seen the news,' Dawn said.

'Shocking, isn't it? It was bad enough when Huw was killed. You'd never think that something like that can happen here. It's not like I knew him well. Do you remember him?'

'I don't think so,' Dawn said.

'Luke Jones' father. Then when Bryn... I'm still in shock.'

Dawn felt her heart thudding in her chest. 'Were you still in contact with him?'

'I saw him now and again,' Pat said.

'What about Teilo? Have you seen him?'

'No. I suppose I should drop a card off or something. So sad. Lost his mother and now his father taken like that. Of course, we can't forget—'

'Don't,' Dawn cut in. She knew what Pat was going to say. She may as well stab her through the heart. She imagined Pat was smirking on the other end of the phone. 'I can't talk about that.'

'Alright, but it makes you wonder. There's been talk.'

'What about?'

'The killer has been blogging.'

'Yeah, I did read about it. Have you seen it?'

'No,' Pat said. 'I wouldn't know where to look. There's been mention of it on Facebook, but my friends aren't the type of people that would share the link or read it themselves. I'm not sure I'd want to read it. Apparently, it goes into graphic details and is very disturbing. All of them died a horrible death.'

'Are people talking about why they were killed?'

'All sorts of theories,' Pat said.

She's not going to volunteer the information, Dawn thought. She'll drag it out like some sort of power game. She decided she wasn't going to play. 'There is nothing in the news about a motive,' she said. 'I guess the police don't know.'

'Well, they're not going to let the public know their theories,' Pat said. 'I have my suspicions.'

'I'm sure you do.'

Pat was quiet for a few moments. Dawn waited. She knew Pat was trying to decide whether to share or not.

'You remember what I told you about Luke Jones?' Pat said eventually.

Dawn remembered the tearful conversation all those years ago. It was the first and only time she had witnessed

Pat lose her confidence. She had been the only one Pat could talk to. While she had kept up a pretence to all those around her, Dawn had known the real reason for Pat's distress. Dawn hadn't been in a good place herself at the time, and it had been a shock. They never spoke of it again.

'Do you think now that Luke was telling the truth about Malcom?' Dawn asked. The thought made her feel sick.

'I didn't back then, obviously. Now I'm not so sure.'

'Do you think he'd kill Malcom?'

'He was violent as a teenager and from what I hear he's still using drugs.'

'Why kill his own father and…' Dawn couldn't bring herself to say his name.

'And Bryn. Don't know, but Huw and Malcom were friends. I've heard they spent a lot of time together. Malcom was there when–'

'Yes, I know,' Dawn cut in. 'I doubt it has anything to do with the murders.'

'No,' Pat agreed. 'But if Luke was telling the truth… Still, I can't believe Bryn would be involved in anything like that, could you?'

Dawn didn't want to say what she thought. 'Have you spoken to the police?'

'Not yet.'

Dawn didn't like the "yet"; it felt like a veiled threat. 'I suppose if you do talk to the police, they are going to wonder why you didn't speak up before, why you kept it to yourself all these years.'

There was silence. Dawn wondered if she'd gone too far. She imagined Pat was seething. It didn't matter. She'd got her point across. She needed to keep herself safe.

Eventually Pat spoke. 'There's a meeting tomorrow evening.'

'What sort of meeting?' Dawn asked.

'It's for the community. The police are going to be there to answer any concerns. I'm going to go and see what they have to say. I expect there will be journalists and maybe cameras. Perhaps you'll see me on the news. If I feel I should talk to the police, then I will. It depends on what they say at the meeting.'

'I'll call you tomorrow to see how it goes,' Dawn said.

'I don't know how long it will go on for. I'll call you when I get back. How about a face-to-face call? It will be nice to see each other. I'll text you a link to the app I use.'

Seeing Pat was the last thing Dawn wanted to do but she needed more information. She didn't have a choice. 'That will be lovely,' she said. 'Speak to you tomorrow.'

Dawn ended the call and went downstairs to join Simon on the sofa.

'Everything OK, love?' Simon asked.

'Yes.' She snuggled up close to him. She could so easily lose all this. She just hoped Pat would keep her mouth shut.

Chapter Twenty-two

Chloe walked through the doors of the church hall and looked around. Chairs had been put out in rows facing a long table. Two arc lights had been placed either side and wires ran under the table, feeding electricity into the microphones. To the side, another two tables held stacks of forms.

Next to her, Anna stiffened. 'I can't do this.'

Chloe felt the same fear, but she wasn't going to show it to her sister. 'It will be OK. You don't have to say anything. Just sit there and look sad.'

'What if the journalists start asking questions?'

'Ignore them,' Chloe said. 'The police will answer any questions. We're just here to appeal for information.' That was the part that worried her. She didn't want anyone coming forward. 'Come on, we better see if we can find someone to tell us what we're doing. I don't know why they wanted us here so early. No one has arrived yet.'

'You sure you got the time right?' Anna asked.

'Yeah. Anyway, what does it matter? We're here now.'

Chloe walked to the front where a technician was testing the microphones. 'Are we supposed to sit down?'

'I don't know. I'm just here to set up.'

Chloe huffed. 'Where is everyone?'

'I expect they'll be here soon,' the technician said.

'Bloody rude,' Chloe said. 'They drag us here and they don't have the decency to meet us. We'll give them two minutes then we're leaving.'

The technician went back to fiddling with the wires.

On the left of the hall a door led into a side room. Meadows could be seen talking to another man with dark grey hair. Chloe turned her back on them.

'Who's that?' Anna asked.

'Another detective. He's the one that called around to ask me to come to this meeting. Chief Inspector Lester, I think he said his name was. He had someone else with him who asked a load of questions. I was tempted to tell them to piss off.'

'Chief Inspector? I got some woman,' Anna said. 'You're obviously more important.'

Or the suspect, Chloe thought.

'Why do you think they want us at Dad's house in the morning?' Anna asked.

'How would I know?' Chloe snapped.

'What aren't you telling me?'

'Nothing.'

'You didn't tell me about Dad blocking access to the holiday park or the stipulation on the land,' Anna said. 'I didn't know what I was supposed to say when the detective asked me yesterday. You could have warned me.'

'It was bloody Huw Jones that got Dad to change his mind about the access. As for the stipulation, I didn't know. There has to be a way around it. Maybe now Bryn Thomas is dead it won't matter.'

'Is that all you can think about?'

'Keep your voice down,' Chloe hissed. 'People are coming in.'

'If you're not careful, they're going to arrest you,' Anna said.

Chloe felt anger spike her veins. 'Why would they arrest me? Why don't you say what you are really thinking?'

Colour rose in Anna's cheeks. 'I'm just worried about you. You're so angry all the time.'

'I think you should be more worried about what they'll find in Dad's house.'

'What do you mean?' Anna asked.

'He always had his camera out. Liked to take photographs.' Chloe felt a sickness in her stomach. She tried to block the images forming in her mind. 'What if he took pictures of—'

'That's disgusting.'

'We need to go to Dad's house and make sure there isn't anything that would make them suspicious.'

'We can't. The police are still there.'

'They're not going to be there all night. We'll go after dark.'

'I'm not going in there,' Anna said.

'You have to. Oh, God.'

'What is it?'

'Look who's just walked through the door.'

* * *

Teilo followed a group into the hall. Most of them had been under the cover of umbrellas and were talking among themselves. So far, no one seemed to recognise him and

158

for that he was grateful. He didn't want sympathy. He knew people only meant well but it was difficult to keep up the pretence of being OK.

He felt Nerys take his hand and give it a squeeze. He was glad she was with him. It meant that she had less sleep before going on the night shift, but she had insisted on supporting him. The room was filling up and the chatter mixed into one loud hum.

'There's Detective Meadows,' Nerys said.

Teilo looked across the room and saw Meadows in conversation with another man. 'They look busy.'

'I expect they are nervous,' Nerys said. 'There's going to be a lot of questions asked.'

Teilo nodded and gazed around the room until his eyes came to rest on Chloe and Anna. As he stared at their faces, the years tumbled away until he was looking at two little girls playing in a field. He felt a wave of nostalgia wash over him, as long-forgotten memories stirred: hot summer days, arid ground, and the cooling water of the stream. He remembered the sounds and the smell of freshly cut hay, the whirring of the blades slicing through the stems. Without warning, an image flashed through his mind. He shook it away. He didn't want to think about that now.

'Are you OK?' Nerys asked.

'Yeah, it's just that I remember those two from when I was young.'

'Who are they?'

'Chloe and erm… Anna, I think. They are Malcom Isaac's daughters. They were mentioned on the news.'

'Oh yeah,' Nerys said. 'I read that he'd been dead for a few weeks. Awful for the two of them.'

'I should go and say something to them,' Teilo said.

He made his way to the front with Nerys. It helped to be moving and focusing on something other than the crowds that were filling the seats. Even though he couldn't make out individual conversations, he imagined what people were talking about. They would have spotted him by now, and were no doubt commenting on his loss and that he'd been the one to discover his father's body. The air seemed to be charged with a collective anxiety mixed with curiosity and a strange sense of excitement. From studying human nature, he knew how easily emotions could be transferred within a group. There was also the idea of being part of something they could tell their friends and family about. A feeling of being special. Teilo didn't want the attention. He didn't want to be singled out.

He was nearing Chloe when she saw him. The expression on her face changed instantly. It was only a fleeting look before she turned away, but Teilo was sure he'd seen fear in her eyes. She whispered something to Anna and moved away. He had almost reached Anna when Chloe turned back. She appeared alarmed that Anna hadn't moved. She stood still, seemingly unsure what to do.

'Hello, Anna,' Teilo said.

Anna turned to look at him and her eyes widened.

'I don't know if you remember me. I'm Teilo.'

'I erm…' Anna looked towards Chloe and back again.

'It's OK,' Teilo said. 'It's been a long time. I'm so sorry for your loss.'

'Oh… yes… erm… the police asked about… well, I didn't remember at the time. I'm sorry for your loss too.'

Teilo felt sorry for Anna. It was clear she was struggling. It was bad enough to be grieving, but to have that grief displayed in public took its toll. On top of that, the shock probably hadn't worn off.

'This is my wife, Nerys.'

Anna gave Nerys a weak smile. 'Nice to meet you.'

Chloe appeared at Anna's side, but she didn't look Teilo in the eyes.

'This is Teilo,' Anna said. 'Do you remember?'

'Should I?' Chloe asked.

Teilo was taken aback but given the circumstances, he guessed she had a lot on her mind.

Chloe seemed to pull herself together and she attempted a smile. 'Oh right, yeah of course. Sorry. It's just all this.' She waved her arms around.

'I understand,' Teilo said.

Chloe cleared her throat. 'Anna, I think we should take our seats. If you'll excuse us. I'm afraid I don't feel like making small talk. If we stay here, then no doubt people will take it as an invitation to chat to us.'

Teilo nodded. 'I think that's a good idea. Have you been told where to sit?'

Chloe shook her head and started to move away.

Nerys leaned in close to Teilo and whispered, 'She wasn't very friendly.'

'I suppose you can't blame her.'

'Yes, but she's not the only one that's suffering. She could have been nicer to you.'

'I'm sure she didn't mean to be rude.'

'I suppose we better sit down,' Nerys said.

'Let's wait a little longer,' he said. 'I don't want to be sitting in front any longer than I have to. You know I don't like crowds. This is worse, as everyone will be looking at me.'

Nerys laughed. 'Call yourself a therapist. You should be comfortable in any situation. Don't you know some magic tricks?'

'Yeah, but they don't seem to work for me. I guess I'm just a pussy.'

'No, you're not.' Nerys took his hand. 'You're the kindest and most compassionate man I know. You can do this.'

Teilo nodded. He tried to comfort himself with the fact that everyone sitting there would be feeling the same. I'll do it for the others, he thought. He saw Meadows moving around the room and his stomach clenched. The police had found out about the farm and he felt like a child caught out in a lie. He should have mentioned it, but it would have led to more questions and he wasn't ready to answer them yet.

'Come on, let's sit down.'

Chloe and Anna were seated at the far end of the table. The moment she saw Teilo approach, Chloe looked away. He guessed it would be awkward to sit next to the sisters, so he took a seat at the other end of the table.

'I expect they will move us around if they want us to sit somewhere else,' Teilo said.

'Hopefully we can stay here. We can make a quick exit when the meeting ends,' Nerys said.

Teilo smiled. 'I like your thinking.'

The rows of chairs were starting to fill up. Teilo watched the people talking. He looked at their clothes, gestures and expressions. He tried to imagine what they were talking about, what lives they led. It seemed strange that everyone around him appeared to be carrying on with life when he felt that his had come to a stop. It was like he was stuck in some strange new reality, and he couldn't find his way back.

His eyes came to rest on a woman in the first row. She was staring intently at him. She was an older woman with sleek bobbed grey hair and bright red lipstick. The woman sitting next to her chatted away, but Red-Lipstick Woman seemed oblivious. Her expression wasn't hostile, more curious. Teilo broke eye contact and looked towards the back of the room.

'That woman is staring at you,' Nerys whispered.

'Yeah, I noticed that. I expect she'll be staring at all of us. I feel like an exhibition.' He tried to sound casual, but he felt uncomfortable.

A feeling of dissociation fell over him. He felt removed from his body, almost like he was dreaming. The chatter became distorted, and he felt a strong urge to get up and run from the room. He knew what the feeling was. It was the mind's way of coping with too much stress. He started to use the grounding techniques he taught his clients. Concentrate on five things you can see: red jumper, microphone, poster on the wall. He stopped. Huw Jones' family had just walked through the door. They looked around, spotted the table, and all three of them stiffened. Teilo looked down the table in time to see Chloe turn her head away. He could see colour rising in her cheeks. Anna fidgeted next to her. Standing by the end of the table, he saw Meadows watching. It was then that he understood why they had all been brought together.

* * *

Lesley was standing just inside the door of the hall. She could see over the heads of the audience to the long table at the front. She looked at the people seated at the table and quickly turned her head away.

'We can't go up there,' she said.

Luke looked at the table and his eyes narrowed. Lesley could almost see the anger emanating from him. Panic constricted her chest and she felt too hot.

'We'll sit right next to them. I don't give a fuck,' Luke said.

Lesley started unbuttoning her coat. 'Please, Luke. Don't make a scene.'

'Don't make this any worse than it is, Luke,' Sarah said. 'Think of Mum.'

Lesley pulled her coat off, but the room still felt too hot. 'The police are watching us.'

'So?' Luke said.

He was jiggling around, and Lesley was sure he had taken something before they picked him up.

'Do you want to get arrested?' Sarah asked. 'You're not going to drag me into it this time. I won't cover for you again.'

'I said I was sorry,' Luke said.

Lesley was starting to feel light-headed. 'I can't do this.' She backed out of the door.

'Don't be stupid,' Luke said. 'You've got to.' He grabbed her arm and pulled her forward.

'Stop it,' Sarah said. 'She's just got rid of one controlling man. She doesn't need another one.'

'Sarah!' Lesley looked around to make sure no one had heard.

'Well, it's true,' Sarah said. 'We're all glad he's gone. Now we have to pretend we're sorry and ask for information.'

'That's enough,' Lesley said as she saw Meadows coming towards them.

'It's OK, Mum.' Sarah put her arms around her. 'We're here with you. You don't have to say anything. Isn't that right, Luke?'

'Yeah,' Luke said. 'Let me do the talking.'

'You best be quiet,' Lesley said. 'I'll be fine.' She had failed to protect her son once. She wasn't going to let that happen again. She needed to be brave. Just sit at the table and say her piece.

'He probably just wants to talk us through what we have to say,' Sarah said.

'That other one already did that. What was his name?'

'Chief Inspector Lester,' Sarah said. 'If the police wanted to know more, he would have asked when he spoke to us.'

Lesley hoped she was right.

'Is everything alright?' Meadows asked.

'Yes, we're fine,' Lesley said. 'There's just a lot more people here than I expected.'

Meadows nodded. 'I'm sure you'll be OK when we start. Chief Inspector Lester will be doing most of the talking and answering questions.'

'We'll take our seats then,' Sarah said.

Meadows nodded.

Lesley felt like all eyes were upon her as she crossed the hall. She focussed on the empty chairs at the table. She didn't want to look at the others. She managed to sit down without making eye contact and Sarah and Luke sat either side of her. The rows of chairs had all been filled and people were standing at the back. A few in the front row were obviously journalists; they took photographs and scribbled away on electronic tablets. Lesley was aware that the whole thing was being filmed. There were even cameras set up around the hall. DCI Lester had explained it was because they wanted to see who attended and record the questions people asked. She knew they were really looking for the killer among them.

She looked around the room trying to locate the cameras then realised that she would be looking straight into them. She didn't like to think about how many times the recording would be watched, every movement and interaction scrutinized. She thought about what she had said to Luke and Sarah since they had come into the hall. What if they were being recorded? What if they had a lip-reader look at the tape? They would know every word they'd said.

The heat was rising up Lesley's neck and she pulled at her collar. If only she had worn layers instead of a jumper, something easy to take off. She was getting light-headed again. What if she fainted? It would be in front of all these people, in front of the cameras. They were probably watching her discomfort now. Act normal, she told herself.

There were bottles of water placed on the table. Lesley grabbed one, twisted off the lid, and gulped. The cool liquid going down her throat felt good. She pressed the bottle against her wrist and tried to slow her breathing.

'Are you OK?' Sarah asked.

'Yes. It's just a bit warm in here.'

'We can go outside for a moment. I'm sure it would be alright.'

Lesley shook her head. 'I'll be fine in a moment.' She set down the bottle and placed her hands on her lap. To distract herself from her thoughts, she looked along the rows of people. There had to be someone she knew, someone who would give her a friendly smile. The members of the WI had sent a condolence card. Some had even called around with flowers. She was sure some of them would be here. Next to her, Luke was fidgeting.

'Look, Luke, there's Joan. You remember her, don't you? Try and look for people you recognise. It helps,' she said.

Luke grunted something but joined in. Occasionally, he would mention a name. Detective Lester was taking his seat and Lesley guessed they would be starting soon. At that moment, she spotted someone she didn't want to see. She'd recognise her anywhere. She was older now, with sleek grey hair cut into a bob, but she still wore bright red lipstick. She was staring at Lesley. Then she smirked. Lesley's stomach flipped. She looked away and was about to distract Luke, but it was too late. He'd seen her.

'What's that bitch doing here?' Luke asked.

'Hush,' Lesley hissed.

Luke folded his arms and stared at the woman. Lesley looked back to the crowd and saw that the woman had a look of pure hatred on her face. It was directed at Luke. Lesley was thankful when Lester called for attention. She could feel the woman's gaze upon her and knew she was waiting for an opportunity to get revenge.

Chapter Twenty-three

Dawn paced the sitting room as she waited for the phone to ring. She had downloaded the app as Pat had requested and made sure the phone was fully charged. She didn't know why Pat had insisted on a face-to-face call. She didn't want to see the woman. It had been hard enough hearing her voice. It had brought up so many memories. Things that she'd put behind her. Things that she thought she would never have to face again. She had felt safe. That was something people took for granted but not Dawn. It had taken her so long to rebuild her life. There were things from her past that her husband didn't know and she needed it to stay that way.

She had sent Simon off to the pub for the evening with friends. There wasn't much time left until he came back and she wouldn't be able to take the call then. She decided to give it another ten minutes then she'd call. It was just like Pat to keep her waiting.

Eight minutes passed, then nine. Dawn grabbed the phone and was about to call when it let out a series of chimes. She hit accept and Pat's face filled the screen. She hadn't changed much. Yes, she was older, but she still had the same hard eyes and thin lips. Her hair was grey and cut just below her chin. It looked thick and glossy. Dawn noticed that Pat still wore her signature red lipstick. She touched her hand to her own cropped hair and wished now she had made more of an effort. She'd put on a little foundation and blusher but had left her eyes and lips bare.

'How nice to see you,' Pat said. 'I'd like to say you haven't changed but we both know we've grown older.' She let out a tinkling laugh.

'You look well, Pat,' Dawn said.

'I try to stay on top of things. We have to make a little more effort at our age. No good letting yourself go.'

'How was the meeting?'

'Very interesting,' Pat said. 'I'm glad I went, although I've had a really busy day. I got my hair done this morning. Then I had to decide what to wear. It took me ages. I knew it would be full and I haven't seen some of the people for years. You know how it works. They check you out.'

Dawn nodded. She wished Pat would get on with it.

'Oh, and that journalist called at my house. Did I tell you about her?'

'Yes. You told me last time we spoke.'

'Nice girl,' Pat continued. 'Although I think she tries too hard. Obviously not from a good background. I would think she's worked hard to get where she is.'

Dawn wasn't interest. 'Good for her,' she said.

'Yes, it's a shame really. There are still telltale signs: short unpolished nails and badly done make-up. She turned up in jeans and a jumper. You'd think she'd wear something smarter to conduct an interview. Not a pretty girl. I did offer some advice.'

I bet you did, Dawn thought. 'So, you spoke to her and went to the meeting.'

'I thought you'd be interested in what she had to say. Given that she's a journalist and has connections.'

That got Dawn's attention. 'What did she say?'

'She's writing an article about changes in the community over the years. She was interested in the old school. I guess I'm the best person to come to for that sort of information. We talked a lot about my time there. Then she started talking about the murders. She asked all sorts of questions about the victims.'

'Such as?'

'Well, she wanted to know if there had been any gossip about Malcom Isaac. There are a lot of things I could have said about him. We both know what type of man he was. It seemed like a good opportunity to put it out there.'

Dawn felt sick. 'You told her about Luke?'

'Of course I didn't. I just gave her some hints. I think she got the picture.'

'You know she's going to write about it.'

'That's the idea. I told her not to quote me. If my suspicions are right, and someone reads the article, they'll come forward. I won't have to get involved.'

The idea appealed to Dawn. 'You're so clever to think of that.'

'I know. It came to me as she was talking. She was also interested in Bryn.'

Dawn's stomach clenched. 'I saw they were painting a picture of a nice, quiet, retired, man in the news,' Dawn said. 'Still, people must be talking about him now and wondering if he did something.'

'Well, they'd be wrong,' Pat said.

It took all of Dawn's strength not to comment. Pat had a smug smile on her face. Doesn't matter, I know the truth, Dawn thought. 'I read somewhere that the police were looking for a woman in connection with the murders. You were—'

'You shouldn't listen to gossip,' Pat cut in.

'It wasn't gossip though, was it?'

Pat's eyes narrowed. 'I don't think you're in a position to judge me.'

'What did you say about Bryn?'

'Nothing,' Pat said. 'I told her I didn't know him. I'd said enough about Malcom to pique her interest. She was happy with what she got. Brought me chocolates and wine. Not any cheap stuff; the chocolates are handmade liqueurs with exotic spices, and look at the box the wine came in.' She held it up for Dawn to see.

'Looks lovely,' Dawn said.

'I'm going to eat the chocolates and have a glass of wine once we've finished.'

'So, the meeting,' Dawn said.

'Oh yes. It was packed.'

'Were any of the victims' family members there?'

'All of them. Chloe and Anna, you know, Malcom's daughters. I didn't talk to them. Chloe thinks herself better than everyone now that she owns Ynysforgan farm.'

The name triggered the ever-present hole in Dawn's stomach to expand. It felt like something was gnawing her from the inside. She pushed her fist into her flesh to try and rid herself of the sensation.

'Why would she want to live there?' she asked.

'She's renovated the place. It looks so different now. She wants to make it into a holiday park. A lot of people are against it. Oh, sorry. I expect that's upsetting news for you.'

The gnawing in Dawn's stomach intensified. 'Well, good for her,' she managed to say. 'Farming is hard work. If she can find another use for the land and make an income, then good luck to her.'

'I suppose,' Pat said.

'Who else was there?'

'Lesley, Huw's wife. Luke' – Pat almost spat his name – 'Sarah. She was always a nice girl, nothing like her brother.'

'Did Lesley speak to you?'

'To me? She wouldn't dare. Luke saw me. You should have seen the look he gave me. It was frightening.'

'I can imagine,' Dawn said.

'Teilo and his wife, Nerys, were there. She's a nurse.'

'What does he do?'

'Some sort of therapist, I heard. It seems to be popular now. People like to talk about their problems. We used to just get on with it without complaining.'

'I think it's a good thing.'

'I don't think I could do it. I like to keep my private life to myself.'

Dawn stifled a laugh. 'It sounds like he did well for himself.'

'Yes, although he did look so sad. No parents now.'

'Did any of them talk at the meeting?'

'Chloe, Lesley, and Teilo read a statement. Just asking anyone with information to come forward, that sort of thing. I thought there would have been tears, but no one was crying.'

'I expect they were holding it in. No one wants to make a spectacle of themselves in front of an audience,' Dawn said.

'Oh, I think it was more than that. Then they all just sat there when the police spoke. The police said there have been developments in the case. They urged anyone with information to come forward. Then they advised us to be extra vigilant. It's supposed to be their job to keep us safe.' Pat shook her head. 'Then there were a lot of questions. A lot of people are angry.'

'What sort of questions?' Dawn asked.

'I can't remember. Oh yes, the police seemed interested in anyone who knew the victims in the mid-eighties and early nineties. They said they were just looking for background information, but I think it's more than that. There were some questions asked about the blog. One of the journalists suggested that the killer was acting out revenge for some past crime.'

'What did the police say to that?'

'They couldn't discuss details of the blog. They wouldn't even confirm it was the killer posting those things. It has to be, though. How else would they know all those details?'

'Was your journalist there?'

'I didn't see her.'

'What were people saying after the meeting?'

'I tried to move around to see what I could pick up, but it was so loud in there. A lot of people were going up to the police after. Your name is bound to come up. Maybe you should–'

'No,' Dawn cut in. 'You know I can't.'

'You could explain.'

'There is nothing I can do to help.'

'Her name will come up.'

'So what if it does? It has nothing to do with what's happening now. How could it?'

'More questions will be asked. People will remember. I won't be able to stay quiet then.'

Chapter Twenty-four

'You're all in early again,' Valentine said as she walked through the office doors.

'That's because some people think five hours' sleep is enough,' Edris said then yawned.

Meadows laughed. 'You're the one that insisted on staying with me. You can go home.'

'No way,' Edris said. 'I'm not leaving you alone when there's a serial killer creeping around your place.'

'Did forensics find anything on the stick doll?' Paskin asked.

'No,' Meadows said. 'Same material that was used on the ones found in Bryn's house.'

The team looked at Meadows and he could see the worry on their faces.

'I think it's some kind of warning,' Meadows said. 'The other stick dolls were left with the victims. If I was the target, the killer would have already tried.'

Chris Harley walked into the office and Meadows was glad of the distraction. He didn't want to dwell too much on the killer's intentions. Especially as Daisy had been in the house the night the stick doll was left there.

They all gathered around a screen as Chris Harley moved through the footage of the meeting.

'Stop it there,' Meadows said. 'Look at Chloe's face when Teilo enters the room.'

'Yeah, definitely someone she wanted to avoid,' Edris said.

'Chloe claimed she didn't know him,' Meadows said. 'Teilo admitted to remembering both Chloe and Anna, yet he claims he hardly remembers the farm. Odd.'

Chris moved the video on and they watched Lesley enter.

'She certainly doesn't want to make eye contact with someone sitting at the table,' Valentine said.

'She looks like she's about to run,' Blackwell added.

'Now look at Luke's face,' Meadows said.

Edris leaned closer. 'I think he's looking at Chloe. Giving her the evil eye. I think you were right. The children of the victims know each other.'

Meadows nodded. 'They could have all gone to school together.'

'Craig-Y-Coed would have been the nearest primary school to the farms but not for Luke,' Edris said.

'We need to check it out. Even if they didn't attend the same school, they could have been friends as children. Maybe one of their friends went missing. OK, can you move the footage forward to when Lesley takes a seat?' Meadows waited then watched them all. 'They are all avoiding eye contact and Lesley looks really uncomfortable.'

'They all look bloody shifty,' Blackwell said. 'All of them look like they haven't slept in a week.'

'So would you, if you were sat in front of that crowd and had to read a statement,' Paskin said.

Something else caught Meadows' eye. 'Can we look at this from a different angle? Lesley is staring at someone, and she looks… well, scared, I think. Now it looks like Luke has spotted the same person. He's angry.'

'Hang on,' Chris said. 'I can pull up the footage taken from the front of the room. It captures the audience's reaction.'

He clicked the keyboard and another video popped up. He ran it forward until it reached the same time as the other one, then paused. The images were side by side.

Meadows studied the screen. 'It's that woman. The one with the grey hair and red lipstick.'

'That's a bitch face if I've ever seen one,' Valentine said. 'Is that look for Lesley or Luke?'

'Looks like she's giving them both the same treatment,' Paskin said.

'Can you run it from the time when Chloe takes her seat?' Meadows asked.

'Yep,' Chris said.

'Same treatment there too,' Edris said. 'She's also starring at Teilo but it's more of a curious look.'

'Valentine, can you see if we can get a name for this woman?' Meadows asked. 'Everyone was given a numbered questionnaire when they came in. You should be able to cross-reference it with the footage. Just a case of counting the people coming in. Uniform should be going through the forms.'

'Will do,' Valentine said.

'I'll leave these with you,' Chris said.

'Thanks for that,' Meadows said.

'What now?' Blackwell asked. 'They clearly know each other and are all lying about it.'

'We don't have any proof,' Meadows said. He grabbed his mug of tea and moved to the incident board. He looked at all the photographs of the crime scenes and the evidence that had been collected. Blackwell, Edris, and Paskin came to stand next to him.

'It's a mess,' Blackwell said.

Meadows took a gulp of his tea. 'What are we missing? The abuser, the child killer, the silent one, the abandoner, and the one that turned their back. Whatever happened is likely to have occurred when Bryn Thomas was living next door to Malcom Isaac. I think Malcom used it to get Bryn to sell the farm. Paskin, do we know how much the farm sold for?'

'I'll check,' Paskin said.

They waited, then Paskin brought up the information.

'Ninety-eight thousand pounds. A few grand over the mortgage.'

'That's cheap for the amount of land,' Meadows said.

'Yeah,' Paskin agreed. 'It's worth 1.5 million now.'

'A lot of money for Teilo to miss out on,' Blackwell said.

'A lot of money for Bryn to lose. He must have been desperate,' Meadows said.

'Lesley's medical report is in,' Paskin said.

'Anything interesting?' Meadows asked.

'She's had treatment for anxiety and depression which goes back a number of years. There are also records of a broken wrist, fractured cheek, and two broken ribs. All were separate visits to A&E.'

'Let me guess: all from falls,' Edris said.

Paskin nodded. 'Something like that. Broken ribs were 1990, the wrist eight years later. It could be innocent.'

'I reckon Huw was the abuser,' Blackwell said.

'If Huw did inflict those injuries, then what else was he capable of?' Meadows asked.

'I have put in requests for the medical records of our other suspects,' Paskin said. 'Nothing back yet but they all use different surgeries. Some are slower than others.'

Valentine came back into the office. 'Got a name for our mystery woman. Patricia Maddox.'

'Maybe the one who left lipstick on the cup in Bryn Thomas' house,' Edris said.

'Paskin, can you do a background check?' said Meadows. 'Find out all the information you can on her. See if there is a connection to the victims. Blackwell and Valentine, I'd like you to go and meet Chloe and Anna at Malcom's house. Search the attic to see if there are any old photographs. It's a slim possibility but I want them to think we have something, or that their father kept some evidence. Edris and I will do the same at Lesley's house.'

'You want to play them off against each other?' Blackwell asked.

Meadows nodded. 'Let them think that we have information or photographs from the other families. Ask about Patricia and see what reaction you get. We'll go to see Patricia after we've been to Lesley's. One of these lot is the killer.' He pointed to the photographs of the suspects. 'One or more are protecting the killer, and possibly one could be the next target. Either way, we need answers and fast before someone else gets killed.'

* * *

Meadows thought Lesley looked exhausted when she opened the door. There were dark circles under her eyes and barely any colour in her cheeks. She stood back to let them in with a resigned look on her face.

Meadows stepped inside and crouched down to take off his shoes. The dog fussed around his feet. 'Hello, Sidney.' He stroked the top of the dog's head.

'Don't bother with the shoes,' Lesley said.

Meadows followed her into the sitting room and noticed the change since his last visit. Huw's armchair had been removed and pictures of Luke, Sarah, and the grandchildren were on display. The coffee table was strewn with a variety of objects and a TV had been placed in the corner. It had a more lived-in feel about it and even the dog seemed more relaxed. It jumped up on the sofa then settled on Lesley's lap. Meadows took a seat in the remaining armchair and Edris perched on the other end of the sofa.

'I hope the meeting yesterday wasn't too stressful for you,' Meadows said.

Lesley ran her fingers through the dog's fur. 'I didn't expect so much anger from people.'

'These things often get heated especially when people don't know the full facts,' Meadows said. 'As far as they can see, we are not doing our job as we haven't caught the killer yet. The problem is, for whatever reason, the people involved are not giving us the whole picture.' He paused and watched Lesley's reaction.

'I see.' She continued stroking the dog, now using both hands.

'There's been an influx of information,' he continued. 'A lot of people came forward to talk to officers after the meeting. We also viewed the footage to see if anyone was displaying particular interest in the families of the victims. We noticed one woman was paying a lot of attention to you and Luke. Patricia Maddox. Do you know her?'

Lesley's hands stopped moving. 'Erm... I don't think so.' Colour rose in her cheeks. 'I mean, the name sounds familiar. Perhaps she knew Huw. Maybe she was one of his old work colleagues. I met so many over the years, I forget their names.'

'Not to worry,' Meadows said. 'We'll be talking to her later today.'

A look of fear flitted across Lesley's face and she nodded before returning her attention to the dog.

'When you walked into the meeting yesterday, you looked towards the table where Anna, Chloe, Teilo, and Nerys were seated. You were startled. You turned away. It looked like you were going to run out.'

'I was nervous. That's all.'

'I think it was more than that,' Meadows said. 'You know the family members of the other two victims, don't you?'

Lesley sighed. 'I don't know them, but Luke and Chloe dated. If you can call it that. They were still in school and...'

'Go on.'

'There's nothing more to it.'

'Judging by the look on Luke's face when he saw Chloe, I would say there is a lot more to it.'

'They had some argument. You know what teenagers are like; it's all drama. They fall in and out of love. Luke was upset at the time. I think Chloe spread some rumours about him. They haven't seen each other for years. I guess when he saw her at the meeting, he was thinking about

177

that. He didn't mention anything afterwards and he seemed fine.'

'What about Malcom Isaac?'

Lesley stiffened. 'What about him?'

'If Luke was dating Chloe then you must have had some contact with him.'

Lesley shook her head.

Meadows gave Edris a nod.

'The reason we called around today is that we are looking for photographs,' Edris said. 'We are interested in ones that would have been taken a number of years ago. The families of the other victims have already given us some to look through. We're working on identifying the people in the photographs and looking for common friends or acquaintances. Bryn Thomas had photographs. Some of them were burnt, but forensics are so clever now, they are able to recreate images. There were also a fair few among Malcom Isaac's possessions. Some were of children, probably friends of his daughters. We'll need to identify them as well.'

Meadows was amazed by how easily and convincingly Edris could embellish the truth. It seemed to work. Lesley looked like she was about to be sick.

'Do you have any old photographs?' Meadows asked.

'No.'

'Are you sure?'

'A lot of people tend to put them in boxes up in the attic,' Edris added.

'There's nothing like that up there.'

'We'll still need to take a look,' Edris said. 'It could be that Huw had some that you weren't aware of.'

'I'll ask Luke to go up when he comes over,' Lesley said.

Edris stood up. 'I can do that for you now. It's no trouble.'

Meadows tried not to smile. Edris was really pushing it. He very much doubted there would be anything to find but Lesley was rattled.

'Fine.' Lesley lifted the dog off her lap, stood up, and smoothed down her skirt.

'I can manage,' Edris said.

Meadows waited for Lesley to sit back down. 'He won't be long,' he said. 'While we wait, there's something I need to talk to you about. We are aware that you had a number of injuries over the years.'

Lesley shrank back into the sofa. 'Everyone has accidents.'

'Professionals can tell when an injury is not accidental.'

Lesley stared at him for a moment. Then tears filled her eyes. 'Huw had a temper. He hit me. There it is. I know what you'll be thinking. Stupid woman. Why did she stay with him?'

'I'm not thinking that at all.' He sat forward in the chair. 'Believe me, I understand. You were a victim of domestic abuse. You're not to blame.'

Lesley wiped the tears from her cheeks. 'It started soon after we were married. We had to get married, you see. I was flattered by his attention. I'd always been a bit shy, and Huw was a strong man who knew what he wanted. I liked that. I wanted someone to make decisions, take control, and look after me.

'The first time he hit me, I was six months pregnant with Luke. It was such a stupid argument. He liked things just so and I hadn't ironed his shirt the way he liked it. He was sorry after and said it wouldn't happen again. It carried on. I had a young baby and nowhere to go. I couldn't go to my parents. I was too ashamed. I guess I wasn't myself after Luke was born. I was so tired, and I let myself go. I couldn't keep up with the housework. I continually made him angry. He said he needed a proper wife and that I was useless. I suppose it was difficult for him. He was working full time, and he should have been able to come home to a tidy house and dinner on the table.'

'No,' Meadows said. 'That's how abusers work. They undermine your confidence and control you. What you needed was help and understanding. He was making impossible demands on you.'

Lesley shrugged. 'That's when I first became depressed. I even thought about ending it all. I was too tired to go out, I had no friends, no one to talk to. The only time I saw my parents was with Huw and then I had to pretend that everything was OK.'

'I'm so sorry, Lesley,' Meadows said.

'Then Sarah came along. I put all my energy into making sure the children were happy and had everything they needed. I thought I could leave him when they got older, but the years just went by and there was never the right time.

'My parents died. I thought that would be an opportunity to leave but I needed help sorting things out. I didn't know about probate and selling a house. Huw took care of it and the money. We used it to pay off the mortgage, then we moved here. Huw wanted a bigger house.'

'Where were you living before?'

'Pont Aber.'

'Did Luke go to Craig-Y-Coed primary school?'

'No. He went to Henllys.'

It wasn't the answer Meadows wanted. 'OK. So, you moved to this house.'

Lesley nodded. 'Huw registered the deeds in his name. I had nothing. Yes, I could divorce him and claim half the property but that would take time. I wouldn't have felt safe.'

'I'm guessing Luke and Sarah knew about the violence.'

'I did my best to keep it from them when they were younger.'

'Was he ever violent towards them?'

Lesley wrapped her arms around her body. 'He was strict, and he did smack them. I tried to protect them and stop him going too far.'

'I'm sure you did,' Meadows said. 'Luke and Sarah must have been worried about you after they left home. I expect they were also angry with their father as well as afraid.'

'Sarah was terrified of him but not Luke. When he was old enough to stand up to him, he did. I think he was past caring if he got hurt. He soon grew strong enough to fight back. It ended up with Luke protecting me. Huw started holding back his temper. He knew if he hurt me Luke would go for him.'

'It's understandable that a son would protect his mother. Luke must have seen years of it.'

Lesley nodded.

Meadows' phone trilled and he hit decline. He didn't want to interrupt Lesley now that she was opening up to him.

'I can imagine the toll that has taken on him,' Meadows said. 'There is only so much a person can take. He snapped. He thought it was the only way to end it. What he needs now is help.'

'What? No! Luke didn't kill Huw.'

'I understand you want to protect him.'

'You don't understand,' Lesley said. 'Luke and Sarah were helping me. I had plans to leave.'

'Did Huw find out?'

'No. I was very careful. I got my own bank account. I was saving as much money as I could. I skimmed a bit off the food bill and I even told Huw I was contributing to a project the WI were working on. I told awful lies.'

'You made plans to go on a trip with the WI.'

'Yes, because I would have left him by then. Luke had given me driving lessons and it gave me a little more freedom. Both of them were giving me money to put away. I only needed enough to be able to rent a place and get a solicitor. I was hoping that in six months things would be settled and I'd have some money from this place. Sarah was looking into it. She said I would be able to get something even though the house was in his name.'

'Why lie to us about what you were doing on Tuesday morning?'

'I don't know. I think I got so used to lying to Huw.'

'What do you do on Tuesday mornings?'

Footsteps could be heard coming down the stairs then Edris stuck his head around the kitchen door. 'Can I have a word?'

'Excuse me a moment,' Meadows said.

He left the kitchen and closed the door behind him. 'What have you found?'

'Nothing,' Edris said. 'Folland was trying to get hold of you. Another body has been found.'

Chapter Twenty-five

Meadows parked behind a police car outside a row of houses in Llandybie. He could see the forensic van with one of the team taking out equipment. On the other side of the road, Hanes was talking to a small group of people. Beyond the road an old stone bridge crossed the River Marlas. A few people could be seen on the bridge. They were still, as if the news of a death had frozen them to the spot. Their eyes watched the house. Above, dark brooding clouds blanketed the sky.

'Has Paskin sent through the details?' Meadows asked.

Edris looked at the screen. 'Yeah, just come through. Looks like she's got a lot of information on Patricia Maddox. You'd already requested it this morning.'

'Let's hope the poor woman was dead by then. If not, and we'd come here to speak to her before going to see Lesley, we may have been able to prevent it.'

Edris shook his head. 'Don't go there. All we knew this morning was that she was staring at the victims' families at a meeting. She didn't give any information. It wasn't a priority.'

'The look she gave them was hostile. Maybe she knew something but was keeping it to herself.'

'Blackmail?' Edris suggested.

Meadows shrugged. 'OK, what do we know?'

'Retired schoolteacher, seventy-two years old. She taught at Dyffryn Du.'

'Do you remember her?' Meadows asked.

'I don't think a Ms Maddox taught me.'

'I don't remember her either. She may have taught there after our time or neither of us were in her class. What else?'

'Never married. She had no record and a clean driving licence. No living relatives. She has a presence on social media. That's about it.'

'Right, let's take a look.'

They got out of the car and Meadows saw a small tent had been erected over the doorway to stop onlookers peeking through the door. Hanes crossed the road to join them.

'Who found her?' Meadows asked.

'That would be me,' Hanes said. 'Her friend Sally Evans was supposed to be meeting Patricia, or Pat as she was known to her friends, for coffee this morning. They were both at the meeting yesterday afternoon. She saw Pat's car parked outside so she was surprised when she didn't answer. She said that Pat was always punctual and would have called if there was a change of plan. She went around the back to knock and tried again at the front. She tried looking through the window, but the curtains were drawn which was another thing she found odd, as Pat was an early riser. She called us as she was concerned. Given that we couldn't get an answer from the door, or the phone, and I could hear the TV, I thought it unusual enough to go in. The neighbour had a spare key for emergencies. I went in and found her on the floor. Sally was understandably upset. They were childhood friends, apparently. I took her details and got Taylor to take her home.'

'So, the house was secure,' Meadows said.

Hanes nodded. 'It was the name that made me suspicious. Valentine was asking about the forms from the meeting and she wanted to see the one Patricia Maddox had filled out. I thought her death might be connected. That's why I called it in.'

'Nice work,' Meadows said.

'I'm just getting details from the neighbours.'

'We'll leave you to get on. Thanks,' Meadows said.

He stepped into the tent and put on protective clothing before stepping through the front door. It opened into a sitting room.

Forensic officers were taking photographs and samples. Meadows recognised Mike Fielding, who gave him a nod. On one side of the room, a dining table was set against the wall with two chairs tucked underneath and a vase of yellow roses on top. A bookshelf was positioned against the other wall and was laden with books. Below was a storage cupboard. The room was divided by a wooden staircase.

Meadows turned his attention to the other side of the room. There was a sofa and armchair facing a large-screen television. Patricia was lying on the floor with Daisy examining her. He stepped across the metal plates to join her.

The first thing he noticed was that Patricia was wearing the same clothes that she had worn at the meeting. She was on her side with her arm stretched out. Just out of reach of her fingers was a mobile phone that had a marker placed next to it.

He felt a stab of pity. It looked like she was trying to get her phone. Did the killer move it out of the way? The thought sickened him. He crouched down next to Daisy and looked at Patricia's face. Her eyes were open, and her lips had a bluish tinge. Brown-coloured dribble stained her chin and the front of her jumper. Her swollen tongue protruded from her mouth. There were no marks on her face or neck.

'Suffocation?' Meadows asked.

'I don't think so,' Daisy said. She took a metal instrument from her bag and inserted it into Patricia's mouth. Using a pencil torch, she looked inside. 'Oedema of the airways. Could be looking at poisoning or a severe allergic reaction, but it's only a guess.'

'So, it may not be murder,' Edris said.

Daisy shrugged. 'Until the post-mortem, there's not much more I can tell you.'

'Time of death?' Meadows asked.

'Roughly twelve to fifteen hours ago,' Daisy said.

'That fits. She hadn't changed from coming back from the meeting.'

Meadows stood up and looked at the table next to the armchair. There was an open box of chocolates and a bottle of wine. The wine glass was lying on the floor. He pointed to the chocolates. 'OK to touch these, Mike?'

'Yeah. They've been photographed.'

Meadows picked up the box. There were five chocolates left and room for six. He lifted the box and looked underneath. The label read "Handmade. Allergen advice: see ingredients." Underneath was the list of ingredients which included brandy, cinnamon, clove, and nutmeg. He lifted them to his nose and inhaled.

'Just smells like spicy liqueurs,' he said. 'They're handmade with no maker on the label.'

'Probably used the spice to cover up whatever was put in there to poison her,' Edris said.

Daisy looked up. 'That's if she was poisoned. I'm not committing myself to anything at the moment.'

Meadows picked up the bottle of wine and examined it. 'So, she comes home from the meeting, settles in front of the television with the wine and chocolate, pops a chocolate in her mouth. Whatever is inside causes a reaction. She tries to wash it down with the wine, but it doesn't work.'

'Likely laced with the same stuff to make sure,' Edris said.

Meadows nodded. 'She drops the glass and tries to call for help. I expect she's panicking by now. She gets up from the chair, drops the phone, then collapses. She tries to grab the phone but it's just out of reach.'

'Or the killer stuffs the chocolates in her mouth and forces down the wine.'

'There are no marks on her face,' Daisy said. 'Nothing to indicate a struggle.'

'OK. So, the killer gives her the chocolates and waits. Maybe they moved the phone just out of reach to taunt her,' Edris said.

'If it is poison then the killer didn't need to be here at all,' Meadows said. 'The chocolates and wine don't look like something you'd buy yourself. They could have been given as a gift or delivered.' He examined the box of chocolates again. 'Maybe one of the ingredients was accidently missed off the list.' He turned to Daisy. 'If that's the case, would a small quantity of an allergen be enough to cause her death? She only ate one chocolate. Most of the wine has been tipped.'

'It depends,' she said. 'If she had a severe allergic reaction, she would've gone into anaphylactic shock. I guess with an allergy that serious, it would only take a small amount of the allergen to cause a reaction. That's why food is labelled with "may contain" if it's produced in the same factory as, say, peanuts; there is a risk of contamination. If someone got a trace of the allergen in their food, then the company could get sued. Someone with that sort of allergy would carry an EpiPen for emergencies.'

'Good point,' Meadows said. 'Mike, did you see her handbag anywhere?'

'There's one on the chair in the kitchen,' he said.

Meadows walked through to the kitchen. The blinds were down but there was still enough light getting through. He located the bag and tipped the contents onto the table. 'Got it.'

'So, it's not murder then,' Edris said.

Meadows went back into the sitting room. 'The EpiPen was too far away but I'm still not convinced that it was accidental. The killer could have known about her allergy. It's clear Patricia knew the family members of the victims. She glared at them all, especially Luke. We were due to talk to her. If we thought she had information, then the killer would be thinking the same thing. They would have been worried about what she could say to us. Right, let's search the house.'

'What are we looking for?'

'Anything that would tie Patricia to the victims. If it is murder, then there will be a stick doll somewhere.'

They started upstairs. Meadows went into the bedroom. He always felt a sense of unease looking though a victim's personal belongings. Their life laid bare for everyone to pick over. No secrets.

The bedroom was nicely decorated with a papered feature wall. The other three were painted a pastel green. The bed was in the centre and had colourful scatter cushions placed on top. Near the window a dressing table displayed bottles of perfume, make-up, and a hairbrush. He opened the drawer and checked the contents. The underwear and socks were all ordered. It was the same in the wardrobe. A section for jumpers, trousers, and skirts. Everything neat.

He noticed the bed had two drawers. He crouched down and opened the first. It was filled with spare bedding. The second drawer had two boxes. The first was filled with paperwork, the second contained photographs. He took them out and looked through them.

Edris came in to join him. 'Nothing of interest in the spare room or bathroom. Did you find something interesting?'

'I don't know yet.' Meadows split the pile of photos and handed some to Edris. 'Have a look through them.'

Meadows flicked through photographs of Patricia on holiday. Always posing alone. There were Christmas parties and other functions, a lot featuring the same people. As he sifted through the pile, the quality of the photographs changed with age. There was one of Patricia standing in front of a stone building surrounded by children of about six years of age. There were a series of these, all containing a board with the year. The last photos were of a man. In one he was posed on a tractor, in another shirtless. One was of the man standing in a crop field. On the back, someone had written "Harvest 1991". The last photo was of the same man sitting in front of a farmhouse. Meadows studied the picture closely then handed it to Edris.

'Interesting,' Edris said.

'Yes. That's Ynysforgan farm. The house has changed but not the original structure or the surrounding area. It's the same man that was in the photos recovered from Bryn's house. We're looking at a young Bryn Thomas.'

Edris nodded. 'Maybe Bryn and Patricia were at it.'

'If that's the case, then she could well have known what Bryn and the other men were up to. Come on, we better check the rest of the house.'

They went back down into the sitting room, searched the cupboards, then went into the kitchen.

'Mike, can we open the blinds?' Meadows called out.

'Yeah, go ahead.'

Meadows pulled the string on the blinds and they rolled up to reveal a view of the garden. There, standing on the lawn, were three stick figures.

Chapter Twenty-six

The team gathered around for the morning briefing. Their usual energy and enthusiasm was muted. Meadows guessed that, like himself, they were also feeling defeated after the discovery of Patricia's body. They had so much information and had worked relentlessly but still, they were no closer to catching the killer. On top of that, there was the looming threat that there would be more killings.

Meadows looked at the incident board then back to the team. 'Patricia Maddox, retired teacher. We are waiting on the post-mortem but given what was found in her garden, I think there is no doubt that she is our fourth victim.

'One stick figure had a cloth tied to make a skirt, the others had blue wool wrapped around them, possibly representing two males and a female. That leaves two dolls if we go by the blog.'

'The dolls around Malcom Isaac seem to represent males,' Valentine said. 'There were fifteen of them. The number of dolls left at the scene have to mean something.'

Meadows nodded. 'I just wish I knew what. Perhaps they represent the amount of people that were hurt.' He thought about the children in the school photograph with Patricia. 'Or children that got hurt. Luke was dating Chloe when he was at school. Anna and Sarah are likely to have gone to the same school. We need to check if Teilo went to Dyffryn Du school before he moved away. Patricia could have been their teacher.'

'She also kept old photos of Bryn,' Edris said. 'Maybe that's her connection to Teilo.'

Valentine raised her eyebrows. 'Could he have been her lover? She might have been seeing him when Teilo's mother was still alive. That would have been a scandal, given her position in the school.'

Paskin nodded. 'Even with Bryn's wife out of the picture, it still wouldn't have looked good.'

'I think our best starting point is the school,' Meadows said. 'Paskin, can you call ahead and ask them to check if the victims' children were taught by Patricia?'

'Will do,' Paskin said.

'Blackwell, Valentine, how did you get on with Chloe and Anna yesterday?'

'We didn't get anything worthwhile out of them,' Blackwell said.

'There were a few photographs of kids around the farm, nothing sinister,' Valentine added.

Hanes walked into the office followed by a group of uniformed officers. 'All yours,' he said.

Meadows smiled. 'Excellent. How did you get on with the neighbours yesterday?'

'No one had seen anyone acting suspiciously and they only had good things to say about Patricia. One did say that a journalist had visited Patricia – a woman. Patricia told her that the journalist was interviewing her for a feature on the community.'

'That's interesting,' Meadows said. 'Perhaps she had information and wanted to sell her story instead of speaking to us.'

'If the killer thought she knew something, they wouldn't want it getting out,' Edris said.

'OK, we need to track down this journalist.'

'I'll get onto that,' Hanes said.

'We also need to check the post office to see if they delivered the chocolates and wine. Talk to everyone in the area to see if they've been approached by a journalist, and check if anyone has doorbell cameras.' Meadows continued with the list of actions while the uniformed officers took notes. 'Paskin, where are we with tracing Patricia's phone calls?'

'Tech unlocked the phone and I'm working my way through the contacts.'

'Great, also look through her social media.' Meadows addressed the room. 'OK, I think that's it for now. Thanks, all.'

The uniform officers left, and Meadows picked up his coat before turning to Edris. 'Let's go to the school and see if they can tell us anything interesting.'

* * *

Meadows walked through the school gates and felt a stab of nostalgia. He had attended the school when his family had left the commune. Over the years, extensions had been added and renovations made to the old, stone, grammar school building. He could still remember the musty smell of the classrooms, the noise of the overcrowded food hall, and the feeling of being an outsider.

Edris looked equally uncomfortable. 'I'm going to be triggered going to the headteacher's office.'

Meadows laughed. 'Spend a lot of time there, did you?'

'I was just a lively kid.'

They entered the reception and showed their identification before being escorted further into the school by a year-six student. The girl led them through a series of corridors and up a flight of stairs before stopping outside a room. She knocked the door.

'Come in,' a woman's voice called.

Meadows thanked the student and opened the door. Inside, two women were sitting. They immediately stood up. One had shoulder-length black hair and was dressed in a suit, the other was older with spiky grey hair, and red-rimmed glassed. Meadows introduced himself and Edris.

'Pallavi Malik. I'm headteacher,' the dark-haired woman said.

'Helen Parsons. I teach mathematics,' the other said.

'I've asked Helen to join us as she has been a member of staff here the longest and knew Patricia. Please, take a seat.'

They all sat around the desk and Edris took out his notepad.

'Were you able to access the student records we requested?' Meadows asked.

'Most of the records from back then were not transferred. Computers weren't what they are now, and only certain data was kept. We do keep old records in storage. I made some enquiries and can confirm that Luke and Sarah Jones and Chloe and Anna Isaac attended school here. Luke and Chloe, from 1993. Sarah and Anna later. Luke and Sarah moved up from Henllys primary school. Chloe and Anna from Craig-Y-Coed. There is no record of Teilo Thomas attending this school. That's the only information I have at present.'

'Thank you,' Meadows said. He turned to Helen. 'Do you remember any of them?'

'I'm afraid not,' Helen said. 'So many pupils go through school over the years. Some stick with you for one reason or another. I don't teach all the classes.'

Meadows nodded. 'What can you tell me about Patricia?'

'She started here not long after me,' Helen said. 'It was 1993, I think. She came in as a teaching assistant, which was unusual.'

'How so?'

'She'd been headteacher of Craig-Y-Coed primary school.'

'Did she say why she'd left?'

'No. It wasn't something you'd ask. Over time, we became friendly. We'd see each other in the staff room and once she let slip that she had taken a year off work as she needed a break. I got the impression she didn't want the responsibility anymore. I thought at the time there must be more to it. There was gossip that she'd had some sort of breakdown.'

'Are you sure it was 1993?' Edris asked.

'I can check her employment records again,' Pallavi said. 'But I'm sure that was when she started.'

'She didn't start at the beginning of the school year,' Helen said. 'It was January. I'd been here over a year by then, and I started in 1991.'

'Did she remain teaching as an assistant?' Meadows asked.

'No, she took the role of English teacher. She became head of department,' Pallavi said.

'Were there any problems when she was here? Arguments with other staff members? Extended leave of absence?'

'No but there were some problems with some of the boys she taught. They were playing up in the class. There was a more serious incident and one of the boys got expelled,' Helen said.

'Do you remember the name of the boy?' Edris asked.

Helen thought for a moment. 'No, sorry. I'm sure it will come to me. I was on maternity leave at the time.'

'Is there anything else you can tell us about Patricia's time here?' Meadows asked.

'I was only here for the last few years that Patricia was a member of staff. Her employment record was exemplary,' Pallavi said. 'She rarely took time off. She was a dedicated, well-liked teacher.'

'Thank you both for your time,' Meadows said. 'If you can find an incident report for the boy who was expelled, that would be very helpful.'

'There will be a record somewhere,' Pallavi said. 'Not on our system but on paper in storage. The problem is, without a name and date, it's highly unlikely I'll be able to track it down.'

'I can work out the year,' Helen said. 'I was on maternity erm… yeah… I was expecting Nia. That would have been 1997.'

'I'll start there,' Pallavi said. 'Leave it with me for a couple of days and I'll see what we can do.'

'That's much appreciated,' Meadows said.

They left the office and walked back through the grounds. They could see children through the classroom windows, all dressed in uniforms, their heads turned towards the teacher.

'Why would Patricia leave a headteacher job and take a lower position?' Edris asked.

'I imagine it paid less as well. Added to that, she took a year off. Something must have happened at her last job.'

'Craig-Y-Coed primary school closed down years ago,' Edris said. 'I remember the petitions to keep it open. I doubt we'll get information now.'

'At least we know they all attended school together except Teilo. He could have gone to Henllys with Luke. There's a connection between all of them somewhere, I'm sure. Let's go and see Patricia's friend, Sally. Maybe she can tell us what happened to make Patricia leave her job and take a year off.'

Chapter Twenty-seven

Sally was still weeping when she opened the door and led Meadows and Edris into her sitting room. She was a tiny woman with curly grey hair.

'I'm so sorry for your loss,' Meadows said. 'I understand Patrica was a good friend of yours.'

'Yes. We went to school together.' She wiped her eyes with a tissue. 'I don't seem to be able to pull myself together. I know at our age you expect one of us to pop off, but she seemed fine Saturday. I've just made myself a cup of tea. Would you like one?'

Meadows could see a cup on the coffee table and a plate of biscuits. 'No thanks, but you go ahead and drink yours before it gets cold.'

Sally sat down and picked up her cup. Meadows and Edris took a seat on the sofa. It was a welcoming room with a stone wall and open-beamed ceiling. Family photos covered the mantle, and a cat was snoozing on the windowsill.

Meadows waited until Sally set her cup down before speaking. 'Are you OK to answer some questions?'

Sally nodded.

'I'm sorry to tell you that at this stage we are treating Patricia's death as suspicious.'

'Oh.' Sally put her hand to her mouth. She took a few moments to speak. 'That can't be right. Who would want to hurt Pat?'

'That's what we are trying to find out. Have you noticed any changes in Patricia recently?'

'No, not really. She was a bit upset about the murders; we all were.'

'Did she talk to you about them?'

'Yes, but everyone is talking about it. I think Pat read everything in the papers and on her computer. I don't use one. I have enough trouble using the phone.'

'Did she say who she thought was responsible?'

Colour rose in Sally's cheeks. 'It was just speculation.'

Meadows sat forward. 'Did she mention anyone in particular?'

Sally pulled her cardigan around her body and crossed her arms. 'It was gossip, nothing else. I wouldn't want to repeat it and get someone in trouble.'

Meadows gave her what he hoped was a reassuring smile. 'I promise you, anything you tell us will be in confidence. We don't arrest people based on gossip.'

Sally picked up her cup and took a sip of tea. She appeared to be considering whether or not to answer. She replaced the cup, sat forward, and lowered her voice. 'At first, she thought it was Luke Jones, but then she changed her mind and thought it was Chloe Watcyn.'

'Did she say why she thought they were involved?'

'She said Chloe was always a precocious child and now she was just a…'

'A what?'

'A bitch,' Sally whispered. 'She thought she would be the type and probably did it for the farm. There was a lot of talk about the holiday park. Councillor Jones talked to everyone in the area. He even came to see me. I told him I wasn't worried about having a holiday park in the area, but he said it would attract the wrong sort of people.'

'What did he mean by that?' Edris asked.

'He said there would be parties – raves, he called them. He thought there would be an increase in crime and lots of noise and drunk people, people who wouldn't care about the countryside. He asked me to sign the petition. I had no idea it was going to be that sort of place.' Sally shook her head. 'So I signed.'

It didn't surprise Meadows that Huw used such tactics. From what he had heard, he was a man used to getting his own way.

'Why did Patricia think that Luke was involved in the murders?' he asked.

'She said he was taking drugs and had been in all sorts of trouble. She hadn't seen him or the other ones she taught for years. That's why she was looking forward to the meeting, to see how they had changed over the years.'

'You went to the meeting with Patricia,' Meadows said.

Sally looked down at her hands. 'Yes, I sat next to her.'

'We did notice she was very interested in the victims' families. At one point, she looked angry. Did she say anything to you about them during the meeting?'

'No, if anything, she was quieter than usual.' Sally looked up and tears misted her eyes. 'It was like she had something on her mind. She was fine on the way in.'

'We've heard Patricia was talking to a journalist. Did she mention that to you?'

'Oh yes, she was very excited. She said there was going to be a feature about the community, and she was being interviewed about the school.'

'Do you know if she spoke to the journalist about the murders?'

'She didn't say she had, but I'm sure it would have come up.'

'Do you know when the journalist contacted her?'

'Erm… I can't remember when she first mentioned it. I'm sure it was before Huw Jones was murdered.' Sally's face creased in concentration. 'It must be over a week ago that she first had a visit. The woman came again on Saturday morning.'

'Did Patricia tell you anything about her? What newspaper she worked for?'

'No. Well, she may have done but…' Sally looked a little embarrassed. 'Pat talked a lot and sometimes I'd just switch off. I know she wasn't that impressed with her. She thought she could have dressed a bit smarter. Pat could be a bit of a snob.'

'Did she say what sort of clothes she wore?' Edris asked.

'Jeans and a jumper. What was it she said erm… oh, yes. "She comes in dressed like she's about to clean the house and sits there like a man", something like that.'

'Did you ever see Patricia with this woman?' Meadows asked.

'No.'

'Did Patricia say if the journalist was coming back?'

'I'm sure she said the article was finished.'

'Did you know any of the victims?' Meadows asked.

'I knew of them.' Sally put her hand to her chest. 'God rest their souls. It's a small community and people talk. I've lived here most of my life. Pat knew a lot of people in the area and taught most of the children. She lived here before she moved.'

'You said she had been upset by the murders, was there one in particular that upset her more?'

Sally thought for a moment. 'She phoned me to tell me about Huw Jones, but it was more for a gossip. I was the one to call her about Bryn Thomas and she sounded like she had been crying. Then when Malcom Isaac was found, she said he probably deserved it.'

'Did she say why she thought that?'

'No, but she could be judgemental and listened to all sorts of gossip.'

'Did she say anything about Bryn Thomas?'

'Only that he was a nice man.'

'Was Pat seeing anyone romantically?'

Sally smiled. 'At our age, the only pleasure is tea and cake. When my husband died, I shut up shop, if you know what I mean.'

Meadows couldn't help smiling. 'What about past relationships? Was there anyone special in Pat's life?'

'She had a lot of boyfriends when she was younger, but none lasted long. She liked her job and said she was more interested in her career than settling down. Her plan was to get married later. I guess she left it too long.'

'We found pictures of a man among her possessions. They were taken some years ago. We believe them to be of Bryn Thomas when he lived on the farm. Is it possible she could have been having an affair with him?'

Sally sat back in the chair and thought for a moment. 'There was a period of time when we didn't see much of each other. Usually when she had a new man, she would tell me all about it. She even brought a few around to meet me. One time though, she was secretive. She said she was busy with work, but she had changed. I'd see her dressed up with her hair and make-up perfect. I did wonder at the time if it was a married man. I suppose it could have been Bryn Thomas but from what I recall his wife died. Yes, I'm sure there was talk of it. I don't remember exactly when. Either way, it wouldn't have looked good if she was dating the father of one of her pupils.'

'We know that Patricia left her job around 1991 and took a year off. Do you know why?'

'Oh, that was very sad. One of her pupils died. Some sort of accident.'

Meadows sat forward and saw Edris do the same. 'At the school?'

'No, it was… Oh… Oh.'

'What is it?'

'The girl who died was Aneira Thomas, Bryn Thomas' daughter.'

Chapter Twenty-eight

Dawn waited patiently for the news to come on. She'd got into the habit of doing this since she'd come back from holiday. If she couldn't catch it on TV, then she googled for updates. Simon had commented a few times, so she had to be careful and only check when he wasn't around. The problem was, with them both being retired, they spent a lot of time together.

Now she was standing in the kitchen preparing dinner. She had slowly changed the time they ate so she could watch the evening news undisturbed.

'Thought we could go to the garden centre on Saturday.'

Dawn turned around. She hadn't noticed Simon coming into the kitchen. 'OK.'

'We could have lunch out and make a day of it.'

'Yeah, that'll be nice. Dinner will be about twenty minutes. I'll give you a shout.'

To Dawn's dismay, Simon sat down at the table. 'I was thinking, we should extend the decking. The weather is supposed to be changing by the weekend. It's a good time to start on the garden. What do you think?'

Dawn wanted to say that she didn't care about the garden or anything else at this time. Instead, she tried to conjure up some enthusiasm.

'Er… yeah, if you like, but it will be a lot of work. We'd have to move the flower bed.'

'It's not like we've got anything better to do. You know I hate being idle. If we extend the decking, we'll have more room for the party.'

'What party?'

'Our anniversary. We talked about it on holiday.'

It had completely gone from Dawn's mind. 'I was thinking maybe we could go away instead. Just the two of us,' she said.

'We can do that as well. I might just have a surprise for you.'

Dawn hated surprises. She turned back to the cooker and stirred the mince. She was hoping Simon would go back to the sitting room, but he stayed. He grabbed a pad and pen and started drawing plans for the decking. The news came on and Dawn turned to watch the headlines. She wasn't expecting any more updates on the murders, so she tried not to get irritated by Simon hovering.

A fourth victim has been confirmed…

Dawn flew across the kitchen and turned up the volume.

'What is it, love?'

'Shush,' Dawn snapped.

The newsreader continued.

The woman named as Patricia Maddox was found in her home on Sunday morning.

'Oh my God.'

'What?' Simon asked.

'I know her.'

On the screen, a photograph of Patricia was shown before it changed to a row of cottages. One had a tent erected over the doorway with a reporter positioned near it.

There remains a heavy police presence in the area. Residents are becoming increasingly concerned. This small community has been left in shock.

The words of the reporter jumbled together as Dawn tried to take it in. I only spoke to her on Saturday, she thought. The police will check her phone, they will see she called me. Panic coiled around her. She wanted to move but her eyes were fixed to the screen. There was a series of interviews with local residents, then photos of the locations of the previous murders. Among them was an aerial photo of the farm. Dawn saw the house, the surrounding fields and properties. Bile rose in her throat. She ran from the kitchen and only just made it to the downstairs toilet before being sick.

'Dawn, are you OK in there?' Simon called.

Dawn wiped her mouth. 'Just give me a few minutes.'

'Can I get you a glass of water?'

'No. I'll be fine.'

She stayed kneeling on the floor. Her hands were shaking, and she felt light-headed. Pat gone. She couldn't believe it. From what she had read online, the other three murders had been violent. The thought made her stomach heave again. Don't think about it, she kept telling herself.

She didn't know how long she sat on the floor, but her legs were going numb. She got up slowly and splashed some water on her face. When she opened the door, Simon was standing outside.

'I was getting really worried,' he said. 'Come here.' He pulled her close and stroked her hair.

Dawn clung to him. She had kept so much from him, and it wasn't fair. She wished she could tell him, but she was afraid of losing him.

'Talk to me,' Simon said. 'You've never mentioned this woman the whole time we've been together. What's upset you so much?'

'I can't go into it now. Can you give me a little time, please?'

'OK.'

'I'm going upstairs for a lie-down.'

Simon's expression was one of sadness and she hated to cause him to worry. She went upstairs to the bedroom and closed the door. She lay looking up at the ceiling. Her thoughts went to dark places from the past. She had tried to bury them and move on with her life. She had been happy with Simon but at what cost? Deep down she always felt that she didn't deserve happiness.

Simon came into the room, placed her phone on the bedside table, and left. She didn't speak. She felt drained. She must have fallen asleep because the trilling startled her. She was confused for a moment then she picked up the phone and hit accept without taking any notice of the number.

'Hello.'

There was silence for a few seconds then the caller spoke. 'I didn't know whether to call or not. I didn't know if you'd want to speak to me.'

Dawn felt like her heart had stopped. She sat up. 'I... is that–'

'Yes, it's me,' the caller said. 'Hi.'

'Hi,' Dawn said. 'It's so good to hear your voice.'

'It's been a long time,' the caller said. 'After what's been happening, I thought... have you seen the news reports?'

'Yes, I've been following it. Are you OK?'

'Not really. It's been hard. With everything that's happened, I got to do a lot of thinking. I don't want to have regrets and time... well, we never know how much we have left.'

Dawn's throat constricted with emotion. 'I'm just so happy you called.'

'I'd like to see you. If you want to, that is.'

Dawn didn't have to think about it. 'I'd like that very much.'

'After the last time we spoke, I thought...' The caller's voice cracked with emotion.

'Don't worry about that,' Dawn said. 'It's in the past.'

'I'm glad you think so. I need your help. There are things I don't know, things I don't understand.'

'You can ask me anything you like,' Dawn said.

'I don't want to do it on the phone. Is there somewhere we could meet? I could come to you.'

Dawn imagined trying to explain the visit to Simon. There was no way she could keep him away. Even if she sent him out shopping or to the pub, there was a risk he would come back and catch them together. She didn't know how much time they would need.

'Maybe it's better I come to you,' she said.

'I know just the place.'

Dawn listened and tears ran down her face. 'I can't believe you remembered.'

'I never forgot,' the caller said. 'I'll see you soon.'

The call ended too soon for Dawn. She wished she could have talked longer; there was so much to say. She walked downstairs to where Simon was sitting on the sofa watching TV.

'Are you feeling better?' he asked.

'Yeah.' She sat down next to him and rested her head on his shoulder.

'I know there are things in your past that you'd rather not talk about,' he said. 'You don't have to tell me. It's just… I'm worried about you. You haven't been yourself since we came back from holiday.'

'I'm sorry,' Dawn said. 'You know I love you. I don't know where I'd be without you. You really did save me.'

Simon laughed. 'I wouldn't go that far.'

'I was in a bad place when we met.'

'I know. That's why I've never asked you about your past.'

'The murders that have been in the news.' Dawn took a breath. 'I know those people.'

'I did wonder why you've been so interested in the news. I take it it's brought up some bad memories for you.'

'Yes, and there is someone I need to see. I think I can help them.'

'Do you think it's a good idea? It must be over thirty years since you've had contact with anyone from your past.'

'It's not been that long.'

'I see.'

'No, it's not like that, I promise you. I kept in contact with Patricia Maddox for a while, the woman who was on the news earlier. It'd been years since I'd spoken to her. It was only ever to keep… to… I just wanted to know…'

'You wanted to keep tabs on certain people?'

Dawn smiled. 'Yeah.'

'Is the person you want to see someone you cared about?'

'Yes.'

'That's all I need to know. When do you want to go? I'll take you.'

'It's probably best I go alone. I can catch the train.'

Simon shook his head. 'With all these people being murdered? It's too dangerous.'

'Nothing is going to happen to me. I'll only be gone a few hours. I'll be back in time for dinner.'

Chapter Twenty-nine

The atmosphere in the office was charged as they all waited for the coroner's report on Aneira's accident.

'Let's just bring Teilo in,' Blackwell said.

'We need to wait for the details,' Meadows said. 'All we know is Aneira died in an accident.'

'It's got to be him,' Blackwell said.

'A dead sister isn't going to be enough for the CPS to bring charges,' Meadows said.

'And he's got an alibi for the morning of Huw's murder,' Valentine said.

Meadows nodded. 'Contact Teilo's client and see if the tyre on his car was vandalised.'

'As far as we know, there is no connection between Huw and Teilo,' Edris said. 'He has no motive to kill him. The abuse was against Lesley and the children.'

'That's a big sticking point,' Paskin said.

'Do we have anything on the journalist that was visiting Patricia?'

'No,' Valentine said. 'All the local papers have been checked, and some of the bigger ones.'

'It could have been Chloe, Anna, or Sarah,' Edris suggested. 'Even Teilo's wife, Nerys. She'd help him. One of them poses as a journalist to see what information Patricia has.'

Valentine nodded. 'It's not a bad theory.'

'The problem with that is if one of them was posing as a journalist, Patricia would have recognised them at the meeting,' Meadows said.

'Sally did say she hadn't seen them for years. So, she pitches up at the meeting and recognises one of them,' Edris said.

'She was giving them the evil eye,' Blackwell said.

'But they all knew the community would be invited and would have known that Patricia would talk,' Paskin added.

Meadows thought for a moment. 'What was it Sally said about the journalist? Didn't dress well and sat like a man, something like that.'

Edris checked his notes. 'Yeah. So, one of them used a disguise. Teilo or Luke. Patricia was staring at them. Maybe she worked it out.'

'What about Patricia's phone log?' Meadows asked. 'Maybe we could trace the journalist that way, if they made contact by phone.'

'She has a lot of contacts,' Paskin said. 'I'm working my way through all of them. There are a few unanswered that I'm waiting on. So far nothing promising. She wasn't in contact with Huw Jones, Bryn Thomas, or Malcom Isaac. I'll keep at it.'

Meadows' phone tinged indicating new mail. He looked at the screen. 'Report from the coroner's office.' He opened the file on his computer.

As he read, he felt a deep sadness wash over him. The details brought vivid images to his mind and churned his stomach. He rubbed his hands over his face, sighed, and turned to the team.

'It's not pleasant reading,' he said. 'Aneria Thomas was six years old at the time. She was either playing in the field or had fallen asleep and didn't hear the machinery. It was harvesting time. Bryn Thomas was cutting the crops with Malcom Isaac's combine harvester. Aneira was caught up in the cutting bar. I don't think I need to go into the details of her injuries.'

'Poor kid,' Blackwell said.

Valentine shook her head. 'It doesn't bear thinking about.'

'According to the inquest report, Malcom Isaac was present at the time of the accident, and Bryn Thomas was driving.'

'So Bryn's the child killer,' Blackwell said.

'Motive for Teilo to kill him and Malcom,' Meadows said. 'What concerns me is the fact that it was a trigger of the killer's memory that started this. The death of a sister is not something you are likely to forget.'

Valentine moved from her desk and started to read out the transcript of the blog pinned to the incident board.

At my feet is a petrol can. I'd like nothing more than to see flames chase away the darkness that surrounds me and the darkness within. It's what I came here to do. To eradicate the place that haunts me.

'It would work if it was Ynysforgan farm.'

'She's right,' Meadows said. 'The accident happened on Bryn's land.'

'What if Teilo knew something about the accident back then? He was just a child himself,' Blackwell said. 'He speaks up, but the adults threaten him somehow. It was Malcom's machinery, he was there. There could be more to the story than what was told at the inquest.'

Meadows nodded. 'It's a possibility.'

'Where does Huw Jones and Patricia Maddox come into it?' Paskin asked.

'It sounds like Patricia had a relationship with Bryn,' Edris said. 'She could have been there that day and been part of the cover-up. She feels guilty, leaves the school and moves from the area.'

'That photograph we found had "Harvest 1991" on the back,' Meadows said. 'Same time Aneira died. That just leaves Huw.'

Everyone shrugged their shoulders.

'He was a friend of Malcom, so he has to be involved somehow,' Blackwell said. 'We know he was abusive.'

'Where do the stick dolls come into it?' Edris asked.

'Children draw them,' Valentine said. 'Aneira was only six years old. Maybe she had been drawing them that day and when Teilo saw them, it remined him of the accident.'

'Teilo would have been on the farm that day. We don't know what he witnessed and may have forgotten,' Meadows said. 'We still have a lot of unanswered questions. Do we have enough to make Teilo our prime suspect?'

'Yeah,' Blackwell said.

The others nodded.

'OK,' Meadows said, 'let's bring him in.'

Chapter Thirty

Meadows entered the interview room and saw Teilo sitting with his solicitor, Andrew Sully. 'Sorry to have kept you waiting.'

Teilo gave him a tight smile.

Meadows took a seat and waited for Edris to tell the time, date and those present for the recording.

'You've been arrested on suspicion of the murder of Malcom Isaac, Huw Jones, Patricia Maddox, and Bryn Thomas,' Meadows said. 'Is there anything you'd like to say before we begin?'

Teilo shook his head. 'I understand that you have a job to do. I'm happy to answer your questions.'

Meadows studied Teilo. While he appeared a little uncomfortable, he wasn't showing outward signs of anxiety. Anyone who found themselves in a police interview room was generally anxious, although there were some who just didn't care. He wondered if Teilo was innocent and therefore not overly concerned, or if he was beyond caring. There had been nothing in Teilo's background check to suggest violence. He was a member of several professional bodies and had glowing reviews on his website. What did stand out was the exhaustion. It showed in his eyes and the pallor of his skin. This didn't come from one bad night's sleep, Meadows thought. It came from continued insomnia like the killer had described.

'You look tired,' Meadows said. 'Are you not sleeping well?'

The question appeared to throw Teilo for a moment. Then he nodded. 'I don't think I've had a good night's sleep since I found… Dad.'

'You can stop the interview anytime you feel you need a break.'

'Sounds fair.'

'I want to ask you about the time you lived on Ynysforgan farm,' Meadows said.

'OK, but as I said before, I was young when I left to live with my auntie and uncle. I don't remember much.'

'You lived there with your parents?'

Teilo rubbed his forearm. 'Yes, until I lost my mother.'

'So, it was just you and your father.'

Teilo shifted in his seat. 'Erm… yes.'

'That's not true though, is it? There was someone else living there.'

Teilo looked down for a moment. When he looked back up, there was a sadness in his eyes. 'My sister Aneira lived with us.'

'Why didn't you mention this the last time we questioned you?'

Colour rose in Teilo's cheeks. 'Honestly? I don't like talking about it. There didn't seem to be a point in bringing it up. It can't have had anything to do with what happened to Dad. It was years ago.'

'Can you tell us what happened to Aneira?'

'Is that necessary?' the solicitor asked. 'My client has already indicated that the memory causes distress.'

'We need to know what your client remembers about his sister's death,' Meadows said.

'It was an accident.' Teilo twisted his hands. 'She fell from the window of the barn.'

Meadows glanced at Edris and saw the look of surprise on his face. 'Were you with her when she fell?'

'No.' Teilo wrapped his arms around is body. 'I was feeding the animals. There was always work to be done but I should have been watching her.'

Meadows wondered if Teilo was lying or if that's what he had been told. He didn't want to cause unnecessary anguish, especially if they were wrong about Teilo's involvement in his father's death. He decided to let it go for now and keep digging. If Teilo was lying, then he would trip up at some point.

'Did you feel guilty about your sister's death?' Edris asked.

Teilo's eyes misted. 'Yes, for a long time.'

'Did your father blame you?' Meadows asked.

'My client can't be expected to know that,' the solicitor said.

'Do you think your father blamed you?' Meadows asked.

Teilo shrugged. 'He never talked to me about it. I don't think he talked to me at all after it happened, he just sent me away. At the time, it felt like he blamed me.'

'Did you talk about it when you reconnected?' Meadows asked.

'No. I mentioned Aneira once and he shut down. He didn't want to talk about her, didn't even keep a photograph of her.'

'That must have made you angry,' Meadows said.

Teilo gave a sad smile. 'I was angry with my father for a long time, angry with myself, and angry at the world. It's why I became a bereavement counsellor. I wanted to help people who have been through the same. I know what it's like to lose someone close, what it can do to you if you don't process the grief.'

'Who told you about Aneira's accident?' Meadows asked.

'Erm… I'm not sure. It may have been my father. I remember I wanted to go to the hospital to see her. I thought she had just hurt herself. It was my auntie who explained it to me in a nice way. She said Aneira had hit her head and fallen asleep; that she wouldn't wake up again. I don't know if she was in a coma and died later or if she died instantly. I'm sure there will be a record at the hospital if you want to check the details.'

'You've never requested the details yourself?' Meadows asked.

'No. I'd like to think that she died instantly. I've learned it's not good to torture yourself with imaginings. Knowing exactly what happened wouldn't change the outcome and bring her back.'

Meadows thought it sounded like a reasonable explanation. If the same thing happened to him, would he want to know the details years later? He doubted it.

'Did you know that both your father and Malcom Isaac were present when your sister died?' he asked.

'You mean they saw her fall?' Teilo sat up a little straighter.

Meadows chose his words carefully. 'Not exactly.'

Teilo's face creased with confusion. 'Are you saying it wasn't an accident? You think Dad or Malcom did something? What? What did they do?'

Meadows could see the flare of Teilo's nostrils and the widening of his eyes. He was breathing quickly. 'We're looking into it. We've only just learned of Aneira's death. Once we know exactly what happened we can discuss it with you, if you wish to know. But for now, that's all I can say.'

'I think my client needs a break,' the solicitor said.

Teilo shook his head. 'I'm OK.'

'Some water?' Meadows asked.

'Please.'

Edris left the room and Meadows gave Teilo a few moments before continuing.

'Tell me about Malcom Isaac.'

'I don't remember him. Dad was always busy on the farm and there were men that came to help out sometimes. Malcom could have been one of them, I suppose. He was just Chloe and Anna's father. I'd catch a glimpse of him now and again but I wouldn't be able to tell you what he looked like.'

'But you do remember Chloe and Anna.'

'Yes, not well though. Chloe was older than me and Anna was younger. She played with Aneira. She was more her age. When I saw them at the meeting, I had a memory of playing with them in a field. There was a stream. It was on Malcom's land. We would play in it when it was hot. It's just snippets that I remember.'

Edris came back into the room and handed Teilo a plastic cup.

'Thank you.' Teilo took a sip then placed the cup on the desk.

'Have you ever been to Ty Gwyn house?'

'Ty Gwyn?'

'Malcom Isaac's house,' Meadows said.

Teilo thought for a moment. 'I think so. I've got a vague memory of Chloe's mother giving us squash and sandwiches. We would sit at the table.'

'What about the rest of the house?'

'I don't think so.'

'You never played inside on a rainy day. Hide and seek?'

'Not that I remember. We were out in all weather. Feeding the animals and walking to school. I don't think we would be allowed to play indoors, even if it was raining. From what I remember, there wasn't a lot of free time until the school holidays. Like I said, I only remember bits. I might have been invited inside to play but I don't remember.'

'Did you know Malcom Isaac kept a shotgun?'

Teilo took another sip of water. 'No, but it wouldn't surprise me. Most farmers have one. My father did.'

Meadows sat back and gave Edris a nod. Edris opened a file and placed three photographs on the desk.

'Do you recognise the man in these photos?'

Teilo looked at them and smiled. 'Yes, it's Dad when he was younger.'

'We found these in Patricia Maddox's house,' Edris said.

'Oh.' Teilo looked thoughtful for a moment. 'That's the woman who was found dead in her house on Sunday. I heard it on the news.'

'Did you know her?'

'No, I don't think so.'

Edris placed a photo of Patricia on the desk.

Teilo looked at it. 'I'm sure she was in the meeting on Saturday. She was staring at me.'

'She was a teacher at Dyffryn Du school and before that, headteacher at Craig-Y-Coed school.'

'I went to Craig-Y-Coed for a little while. I don't remember her though.'

'We think it's probable that she was in a relationship with your father.'

'Really? Well, I suppose she could have been. He was on his own at the farm when I left.' Teilo sat back in his chair.

'We think you would have still been with your father at the time,' Meadows said. 'Do you remember any women visiting?'

'No. We didn't have any visitors except my auntie and uncle. They would come sometimes.'

'We know you would have been at school with Chloe and Anna, but how do you know Luke Jones?'

'I don't.'

'You spoke to Luke at the meeting briefly,' Meadows said.

'Just to say sorry for his loss.'

Meadows thought about the interaction he'd seen on the recording. It did appear that the men didn't know each other. 'What about Sarah Jones? Do you know her?'

'I met her for the first time at the meeting. I don't know the family. Dad may have, but he never mentioned them.'

Meadows took a series of photographs from the file and placed them on the desk. 'What can you tell me about these?'

Teilo looked down at the stick dolls and recoiled, as if he'd been stung. 'You already showed me the ones found in Dad's house. Were these things found with all the victims?'

'Yes,' Meadows said. 'You appear bothered by them.'

'Wouldn't you be if it was your father?'

Fair point, Meadows thought. 'Have you seen them before?'

Teilo shook his head.

'What can you tell me about inner-child therapy?'

'It's a method used to try and heal childhood trauma. The idea is you connect with your inner child and explore the time when that child was damaged. Some refer to it as "reparenting".'

'Have you used this method in your work?'

'No. I came across it during my training but it's not really applicable to grief counselling. Why?'

'It's something that came up during our investigation,' Meadows said. He gave Edris another nod.

'Can you tell us about your movements on Saturday just gone?' Edris asked.

'I had breakfast with Nerys when she came home from her shift, caught up with some paperwork, then visited my auntie in hospital.'

'How long did you stay?'

'About an hour. I came home, had food, then went to the meeting.'

'Did you stop off anywhere on the way to or the way back from the hospital?'

'No.'

'What did you do after the meeting?'

'I went straight home.'

'Alone?'

'Nerys went off to work about half an hour later.'

'Did you see or speak to anyone after Nerys left for work?'

'No.'

Edris wrote some notes then sat back in his chair.

'Can I go now?' Teilo asked.

'We will need to check with the hospital that you were there at the times you gave us,' Meadows said. 'As was explained to you earlier a search is being carried out at your property. Any items of clothing or shoes recovered will need to be processed, as well as any devices.'

'How long will that take?'

'It will be given priority.'

'So, I've got to stay here? In a cell?'

'I'm afraid so,' Meadows said.

'I really must object,' the solicitor said. 'My client has answered all of your questions and you have no evidence to tie him to the crimes. Unless you are going to charge him, release him pending further investigation.'

'Given the nature of the crimes committed, we will be holding your client for the maximum period. As you are aware, we can apply for an extension after that.'

The solicitor turned to Teilo. 'I'll see what I can do about getting you released as soon as possible.'

'I've already missed appointments,' Teilo said. 'I don't like letting people down.'

'I'm sure they will understand,' Meadows said.

While Teilo didn't look happy about the situation, he didn't protest about being taken to the holding cell.

* * *

'Do you think it's him?' Edris asked as they made their way back upstairs.

'Honestly?' Meadows said. 'I don't know. He was polite, answered all our questions, and was honest about being angry with his father. His account of his sister's death is very convincing.'

'But?'

'Did I say there was a but?'

Edris smiled. 'I can tell.'

'I just have a feeling that he is involved. Maybe he's *too* nice.'

Edris laughed. 'Says Mr Nice Guy himself.'

'I'm not that nice.'

'I don't think I've ever seen you lose your temper.'

'Yeah, well, getting angry doesn't get you anywhere.'

As they reached the top of the stairs they met up with Paskin.

'I was just coming to find you,' she said. 'There's another post on the killer's blog.'

Chapter Thirty-one

I'm not a monster. I've seen what's been written about me. Reporters, who don't know the real story, talk of a maniac randomly killing pensioners. They should be writing about what these people have done.

A child only has to have basic needs met to survive: food, water, shelter, love, and protection. It's not much to ask. So many times, these needs are not met. The parents fail them, the system fails them. Blame and shame fall on them. It takes its toll.

These so-called victims are not innocent. Any one of them could have stopped it. I never asked for this, the endless pain and torment. Neither did the others. Even now that invisible gag is so tight they cannot speak out. It's just as well, for if they did, I wouldn't have a chance to finish it. At least, they will be free now.

All around me people are talking about Patricia Maddox. They paint this picture of a wonderful woman who dedicated her life to teaching children. That's not what she was. She was in a position of trust. An adult that children looked up to. She betrayed that trust.

I couldn't stay to watch her die, I've seen enough. It was a big risk, but it worked. She'd lived a long life with no guilt or shame. I know this as she talked so much. She was so arrogant she didn't see it coming. There was an excitement in her eyes as she talked about the murders. She was quick to talk of the fault in others and point out the splinter in their eyes while not seeing the plank in her own. Hypocrite, as the Bible says.

You probably think the same of me. The difference is I know what I've done, what I've become. The secrets and lies will end with me.

I'm going to tell you my story, but first I have the two little stick dolls left. I kept them for the one it started with.

* * *

Meadows read through the blog again then sat back in his chair. The team came in one by one.

'It feels like we haven't been home in days,' Edris said.

'You haven't,' Meadows said.

'I meant, away from this place.'

Blackwell was the last in, having stopped off with forensics. Meadows could tell by his face that it wasn't good news.

'Nothing then?'

Blackwell shook his head. 'Everything taken from Teilo's house has been tested. There was something interesting. Mike Fielding said fibres found on one of the armchairs in Patricia Maddox's house matched fibres caught in one of the bolts used to kill Huw Jones. There was also synthetic hair.'

'We had a suspicion that the killer is using a disguise,' Meadows said.

Before anyone had a chance to respond, Lester appeared.

'Why have you still got Teilo Thomas in custody?' Lester asked.

'We were waiting on forensics.'

'And?'

'We've got nothing on him,' Meadows said. 'We had limitations to the warrant because of client confidentiality. We can't touch the files unless we have good reason to believe that the killer is one of Teilo's clients. There was nothing of significance taken from his house. Shoes and items of clothing have been tested and a thorough search was made for any hidden devices.'

'Do Teilo's alibis check out?' Lester asked.

Meadows nodded. 'The client said the flat tyre was just that. No damage, but Teilo could have let it down. He was also at the hospital at the time he gave. The problem is, Malcom and Bryn were killed at night. Teilo's wife works the night shift so we can't rule him out for those murders. Same with Patricia. She could have been given the wine and chocolates at any time.'

'What about this latest blog post?' Lester asked.

'Could have been scheduled,' Meadows said. 'Chris is working on tracing it.'

'Have you spoken to the auntie?' Lester asked.

'The doctor said she should be well enough to talk to in a couple of days. Perhaps we can push to see her sooner and hold Teilo until then.'

Lester shook his head. 'Release him. CPS are not going to agree to a charge.'

Meadows wasn't happy about it but he agreed to the release.

'He could have an accomplice,' Valentine said. 'The child-killer reference has got to relate to the death of Aneira Thomas.'

'The blog refers to others suffering. It makes me think there is more to it. There are still missing pieces of the puzzle,' Meadows said.

'Or a missing person of the puzzle,' Paskin said. 'We've got the child killer, Bryn Thomas; the abuser, Huw Jones or Malcom Isaac; the one who kept quiet, possibly Patricia Maddox; and the one who turned their back, I suppose that could be Malcom Isaac. Perhaps he was supposed to be making sure the machinery was safe. That leaves the abandoner.'

'Bryn abandoned Teilo,' Blackwell said. 'Maybe Malcom was the one who was driving the combine harvester. That would make him the child killer.'

'Why would Bryn keep quiet about that?' Valentine asked.

Blackwell shrugged. 'Malcom had money so maybe he paid him off.'

'I thought Malcom was the abuser,' Edris said. 'Given all the dolls that were left with his body.'

Valentine shook her head. 'We know that Huw was physically abusing Lesley.'

'Either way we are still missing one,' Paskin said.

'It all leads back to Teilo, he's the one who lost his sister. We just can't find a motive for him to kill Huw Jones. Unless...' Meadows rubbed his hands over his chin. 'What if someone else witnessed the accident and was traumatised? Teilo said that Aneira and Anna played together. One of the girls could have been out in the field that day. Chloe also has motive for killing Huw and her father but not Patricia. Then there is the Joneses but I can't see a connection between them and the death of Aneira.'

'Yeah but the forty-one bolts tie Lesley, Sarah, and Luke to Huw's murder,' Blackwell said.

'I take it all these people have alibis,' Lester said.

'Luke and Sarah were with Lesley on the dates in question apart from for the murder of Huw Jones.'

'Mother protecting her children,' Lester said.

'Or the other way around,' Meadows said. 'Chloe claims she is always either at the farm or on school runs.

Her sister, Anna, was at home. We only have their husbands' word that they didn't go out at night.'

'No other viable suspects?'

Meadows shook his head. 'Teilo was our prime suspect. We've gone through every family member and anyone connected to the victims. We're still working on eliminating those connected to Patricia.'

'Keep me updated,' Lester said. 'I'm going to the incident room. Last time I checked, they were inundated with calls. I'll see if they need more resources to help process the information. Then I'm due to talk to the press.'

'I don't envy you that,' Meadows said. 'Good luck.'

'We should arrest them all,' Blackwell said.

'Tempting,' Meadows said. 'If it would make them talk, then I would. I'm sure they're all holding back information, Teilo included. That information could crack the case. Can you chase up the transcript for Aneira Thomas' inquest? I want to know who attended and who gave evidence.'

'I'll get on it,' Paskin said.

'Blackwell and Valentine, interview the neighbouring farms. See who remembers the accident. There may have been talk at the time. It would be good to place Huw Jones there. We need a motive that ties to all four victims.' Meadows checked the time. 'Let's head to Patricia's post-mortem and see what we can find out.'

* * *

Not enough time had passed since their last visit to the morgue for Meadows' liking, though he was pleased to be seeing Daisy. It was the only place he felt was safe for them to meet.

Daisy gave them a smile when they entered her office.

'Only one week to go for the wedding,' Edris said. 'You must be getting excited.'

'I haven't had time to get excited,' Daisy said.

Meadows felt a pang of guilt. The wedding was the furthest thing from his mind at the moment. It should have been a time filled with preparations for the approaching day.

'Well, I can't wait,' Edris said. 'I've got two days off to recover.'

Meadows laughed. 'How much are you planning on drinking?'

'I want to enjoy myself and Rain said I could stay.'

Daisy arched her eyebrows. 'You're going to stay in the commune? In this weather?'

'There will be a fire, won't there?'

Meadows grinned. 'Oh yeah, you'll have all the comforts of home.'

'OK, enough chatter. I'll take you through,' Daisy said.

They entered the morgue and saw Patricia laid out on a metal gurney. A sheet was pulled up to her shoulders.

'For her age, she was in good health,' Daisy said. 'It makes it all the more tragic. There isn't a lot to tell you. No physical injuries or defence marks. There is scar tissue in her uterus. Nothing in her medical history to suggest gynaecological problems. It's possible she had a termination or miscarriage.'

'It could be another reason why she took a year off teaching,' Meadows said. 'I imagine if she'd lost a baby, it would be hard being around children all day.'

Daisy nodded. 'The official cause of death is anaphylactic shock. There was a note in her records that she had a severe allergy to chilli. Test showed that chilli was present in the wine and chocolates.'

'The killer was making sure,' Meadows said.

'The chilli apparently is one of the hottest. Appropriately named Dragon's Breath. I imagine she ate a chocolate, felt the burn, and tried to calm it by drinking the wine. Her airways would have swollen quickly.'

'So, she effectively suffocated,' Meadows said.

'Yes.'

'The killer would've had to know about the allergy,' Edris said. 'So, it's someone who knew her well.'

'Not necessarily,' Meadows said. 'If our journalist and killer are one and the same, they could have easily found out that information. All they would have to say is they wanted to give her a thank-you gift, then ask if she had any allergies. Or she could have volunteered the information, and that's what gave the killer the idea.'

'Time of death?' Edris asked.

'Anytime between 8 p.m. and, say, 11 p.m.'

'Problem is the killer didn't have to be anywhere near,' Meadows said. He looked at Daisy. 'Thanks.'

Daisy smiled. 'No worries.'

* * *

Outside, heavy rain bounced off the tarmac. The detectives ran for the car but were soaked by the time they shut the doors.

'What now?' Edris asked.

'Ynysforgan farm,' Meadows said. 'I want to ask Chloe what she remembers about Aneira's accident. I'm also interested in what she has to say about her relationship with Luke and why she didn't tell us.'

Meadows pulled out of the car park and switched the wipers to double speed.

'I wonder who the father of Patricia's baby was,' Edris said.

'I'm betting Bryn Thomas. If she was seeing him at the time of Aneira's death, then perhaps he didn't want another child when he had just lost his daughter.'

'Or maybe Patricia was jealous of the children. Angry she'd lost the baby. Maybe she did something to Aneira. Could have placed her in the field knowing Bryn would be harvesting. With her injuries, they wouldn't be looking for any other cause of death.'

Meadows' phoned trilled through the car speakers and Paskin's name flashed up on the screen.

'What have you got for us?' Meadows asked.

'Just had a call from Pallavi, Dyffryn Du school. She found the name of the pupil that attacked Patricia. It was Luke Jones. She also confirmed that he attended Craig-Y-Coed before moving to Henllys primary school for the last year.'

'Thanks.' He ended the call.

'So Teilo and Luke went to primary school together,' Edris said. 'Interesting.'

'Yeah, and Lesley lied about it. Luke attacked Patricia when he was in school. He was a teenager. What if he decided to finish what he started? We need to bring him in.'

Chapter Thirty-two

They had no luck finding Luke and now their last hope was a known squat where Hanes and Taylor were waiting for them.

The house looked derelict and had blankets hanging in front of the windows.

'Looks like a crack house,' Edris said when they arrived.

'That's exactly what it is,' Hanes said. 'What's the plan?'

'I just want to see if Luke is inside,' Meadows said. 'If you want to arrest anyone, that's your call. OK, let's do this.'

Hanes moved to the door and banged loudly. 'Police!' he shouted before flinging open the door.

Meadows was hit with the strong aroma of cannabis.

They moved into the sitting room, which was a haze of smoke. Two women and four men looked at them but made no effort to move.

Meadows looked around. The occupants were sitting on various beaten-up chairs. The carpet was littered with debris. Glass pipes, bits of tin foil, and syringes were strewn across a table illuminated by candlelight.

'You can't come in here,' one of the women said. She had a gaunt, pockmarked face and several missing teeth.

'Own the place, do you?' Hanes asked.

'No but we have rights.'

'We're only here to have a chat with Luke,' Meadows said. 'My advice would be to sit quietly. If you play nice then PC Hanes won't take your sweeties away.'

The woman scowled but didn't make any further comment.

Meadows walked over to Luke, who was slouched in a chair. His head was resting to one side and the sleeve of his jumper was pulled up.

Meadows crouched down. 'Luke, we need to speak to you.'

Luke looked at him through hooded eyes. 'Go away,' he mumbled.

'He's off his tits,' Edris said. 'We're not going to get any sense out of him.'

'Yeah, you're right,' Meadows said. He stood up and grabbed Luke by the arm. 'Come on, get up; we're going for a ride.' He turned to Edris. 'Grab his jacket.'

Luke put up little resistance as Hanes grabbed his other arm and hauled him to his feet. Together, they walked him outside. Taylor opened the back door to the police car.

'I'll book him in,' Hanes said. 'He'll sober up by the morning.'

'We haven't got time to mess around,' said Meadows. 'Stick him in my car. We'll take him to his mother's house; let her see him in this state. Maybe it will give her some incentive to talk.'

'What if he's the killer?' Edris asked.

'The only person he's capable of killing at the moment is himself,' Meadows said.

Hanes bundled Luke into the back of the car and Edris climbed in beside him. Meadows drove away from the house and Luke rested his head against the window. Edris was as close to the other door as he could get.

'He's drooling,' Edris said.

'He's fine.'

'What if he pukes?'

Meadows lips twitched. 'Then catch it in something. I don't want it all over the car.'

They had only driven a couple of miles when Luke took a tin from his pocket and took the lid off. The car filled with the smell of weed.

'Don't even think about skinning up in here,' Edris said. 'I already stink of the stuff from that house.'

'Sergeant Edris is not in favour of hotboxing it,' Meadows said. 'You can put it away and we'll drop you with your mum or we can put you in a cell.'

Luke ignored him and tried to take out the papers, but he had no coordination. The tin tipped and the contents emptied over his lap and the back seat.

'No,' Edris groaned. He started to brush at the seat next to him with his hand. 'I think some has got on me.'

Meadows tried not to laugh. 'Shake it off when we stop.'

The rest of the journey was spent with Luke trying to salvage the cannabis, but he was too out of it to clear up.

Edris was out of the car as soon as Meadows pulled up the handbrake. Meadows got Luke out then scooped what he could of the cannabis back into the tin before handing it to Luke. They walked Luke to the front door of Lesley's house and Meadows knocked loudly. It took a few minutes for the door to be opened.

Lesley was in her dressing gown. 'What's going on?' She looked at Luke. 'What have you done to him?'

'We haven't done anything to him,' Meadows said. 'He's done this to himself. The question you should be asking is, why is he doing this? I think we better get him inside.'

They followed Lesley into the sitting room and Luke plonked himself down on the sofa.

'What's he taken?' Lesley asked.

'My best guess is heroin,' said Meadows. 'Possibly some other stuff. In my experience people who inject it into their veins do so to escape some sort of torment. Maybe it's time you told us the truth so he can get some help.'

'I've told you what Huw was like.'

'I think it's more than that,' Meadows said. 'Why did you lie about Luke attending Craig-Y-Coed primary school?'

'I didn't lie.'

'I asked you if he attended that school and you said no. Why did he change school?'

Lesley looked at Luke then back to Meadows. 'Huw thought Henllys was a better school. He thought Luke would do better there.'

Meadows shook his head. 'Why do you keep lying to us?' He moved to the sofa and crouched down next to Luke. 'Your mother told us how your father abused her, abused you all. We know you tried to protect her. What else happened?'

'You can't ask him questions when he's in this state,' Lesley said.

Meadows knew she was right, but he carried on. 'What happened to Aneira Thomas? Luke!'

Luke looked at him. 'Dunno.'

'Teilo's sister.'

'Who's that?'

'You went to school together. Aneira had an accident. What do you know about it?'

'Dunno what the fuck you're talking about.' Luke's eyelids drooped.

'Luke! Why did you attack Patricia Maddox when you were in school?'

'She was a bitch, innit. Didn't listen.'

'Didn't listen to what?'

'He struggled in school,' Lesley said. 'He told her he couldn't do the work. She kept picking on him.'

'Luke?'

Luke nodded.

'You and Chloe went out together. Why did you argue?'

Lesley took a step forward. 'I told you that–'

'I need Luke to answer,' Meadows snapped. 'Luke, listen to me. You had a strained relationship with your father, and you attacked Patricia Maddox. Both are dead. It doesn't look good for you.'

'Shit happens,' Luke said.

'You and Chloe. What happened between the two of you?'

Luke rubbed his eyes. 'I'm done.'

'Not yet,' Meadows said. 'Just tell me what you and Chloe argued about.'

Despite the effect of the drugs, Luke's eyes narrowed and he clenched his jaw.

'We can't help you if you won't tell us,' Meadows said.

'Why don't you ask Chloe what her father did?'

'I think I'd like you to leave,' Lesley said.

Meadows nodded. 'I suggest you keep him here and sober him up. We'll be back in the morning. If he's not here then I'll put out a warrant for his arrest. If I find out either of you is harbouring a killer, then I'll arrest you for perverting the course of justice. You could end up with a life sentence.'

Meadows left the house and jumped in the car.

'I don't think I've ever seen you so angry,' Edris said.

'I'm not angry. I'm just fed up with playing games. Anyway, you told me I was too nice.'

'Yeah, well, you are, usually.'

Meadows smiled. 'I figured we needed to shake things up. First thing in the morning, we're going to Ynysforgan farm. They should all be up early. I'll let you play the angry one if you like.'

'Nah, it will be more fun watching you trying to be tough.'

'At least we know Malcom did do something. What we need to find out is why Chloe would protect the name of a man she claims to hate.'

Chapter Thirty-three

'This car still stinks of weed,' Edris complained. 'If someone smells it, you could be in a lot of trouble.'

'Nah, I'll tell them you dropped your bag.' Meadows saw the horror on Edris' face and laughed. 'Don't worry. I'll hoover it as soon as I have time.'

'As soon as we get back to the office, I'm putting it in for valeting,' Edris said.

If this was Edris' reaction, Meadows worried about what he'd be like at the commune. 'You know that some people like the odd joint up at the commune,' Meadows said. 'Maybe staying after the wedding isn't such a good idea.'

Edris laughed. 'How thick do you think I am? I'd be more surprised if people weren't stoned. I won't be on duty. It's the dealers I hate, and traffickers who use slave labour on cannabis farms. If some old bugger wants to smoke it for his arthritis, then good luck to him. What I don't like is sitting in a car smelling of the stuff and molecules penetrating my suit.'

They arrived at the farm and were told by a man on a quad bike that Chloe and Anna were at Malcom's farm tending to the sheep.

'Great, now we're going to have to traipse through a muddy field,' Edris complained.

'You'll be fine. Put your boots on.'

Meadows drove to Malcom's house and parked up in the yard. 'Come on then, they can't be far. We went through a field of sheep when we were looking for Malcom. This way.'

'I was thinking,' Edris said. 'All the angst between Chloe and Luke could be a front. Maybe they're banging.'

'Banging?'

'Yeah, you know, having an affair.'

'I know what banging is,' Meadows said. 'I just can't see it.'

'It would make sense. Chloe wants to get rid of Malcom so she can have access to the land, and Luke wants to get rid of his father. Bryn has some document on the stipulation, so they kill him and Patricia... well, she did something to piss them off.'

'What about the blog?'

'Huw's the abuser, Malcom stayed silent about the stipulation of the land, they say Bryn is a child killer because they know about Aneira and...'

'Well, don't stop now,' Meadows said. 'You've nearly solved the case.'

'We just need them to tell us why Patricia died.'

'That's the problem. There is always a sticking point. Teilo doesn't have a reason to kill Huw Jones or Patricia. Chloe or Anna don't have a reason to kill Patricia. Lesley, Luke, and Sarah don't have a reason to kill anyone except Huw. Yet one of them had a reason to kill them all.'

By the time they reached the field with the sheep, they both had mud splattered up their trouser legs.

Chloe and Anna watched their approach.

'What now?' Chloe asked.

Meadows regarded the two sisters. 'Now you can tell me about Aneira's accident.'

Chloe stiffened. 'Anna, go back to my house and wait there.'

'No.' Anna looked at Meadows. 'I'd forgotten about Aneira until–'

'This lot started dragging things up,' Chloe said.

'Why didn't you tell us?' Meadows asked.

'What was the point? It was years ago,' Chloe said.

'I want you to tell me what happened.'

'I don't bloody know,' Chloe said. 'Aneira was in the field and...' She looked at Anna. 'She was hit by the combine harvester.'

Meadows looked at Anna, then back to Chloe. 'Did one of you witness the accident?'

'No,' Chloe said. 'Dad told us. He used it as a way to keep us from going into the crop fields. He said Aneira had... had been chopped to bits. Anna had nightmares for weeks. That's the kind of bastard he was.' Chloe turned to her sister. 'I'm sorry, Anna. I didn't want to remind you of it. She was your friend.'

All the colour drained from Anna's face. 'Oh God, I remember now.'

'What else?' Meadows asked.

Chloe huffed. 'There is nothing else to tell.'

'Your father was with Bryn that day.'

'Yeah.'

'And Patricia Maddox?'

'What? No... well, I don't know. Why would she be there?'

'Who else was there?'

'I don't know!'

'Do you think that your father was in same way responsible?'

'Why would I think that?'

'You know something,' Meadows said. 'You're not protecting your father so who are you protecting? Your sister?'

'What? I... I haven't done anything,' Anna said.

'We spoke to Luke last night. He told us what your father did. Enough pretending. Either you talk now or I'm arresting the two of you on suspicion of murder.'

Anna looked terrified. 'Chloe, you have to—'

'They're not going to do that,' Chloe said.

'We know you've deliberately withheld information that could have prevented the death of Bryn Thomas and Patricia Maddox. That's enough to take you in.' Meadows turned to Edris. 'Go ahead.'

'Fine,' Chloe said. 'You want to know if Luke is telling the truth? Then yes, he is.'

Meadows had to think quickly. 'I'd like to hear your version. You kept it a secret all these years. Why?'

'Why! Why!' Chloe's eyes were wild. 'You're unbelievable. It was bad enough when Luke brought it up, but to have everyone know – can you imagine what that would do to us in a place like this?'

Anna started to cry.

'Why don't we calm things down?' Meadows said. 'Perhaps we can go back to your house and talk about this.'

Chloe nodded. 'We'll cut across the fields and meet you there.'

* * *

'Do you think we should have let them go off on their own?' Edris asked.

'They've got nowhere to run but open fields. They'll probably get back to the house before us,' Meadows said.

Edris nodded. 'Great trick, by the way. You got Chloe talking. You sounded so convincing, I almost believed it myself.'

'Now Chloe thinks we know whatever it is we don't know. We're going to have to be careful. Let her think we know everything; it's the only way we're going to get answers. Best just let her talk when we get to the house.'

As they parked in the yard, Chloe and Anna arrived. It made Meadows realise just how close the neighbouring farms were if you knew the shortcut through the fields.

The two women didn't wait to invite them in, so Meadows and Edris used the door that led to the kitchen.

231

'Shall I make us a cup of tea?' Edris asked.

'Please yourself,' Chloe said. 'I need something stronger.' She grabbed a bottle of brandy from the cupboard and poured a glassful. She knocked it back then poured another. 'You want one?' she asked her sister.

'I'll have tea,' Anna said.

Chloe grabbed the glass and bottle and sat down next to Anna. Meadows took a seat and Edris filled the kettle.

Chloe took another gulp from the glass. 'Don't judge me. I need something to get me through this.'

'No one is judging you, Chloe,' Meadows said. 'I just want the truth, so we have a chance of catching the person responsible for killing your father. Sergeant Edris thinks you are responsible, that you and Luke are working together. You need to convince me otherwise.'

Chloe took another sip and set the glass down. 'I told you my father was a dick, and I wasn't lying. He took no interest in me and Anna. We were just an inconvenience. What hurt the most is he encouraged us to have friends over to play and he paid them lots of attention. He used to take the boys for rides on the quad bikes.'

'Luke and Teilo?' Meadows asked.

'Yeah. It stopped for a while after Aneira's accident. Parents didn't want their kids playing near the machinery.'

The picture was becoming clearer in Meadows' mind and an uneasy feeling crept over him. He noticed Anna had remained silent throughout.

'The accident was soon forgotten,' Chloe continued, 'and things went back to normal. Not for me, though. In school, Luke was mean to me and some of the other boys joined in. Then Luke moved schools and I didn't see him again until I went to Dyffryn Du.' Chloe picked up her glass and drained it.

Edris quietly placed a mug of tea in front of Anna and Meadows. He then grabbed another mug before taking a seat. There was silence for a few moments, then Chloe continued.

'Luke mostly ignored me for the first few years, then he talked to me again. We ended up dating. It was good at first then he started acting odd. One night, we got a flagon of cider and took it up the field to drink. Luke drank most of it, then he got angry. It came out of the blue. He told me what my father did to him and some of the other boys – all the sick details. I didn't want to believe it at first but then I remembered something, and I knew he was telling the truth. I was so ashamed and afraid of what people would say. Imagine the gossip, even now. It would ruin mine and Anna's life. Our children would be tainted.'

'Was it only boys?'

Chloe nodded.

'Do you think Aneira might have seen something?'

'I honestly don't know. I didn't see Teilo or his father after the accident. I don't think Dad went over there. I have wondered if there was more to the accident than he said. My father wasn't a nice man. Nothing he did would surprise me.'

'Anna, you were friends with Aneria. Do you think she could have seen something? Do you remember a time when she was afraid? Did she ever tell you she had a secret?'

Anna shook head. 'I was only seven at the time. Aneira was a year younger. I remember being scared of going to the field after what Dad told us. The nightmares went on for a long time.'

'My mother took her to the doctor. That's how bad it was,' Chloe said.

'Do you remember seeing your father with any of the boys?'

'No,' Anna said. 'Chloe only told me after I had my boys. She wanted to protect them from Dad.'

'Chloe, you said that you believed Luke because you remembered something. What was it?' Meadows asked.

'I was ill one day so I stayed home from school. I heard shouting so I sneaked downstairs. It was Dad and a woman. No one ever stood up to my father. He had land, money, and equipment which gave him power over the other farmers so they needed him. I peeked through the door to see what was happening. The woman was screaming at him about what he had done to her son. Called him all sort of names I didn't understand at the time.'

'Do you know who the woman was?'

'Yes, it was Lesley Jones.'

Chapter Thirty-four

'I wouldn't have thought that Lesley would stand up to Malcom like that,' Edris said.

'She wouldn't fight for herself but her whole life has been about her children,' Meadows said.

'I suppose it makes sense now. She goes to confront Malcom. She needed the gun so he couldn't intimidate her. It goes off by accident, and she figures she's got nothing to lose so she goes on and kills her husband.'

'What about Bryn and Patricia?'

'Patricia was headteacher. Maybe she knew about the abuse. One of the boys could have told her. Bryn and Malcom hung out together, maybe Bryn was just as sick in the head.'

A car came around the bend, forcing Meadows to brake. He reversed to the nearest lay-by and let the car pass. 'I'll be glad to get on the main road,' he said.

'Let's hope Lesley hasn't run.'

'I don't think she will. What I don't understand is the blog. The writer said they were triggered by the drawing of a stickman. Lesley isn't likely to have forgotten what Malcom did.'

'She may have remembered but Luke might have forgotten. He might be the one that's triggered,' Edris said. 'Look at the state he's in. Lesley could be trying to help him. She confronts Malcom to get him to confess. She could be writing the blog through Luke's eyes.'

'I still think Aneira's accident has something to do with the murders.'

'Malcom was twisted,' Edris said. 'Look what he told his own daughters about the accident. Maybe he told Luke the same sort of thing. Told him the same would happen to him if he didn't keep quiet. Maybe he put it in Luke's mind that Bryn ran the girl over deliberately.'

'I still don't think we've got the whole story.' Meadows pulled out on the main road and put his foot down.

They reached Lesley's house and Meadows was relieved that both she and Luke were there. Lesley led them into the kitchen where Luke was sitting with a plate of bacon, eggs, and toast.

'We've spoken to Chloe,' said Meadows. 'We know what Malcom did. I'm so sorry, Luke.'

Luke looked at Lesley then back to Meadows. 'Let me finish my breakfast then you can take me in.'

'What? No!' Lesley said.

Meadows was as taken back as Lesley. 'Are you confessing to the murders?'

'Yes,' Luke said.

'No, he isn't,' Lesley said. 'I did it. I killed Malcom, Bryn, Patricia and Huw. If Chloe told you everything then you know why.'

Luke slammed his knife and fork down. 'Fuck's sake, Mum. Shut up, will you?'

'I think it's a bit late for that,' Meadows said.

'Do you want to put handcuffs on me?' Lesley asked.

Luke jumped up from the chair. 'You can't arrest her. You have no evidence. Mum, just keep your mouth shut.'

'It's alright, Luke,' Lesley said. 'It's over now.'

Luke shook his head and his eyes filled with tears. 'It's not alright. Do you know how hard Sarah and I have tried to protect you? You should have let me take the blame. My life is completely fucked up anyway.'

Meadows watched the interaction with interest. 'You'd take the blame for your mother?'

'Yes,' Luke said. 'She did it for me.'

'What?' Lesley looked confused. 'I thought…'

'What did you think?' Meadows asked.

'Nothing. Let's get on with it?'

'How did you manage to write the blog posts and stop us from tracing them?' Meadows asked.

'Well… I… it was tricky.'

'Did you use a QLC?'

'Yes,' she said.

Luke shook his head.

'Actually, there is no such thing. I just made that up,' Meadows said. 'You're confessing because you think Luke killed them.'

'What? You thought that I… Why would you think that?' Luke asked.

Lesley looked at her son. 'Didn't you?'

'No.'

Meadows sighed. 'Everyone, just sit down. Lesley, do you want to withdraw your confession?'

'Yes,' she said.

'Luke?'

Luke nodded and shovelled some bacon into his mouth.

'I think it's time for some honesty here,' Meadows said. 'Luke, why did you think your mum killed four people?'

Luke shrugged. 'I was fine with it. Dad, Malcom, and Patricia deserved it. I just didn't want to see her go down for it.'

'I should arrest you both for perverting the course of justice. You both withheld vital information that could have saved a life, maybe more than one. Right now, I have more important things to worry about. Luke, why did you attack Patricia when you were in school?'

'Because she didn't believe me.'

'About Malcom?'

'Yeah.'

'It was my idea to involve Patricia,' Lesley said. 'I knew something was wrong. Luke changed.'

'I can't listen to this.' Luke pushed his plate away and stood up. 'I'm going out the garden for a smoke.'

'I'll go with you,' Edris said.

Meadows waited for Luke and Edris to leave then turned back to Lesley. 'Go on.'

'Luke changed from a happy normal boy to a miserable, angry one. I thought it was because of what was going on with Huw, but nothing had changed. He started wetting the bed and didn't want to go out to play. I eventually coaxed it out of him. He'd been up the farm playing with Chloe, Anna, and some others. Malcom...' Lesley's voice cracked. 'He did things to Luke. I told Huw but he said Luke was making it up. He punished him. I was so angry. I went to confront Malcom at his house. He denied it, of course. I remember screaming at him. He grabbed me and threw me out. He said no one would believe Luke. He must have told Huw because he came home in a rage not long after that. He said I'd humiliated him. That's when I ended up in hospital with broken ribs.

'Huw made Luke go there to apologise. Malcom said Luke could come and do chores for him on the weekends to make up for it. Huw just left Luke there, turned his back on him.

'I thought Patricia could help. She was headmistress of the school so I was sure the police would listen to her. I thought maybe she'd be able to talk to some of the other boys that went to the farm; get an idea if Malcom had done the same to them. I persuaded Luke to talk to her. I told him that she would help. She told him off for making up stories. Started keeping him in at playtime. I took Luke out of school and moved him to Henllys. I didn't care what Huw did to me. I thought Luke would settle down but the older he got, the more trouble he seemed to get in. Then Patricia started teaching at Dyffryn Du. He lost it one day and attacked her.'

'Who else knew about this?' Meadows asked.

'No one. Just Huw, Malcom, and Patricia. I couldn't go to the police. Huw said he would kill me.'

Meadows could understand that Lesley had been scared but he still felt angry. She could have gone to the police and reported the abuse, even if that meant she went to a refuge. She could have put a stop to so much suffering.

'What about Sarah? Did she know about the abuse?'

'She knew something was wrong with Luke at the time, but I tried to shield her from it.'

'I told her after Malcom was found,' Luke said.

Meadows hadn't noticed Luke and Edris slip back in. 'Do you think she knew before that?'

'No. She thought Mum had killed him as well.'

'Who else did you tell?'

'No one,' Luke said. 'Do you think I'd want anyone to know? It was bad enough that Chloe knew. I hated her at the time. I had this idea to use her to get at Malcom. I went out with her, and I was going to do to her what he'd done to me. Then I got to know her. I realised her father didn't care for her and that she hated him. I started to have feelings for her. I was so messed up. I told her what her father had done, that she was as sick as him and knew what he got up to. We never spoke again. I heard one or two boys refer to Malcom as a pervert, so I suppose one of them could have gone after him.'

'They wouldn't have known about the part your father played,' Meadows said. 'He caused harm to you, but no one else we know about. Lesley, you used the phrase "turned his back" when you talked about Huw. It's a phrase that came up in our enquiries. Think, it's really important. Who else would you have said that to?'

'I… I didn't…' Lesley thought for a moment then bit her lip. 'About a year ago I was in a dark place. The depression was so bad I wanted to end it.' She looked at Luke. 'I never wanted you and your sister to know that I thought about leaving the two of you. That I couldn't cope anymore. I couldn't see a way out. I'd lost my confidence over the years and I didn't think I'd ever be able to leave Huw. I was ashamed of how weak and pathetic I felt. I heard someone talking about therapy, so I decided to give it a go. He was so good at listening. It all just came out. Everything.'

Meadows already knew the answer, but he asked anyway. 'Who was the therapist?'

'Teilo Thomas.'

Chapter Thirty-five

Dawn had only just broken when Meadows arrived at the police station. Folland shook his head before Meadows opened his mouth.

'Lester is already in,' Folland said.

'OK,' Meadows said. He took the stairs two at a time and headed straight for Lester's office.

Lester was on the phone barking orders. He ended the call and huffed. 'Helicopter is about to take off and search teams are on the ground, but he could be anywhere. Did you get any more from Nerys Thomas last night?'

'No,' Meadows said. 'She stuck to her story. Teilo came home when we released him. He said he needed a few days away and took his camping equipment. I think she's telling the truth. She thought he was still grieving for his father and a few days away from it all would do him good. She won't believe that he is responsible for the murders.'

'We've organised a trace on her phone. If he does contact his wife, we'll be able to find him.'

Meadows nodded. 'I think it likely he'll hide out until he's ready to go after the next victim. I'm sorry. We had him.'

'You released him on my orders.'

'We didn't have the information. We couldn't connect him to Huw Jones until now.'

'When this is over, I want the lot of them charged.'

'I think they've suffered enough,' Meadows said. 'They were all afraid to tell the truth. Like Teilo wrote in the blog, it's an invisible gag. Shame keeps the victims silent. It's how abusers get away with it. Even Chloe Watcyn was too ashamed to speak up. What we need to do now is find the next intended victim.'

'Keep me updated,' Lester said.

Meadows took that as a sign he was dismissed. He went to his own office and started trawling through all the information. He was sure there had to be something that stood out. One by one, the team came and joined in. Meadows put down a statement he was reading.

'We were wrong about Huw being the abuser,' he said. 'He was the one who turned his back. Malcom was the abuser.'

'Bryn, the child killer,' Valentine said.

'Patricia, the one who kept quiet,' Edris added. 'That leaves the abandoner.'

'Bryn abandoned Teilo,' Meadows said. 'So, who does he blame for Aneira's death? Even if he did blame his father, it leaves the question of whom he considers abandoned him.' He picked up the notes from the first interview with Teilo and read through them. 'The auntie, Rhoda Williams,' he said.

'She didn't abandon him,' Paskin said.

'No, but she might have an idea of who else Teilo blames for his sister's death or who he feels abandoned him. It doesn't matter if the doctors think she is fit enough, we need to talk to her now. Blackwell and Valentine, go to the auntie's house and take back-up. The house has been empty since she's been in hospital. Maybe he's hiding out there.'

'Then why would he take camping equipment?' Blackwell asked.

'He's not stupid. He knows we're onto him. Telling Nerys he's going camping would buy him more time. If I'm wrong, we've nothing to lose. Edris, grab Hanes. He can give us a blue light to the hospital.'

* * *

A nurse was waiting for them at the hospital entrance. She led them to Rhoda's room and stopped outside.

'She's very frail now,' the nurse said.

'We'll do our best not to distress her,' Meadows said.

The nurse smiled. 'Frail in body, not in mind. She's a tough one. I told her you were coming.'

Meadows entered the room with Edris. Rhoda was skeletal with her scalp showing through what was left of her white hair. She was propped up in the bed with a shawl around her shoulders. A drip was attached to one arm and dressings could be seen on her neck and head. Her watery blue eyes looked from Edris to Meadows, and she gave them a smile.

Meadows introduced himself and Edris.

'Come and sit so I can see you better,' Rhoda said. The left side of her face had a slight droop, but her speech was not impaired.

'We're sorry to disturb you,' Meadows said. 'Are you up to answering a few questions?'

'No need to pussyfoot around,' Rhoda said. 'I'm old, not stupid. Two detectives visiting me; it must be serious. Spit it out.'

'We are trying to find Teilo. When was the last time you saw him?'

'He was here yesterday. He comes as often as he can. Every two to three days. Why? Is he OK?'

'We are concerned for his welfare,' Meadows said.

'You think he's lost the plot again?'

'He's had problems before?'

'Yes, but that was years ago. I did wonder if this business with his father was too much for him.'

'Can you tell us what happened last time?'

'It was after his sister, Aneira, died. I got a call, so I went down to the farm. Malcom Isaac was with Bryn. He was in a state. The police were still there. I asked where Teilo was and if anyone had told him. That's when Malcom told me Teilo had seen the accident, and that he'd taken him to his house. His wife was looking after him. I forget her name now.'

'Rachel,' Edris said.

'Yes, that's right. There wasn't anything I could do for Bryn. Malcom had poured him a whisky and I imagine that wasn't the first glass he'd drunk before I arrived. I went over to see Teilo. He was in the kitchen. Rachel had wrapped him in a blanket. He was covered in blood. She said she'd tried to clean him, but he wouldn't let her touch him.

'I took him home with me. He didn't say a word. Not for weeks after. We didn't want to put him through the ordeal of questions and the inquest, so we never told anyone that he was in the field that day.

'He had terrible nightmares and was very withdrawn. Then, one day, he tried to hurt himself. That's when we decided he needed professional help. We took him to a private therapist. She was good but progress was slow. She wanted to try a new type of therapy. Altered memory, something like that. The idea was to try and replace his memory of the accident. We took away all pictures of Aneira and we came up with a story that she had fallen from the barn window. With the help of the therapist, he began to believe it. He was told that he was so upset by his sister's death that he'd had a nightmare and was confused.

It worked in the end. We were warned to watch out for triggers. That's why he never went back to the farm.'

'We think something may have triggered his memory,' said Meadows. 'Is there someone other than his father that he might blame for Aneira's death?'

'Blame? It was an accident.'

'I don't think Teilo is seeing it that way at the moment.'

'I hope you're not thinking that Teilo would... that he did something to his father. He's a good boy.'

'What Teilo needs now is help,' Meadows said. 'Is there someone who Teilo would think abandoned him or contributed to his sister's death?'

'His mother,' Rhoda said.

'We understood his mother died before the accident.'

'Dawn isn't dead. Well, not that I know of,' Rhoda said. 'That's what Bryn told the kids – what he told everyone – but she left him.'

'Where is she?'

'I don't know.'

'Does Teilo know she's alive?'

Rhoda shook her head. 'There was another time he went off the rails. He was about nineteen. We were worried that something had happened to bring up the past, but he wouldn't speak to us. He had a period of drinking and, I suspect, taking drugs, but he sorted himself out. I suppose she could have tried to contact him. It would have been a shock.'

'It's really important that we find Dawn. Is there anyone you can think of who may know where she is?'

'No. Even if Teilo found out she was alive, he'd never hurt her. He idolised his mother. He talked a lot about the last time they were together. She'd taken him out for his birthday. We let him have those happy memories.'

'Where did she take him?'

'Erm... A castle near the farm. They'd gone up a tower and spread their arms pretending to be birds. She told him she'd like to be a bird, free in the sky. He used to like watching the birds. He used to say that his mother was an angel and she'd got her wish. He will be OK, won't he?'

Meadows didn't like to make any promises. 'We'll do our best to find him.'

Chapter Thirty-six

The police car sped along with its blue lights flashing. Hanes' face was set in concentration. Meadows was on the phone to Paskin while Edris talked to Blackwell.

'Patricia was in contact with someone called Dawn,' Paskin said. 'It's one of the contacts that haven't got back to me.'

'It's got to be her,' Meadows said. 'See if you can trace the number and get an address. Keep calling her. We need the search team to move to Dinefwr Park. I think that's where he'll take her. He mentioned the castle in the blog and also talked about it with Rhoda. Best get an ambulance on standby.'

'On it,' Paskin said.

Meadows hung up and turned in his seat to speak to Edris. 'What did Blackwell say?'

'Teilo's been staying at Rhoda's house. They found the missing laptops, one switched on. Evidence of chocolate making. They even found sticks, and wool. The neighbour said they'd seen him leave early this morning. He's been driving his auntie's car. It's no wonder Teilo's car wasn't picked up travelling to the locations of the murders. Blackwell is going to send through the registration.'

'They could already be there,' Meadows said. Every muscle in his body was tensed. Cars moved out of their way and Hanes floored the accelerator, but still Meadows felt the time slipping away. Every second that went by brought Dawn nearer to death. Each time the radio crackled to life Meadows held his breath for bad news.

'Better turn off the siren,' Meadows said as they neared the park. 'I don't want Teilo getting spooked.'

'I'll get you as close as I can,' Hanes said. He drove past the car park and followed the track downwards until they reached the gate. Beyond was a field that sloped up towards the castle.

'Tell search and rescue to head for the castle with caution,' Meadows said. 'Keep me updated.' He turned to Edris. 'Let's go.'

Meadows took off at a sprint with Edris keeping pace. The castle loomed in front of them. He could feel the muscles in his thighs burning as he pushed on up the hill. Another gate led them into the woods.

Meadows slowed to catch his breath. Edris was panting heavily beside him. They jogged along through the woods then sprinted to the main path that led into the castle. They walked the last of the track silently and entered through the castle gates.

'Doesn't look like they are here,' Edris said.

Meadows looked around. To their right, a set of steps led up to the keep. On their left, another set of steps led to the parapet. Ahead, a square tower marked the highest point of the building. As he looked up at the tower, two figures appeared.

Meadows pulled Edris back. 'It's them.'

'Do you think he's going to throw her off the top?'

'Not if I can help it,' Meadows said. 'I'm going to try and keep him talking until help arrives. Even when it does, I can't see how they will be able to surround the tower with something to break her fall. Our only chance is to talk him down. Stay here and see what you can do.'

Edris nodded.

Meadows moved across the courtyard, under an arch, and onto a set of metal steps. He moved as quickly and quietly as he could. He reached the first landing and moved on to the stone spiral staircase. The ancient treads were worn and uneven, so he grabbed the railing that had been fixed to the wall. The staircase was narrow, with only enough room for one person. He reached the second landing and moved onto a straight staircase. Arrow slits lit the way and Meadows could see the Tywi valley below as he rose higher. The staircase twisted to the right, and he heard voices.

'This was where I last saw you,' Teilo said.

'I wanted to make the day special for you.'

'You left us. You knew what Dad was like.'

'I had to leave,' Dawn said. 'I couldn't take you with me. I didn't have anywhere to stay.'

'He told us you were dead. I cried for you.'

'I'm so sorry. I was going to come back but then...'

Meadows was nearing the top of the staircase. He could see Teilo and Dawn looking out over the valley from the top of the tower. The platform was only three feet wide and stretched to around ten feet in length. A low railing ran the perimeter covering the crumbling walls.

'You can't say her name, can you? Aneira, your little girl who cried for you. Aneira, who would still be alive if you'd cared enough to stay. Do you know how she died? Do you know how scared she must have been?'

Dawn put her hands to her head. 'Teilo, stop it. Please.'

'She was torn to shreds!'

Meadows inched closer. They were too close to the edge. Teilo put his hand on Dawn's back.

'Teilo, don't,' Meadows said.

Teilo spun around and Dawn scurried to the corner, her eyes wide with shock.

'Don't come any closer,' Teilo said.

There was no way Meadows could get to Dawn with Teilo blocking the way and he couldn't risk a struggle. He held up his hands. 'I just want to talk. To help you.'

'No one can help me,' Teilo said.

'Everyone lied to you,' Meadows said. 'I can't imagine how that made you feel, but they only did it to protect you. Even your father probably didn't know how to tell you that your mother had left.'

Teilo looked at Dawn. 'Why did you even bother trying to contact me? Imagine what it did to me to find out you were alive. I'd grieved for you.'

'I'm sorry,' Dawn said. 'I wanted to explain.'

Teilo's eyes narrowed. 'Explain. How do you explain abandoning your children?'

'Can we go down now?' Dawn asked. 'I'll answer all your questions.'

'You want to go down?' Teilo lunged at Dawn and grabbed her by the arm. 'Do you want to be free?' He yanked her until her legs collided with the railings.

Dawn let out a scream.

'Teilo, look at me,' Meadows said.

Teilo moved behind Dawn. In a flash, he whipped out a knife from his pocket and held it to her throat.

'Dawn, don't move,' Meadows said. 'Teilo, don't you want to tell her why? Tell her how you feel. I read your blog. You're better than this. It won't make the pain go away, won't stop the torment. You need help. Tell me about the drawing. The one that started this.'

Teilo ignored him. 'Step over the railing,' he said to Dawn.

Dawn was trembling and Meadows could see the terror in her eyes. If he made a move now, he was sure Teilo would kill her.

'Don't do that, Teilo,' Meadows said.

Teilo looked at Dawn. 'You want me to tell you? Then step over. I want you to know how it feels to be terrified.' He pushed the blade against her throat.

'OK,' Dawn sobbed. Slowly, she climbed on the railing. Her legs shook as she swung them over.

Teilo did the same, so they were standing side by side with their backs against the railing. Teilo put the knife back into his pocket and gripped Dawn's upper arm.

Meadows was trying to work out how he could stop them from going over the edge. The ledge they were standing on was uneven and loose stones lay under their feet. He heard Edris behind him.

'Search and rescue are here,' Edris whispered. 'They're working on a way to break the fall.'

Meadows hoped it wouldn't come to that. There was still a chance he could talk Teilo down. 'The drawing,' he said. 'Why did it upset you?'

'I was trying to help a child,' Teilo said. 'He'd lost his father. He was drawing a picture of his family. They were stick figures. I felt sick. I didn't know why. Then the nightmares started, and I would wake up screaming. I felt like I was losing my mind.'

'Why didn't you get help?'

'I couldn't. I was too ashamed. All I ever wanted to do was help people. How could I do that if I couldn't even help myself? That's why I went on the forum. It was my way of being able to talk about it.' Teilo gripped the rail and looked down. Next to him Dawn was deathly pale.

'It helped you remember,' Meadows said.

'No. I took on a new client. I was trying to help her overcome her anxiety. She came every Tuesday morning. At first, she told me about her husband and how cruel he had been. Then she told me about her son.'

'Luke,' Meadows said.

Teilo looked back at Meadows. 'Lesley let slip Luke's abuser's name. The name gave me a flashback. Malcom carrying me over his shoulder and me screaming. Then I started to remember more. I remembered what he'd done. Then Lesley told me how Patricia had let her down. It was another name I remembered, another name I associated with something bad happening.'

'I didn't know,' Dawn said. Tears ran down her cheeks and her lips trembled. One hand was behind her back as she griped the rail.

Meadows' legs were starting to cramp. He moved his weight to his back foot. He had no idea what was going on below. 'I know you didn't mean to kill Malcom.'

'I only wanted to confront him. Chloe had told me about the gun when we were kids. She showed me once. I got the gun so he would feel powerless, like I had. I wanted him to show some remorse. He didn't. He wasn't ashamed. The gun went off by accident. Blood splattered everywhere. It stirred something in my mind. Something far worse than what Malcom had done to me.

'I thought someone would come for me, but they never did. I went back to move Malcom.'

'Why did you go after Huw?'

'Because of what he'd done. He not only turned his back on his own son but the rest of us. He could have stopped it. I started to follow him in the mornings. Nerys had a wig that she had worn to a fancy-dress party; I put that on with one of her jumpers. I didn't want to be recognised. I ordered the crossbow from Dad's computer using his card. I told him I was buying a surprise present for Nerys and gave him the cash. That morning, I let the tyre down on my client's car. If you've read the blog, then you know the rest. When I saw the blood again, that's when I remembered everything.'

The wind picked up and Teilo swayed. Dawn let out a squeal.

Meadows didn't know how much longer Dawn could keep gripping the rail. 'Why forty-one bolts?'

'For Lesley. That's how long she suffered. I dipped the bolts in ammonia to intensify the pain. I wanted him to feel helpless, afraid, and in agony.'

'But you implicated Lesley in his murder. Caused her more suffering.'

Pain filled Teilo's eyes. 'I didn't mean for that to happen.' He looked away.

'You didn't write about killing your father.'

Teilo spoke into the wind. 'No, because that would have given me away. I'd asked him to get the old photographs down from the attic. I wanted photos of Aneira and to give him a chance to talk about her. There were no photos of her. He'd destroyed them. We argued. He still blamed me. That's when I decided to go through with my plan. I gave him night nurse in a hip flask. Told him to drink it before bed and it would help with his cough. It worked. He didn't hear me come in. I made him feel the pain Aneira felt. Then I burned every photo of him. I took the laptops so I could write the blog. I couldn't risk you finding something on mine.'

'What about the cup we found in his house with the lipstick?'

'It was one of my clients'. I waited until they were gone then used gloves to put it in a plastic bag. I thought it would confuse you.'

'It did,' Meadows said. 'What about Patricia?'

'I put the wig on and went to see her. She loved talking about herself. That's how I learned about the chilli. It made things easier. I thought she'd worked it out at the meeting. She kept staring at me, but she let me in that evening.'

Teilo kept talking. Every now and then he would look down. Dawn was shaking uncontrollably. Meadows was trying to work out if he could reach Dawn before Teilo had a chance to push her.

'I understand,' Meadows said. 'You were traumatised by what happened.'

'They should never have convinced me that it was all in my head. I never had the chance to process it. It lay dormant inside, eating away at me until it was too late.'

'It's not too late.' Dawn looked at her son. The fear in her eyes had been replaced by guilt and pity.

Teilo shuffled on the ledge and the loose bits of stone tumbled over the edge, clattering down the tower and hitting the ground. Dawn tried to twist around to scramble back to safety but Teilo pulled her back.

'Stop!' Meadows said. 'You need to stay still.'

Dawn stopped struggling but Meadows could see she was breathing heavily. He knew she was fighting against the fight-or-flight instinct.

'Teilo, please come back over the railings. We can just talk,' Meadows said.

'No. I've got to finish this,' Teilo said.

'Tell me about the stick dolls,' Meadows said.

'It was Aneira's birthday. She wanted a doll, but Dad said we didn't have money to buy toys. She had no birthday party, cake, or presents. I made her a doll from the twigs of the sycamore tree. I unravelled the wool on my jumper, then I cut a piece from a curtain to make the skirt. Aneira loved it. Children don't need much. Food, water, shelter, and love.' He looked at Dawn. 'Why didn't you love her?'

'I did.' Dawn's voice quivered. 'I loved you both so much.'

'Don't lie to me.'

'Go on,' Meadows said.

'She asked me to make her another one. She wanted her doll to have a brother. She took them everywhere.

'Patricia was always coming around the house. She made us call her Miss Maddox even in our own home. The night before the accident, I heard her downstairs. She was arguing with Dad. She stayed for a long time shouting and crying, then she left. She slammed the door.

'The next morning Aneira was ill. She was crying so I took her downstairs as I didn't want to wake Dad. It was harvesting time, but he hadn't bothered going to the fields or feeding the animals. He was drinking all the time. It was better to leave him to sleep.

'Patricia came around again. She woke Dad up. They started arguing again. I went to the kitchen to see what was going on. Dad had poured himself a drink and I knew how angry Dad got after drinking so I scuttled back into the sitting room. Patricia came in after me and told me to go out and play. I told her Aneira was sick. She said to give her some Calpol then take her out as the fresh air would do her good.

'I went into the kitchen to get the Calpol. Dad said something to Patricia – I can't remember what exactly – something about not having enough for two kids. Patricia started to cry so I gave Aneira the medicine and took her out. She took her stick dolls with her. We went to the barn, but Malcom came over. I saw him walk past on the way to the house. I thought he was looking for me, so I took Aneira to the top field to play. The crops were high, and he wouldn't see us there.

'The combine harvester was at the top of the field. Malcom said I could ride on it with him, but I didn't want to. I knew what he would want in return. I played about for a while with the harvester and when I went back to Aneira, she had fallen asleep. Her cheeks were bright red. I felt her head. She was so hot. I knew this wasn't good so I went back to tell Dad and get her some water. I went down through the field so I wouldn't run into Malcom.

'When I got back to the house, Dad wasn't there. I filled a glass of water then started to make my way back. That's when I heard it. The engine. The whirring of the cutting bar. I dropped the glass and ran.

'I got to the bottom of the field. Malcom and Dad where in the cab and they were heading towards where I'd left Aneira. I was shouting and waving my hands as I ran. They didn't see me. They looked like they were arguing. They weren't watching where they were going. The crops slowed me down. I tried so hard to reach her. The cutting blade hit Aneira and they must have felt a jolt because they stopped. She was… she was… I tried to pull her free.

'I remember Malcom picking me up and throwing me over his shoulder. I was screaming. I saw the stick dolls on the ground. One of them was broken, like Aneira, and the other was covered in blood.

'I think Malcom took me back to our house first to call for help. All I remember after is being with Chloe's mum in their kitchen. The silence and the sticky blood on my hands.'

Both Teilo and Dawn were crying; the pain mirrored on each other's faces. Meadows put his weight on his front foot, ready to spring forward.

'You all killed her,' Teilo said. 'If Huw had spoken out about Malcom, he would have been locked up where he belonged and that machine would never have been in the field. If Malcom wasn't a pervert, I wouldn't have had to hide from him that day. If Patricia hadn't sent us out to play. If Dad wasn't drunk.' He glared at Dawn. 'All of it started with you. If you hadn't left, none of this would have happened. I left stick dolls for all of them. For all the boys that Malcom damaged. I left one for Luke with Huw. The brother and sister dolls watched Dad die for me and Aneira. I left three with Patricia for the three little children she failed to help: Aneira, Luke, and me.'

'What about the one you left with me?' Meadows asked.

'The police didn't look into Aneira's death. I wanted to scare you. Give you some incentive to uncover the truth. I've written my final blog post. It's scheduled to go out tonight.' He looked at Dawn. 'Open my rucksack.'

Dawn's hands were shaking as she pulled the zipper while trying to keep her balance. She plucked out two stick dolls.

'A boy and girl,' Teilo said. 'The children you deserted.'

Dawn nodded. 'You're right. Nothing I can say will justify my actions. I don't deserve to live.' She pitched forward.

Teilo, caught off guard, grabbed hold of the railing in an act of automatic reflex. His other hand clutched Dawn's coat. At the same time, Meadows sprang forward with his hands outstretched. He just manged to grab Dawn's ankles before she went over. His body collided with the wall.

Teilo looked down at Meadows for a moment. In his eyes, Meadows saw despair. 'Don't,' Meadows said.

Teilo let go of the rail and let himself fall.

Chapter Thirty-seven

Dawn was sitting in the back of the ambulance with a blanket placed around her shoulders and a hot drink in her hands.

'How is she?' Meadows asked the paramedic.

'Just some nasty scrapes to her legs and stomach. Mostly shock but she'll be OK.'

'Can I have a quick word with her before you take her in?'

The paramedic nodded.

Meadows climbed into the back of the ambulance and sat opposite Dawn.

'I thought you'd like to know that Teilo is going to be OK. Firefighters managed to break his fall with a net.'

'It's all my fault,' Dawn said. 'You shouldn't have bothered pulling me back.'

'You can't blame yourself,' Meadows said. 'Teilo went through a traumatic experience. He never fully recovered. His mind is in torment. He did try hard to make a life for himself and help other people.'

'What will happen to him?'

'I don't know,' Meadows said. 'I don't think he'll be fit to stand trial so, likely, he'll serve his time in a secure psychiatric hospital. You'll have a chance to visit him if you want to.'

'He's my son. It doesn't matter what's he done. I still love him.'

Meadows nodded. 'Everyone believed you were dead. If we'd known, we could have warned you.'

'Bryn told the kids I was ill at first, then he told them I had died. He even told my parents that I had run off with some man and had an accident in Spain. Pat took great pleasure in spreading the rumour, I'm sure. Everyone believed it.

'I had to leave. Bryn was a violent man after a few drinks. We had no money, and we were struggling to keep the farm going. The less we had, the more he drank. I was sure he was going to go too far and kill me one night.'

Meadows thought of Lesley. She had stayed and endured years of abuse. Damned if you do and damned if you don't, he thought. These women had to make difficult choices and suffered either way.

'You did what you had to do to survive,' Meadows said. 'No one can blame you for that. You weren't to know.'

'I thought they would be alright. I knew Bryn was seeing Pat. He didn't make a secret of it, and she was in love with him. I saw it as my chance to escape. She gave me some money, just enough to travel and for some food. She said she would keep watch over the children until I could come back to get them. That was always my intention.'

'We think at some stage Patricia was pregnant and either lost the baby or had a termination.'

'That doesn't surprise me. She would have seen it as a way to bind herself to Bryn.'

'What happened when you left?' Meadows asked.

'I tried to get work but ended up sleeping rough. I couldn't look after myself, let alone the children. Many times, I felt like giving up and going back, but I knew what would be waiting for me. I only kept in contact with Pat to find out how the children were doing. She told me they thought I was dead. That hurt so much, but I thought there would be time to put it right. When I heard the news about Aneira, I… I gave up caring. I started drinking and taking drugs, anything to numb the pain. I didn't speak to Pat for a few years after that.'

'Did you know about Malcom?'

'I didn't know what he was doing. I asked Pat to look after the children for me. She never mentioned anything about Malcom. The first I heard of it was when Luke attacked her. She had no one else she could talk to about it. She was in a state and told me why he'd done it, what he'd told her years before.'

'Why didn't she report him?'

Dawn shrugged. 'I can only guess. Pat was a selfish woman. I don't think she cared about the children she worked with. She enjoyed being a figure of authority. Bryn needed Malcom to work the land and Pat wouldn't have caused problems for Bryn. When Luke attacked her, she was afraid it would come to light that she never acted at the time and she would lose her job. So she covered it up and made out that Luke was on drugs and out of control. She wasn't ashamed about keeping quiet.'

'You could have made an anonymous call.'

'Teilo had gone to live with Rhoda after Aneira's accident. He was safe.'

Meadows felt a spike of anger. 'Others weren't safe. You could have put a stop to it; saved other young boys from that trauma.'

Dawn nodded and tears tracked down her face. 'I wish I could go back and change things. I wish I'd never left. Even contacting Teilo when he turned eighteen only did more damage. I cut all ties then. I didn't speak to Pat after that.'

'Her phone records show that you'd been in contact recently,' Meadows said.

'I heard about the murders on the news. I wanted to make sure that Teilo was OK. Pat was worried that Luke was involved. She wouldn't go to the police because she knew too many questions would be asked. She'd kept her relationship with Bryn secret, and then there was Malcom.'

'Why didn't you come forward?'

'I never for a minute suspected that Teilo was involved. I could have given you information about Malcom, but I couldn't come back because... well... I...' She rubbed her hands over her face. 'When I was at my lowest someone helped me. His name was Simon. He volunteered at a homeless shelter. He got me off the streets, helped me find work, and a place to live. I wanted to give something back, so I became a volunteer. Simon and I got together. He asked me so many times to marry him. I ran out of excuses, so I agreed. I wanted to make him happy. I had taken my birth certificate from home and the rest was easy. It was only a registry office, but I was still afraid I'd be found out. I guess you'll have to arrest me now.'

'Technically you're a widow, and I think there's been enough suffering. Though your husband deserves an explanation. Not just for his sake but for yours. It's time to stop hiding.'

Dawn nodded. 'Thank you.'

Meadows stepped out of the ambulance to where Edris was waiting.

'Ready to go?'

'Yeah. There's nothing else to do here. I'm going to pick up my future wife and take her home.'

Chapter Thirty-eight

It was a crisp, clear night. The stars were out, and a three-quarter moon lit up the sky. Meadows could hear laugher and feel the excitement of those gathered in the commune. Incense sticks filled the air with the aroma of jasmine and sandalwood, and strings of twinkling lights added to the festive mood.

'Ready?' Rain asked.

Meadows felt a fluttering in his stomach. 'Yes. I can't wait.'

They walked side by side, passing the large bonfire before reaching the pagoda. Friends and family had formed a line to make the aisle. Each one held a candle which cast a soft glow on their faces. Their eyes danced with excitement and their smiles were full of love and warmth.

A cheer went up as Meadows walked the pathway of light. He saw his team standing in the line. Even Blackwell was cheering and smiling. At the end of the aisle, Iggy, the commune elder, was standing next to the registrar. Meadows came to a stop in front of him. His mother stepped out of the line and gave him a kiss on the cheek.

Music started up and he turned. Daisy began her walk with her father beside her. She was dressed in a forest-green corseted gown. Her long black hair cascaded over her shoulders in soft curls. Her face was aglow. She came to stand next to Meadows and the guests fell silent.

Iggy cleared his throat. 'Tonight, we celebrate the spring equinox, and we will greet the dawn with the start of spring. It is a time for new beginnings.' He looked at Meadows and Daisy. 'It is the beginning of your life together.'

Meadows took Daisy's hand. His winter was over.

List of characters

If you enjoyed this book, please let others know by leaving a quick review on Amazon. Also, if you spot anything untoward in the paperback, get in touch. We strive for the best quality and appreciate reader feedback.

editor@thebookfolks.com

www.thebookfolks.com

Also in this series:

THE SILENT QUARRY (Book 1)

Following a fall and a bang to the head, a woman's memories come flooding back about an incident that occurred twenty years ago in which her friend was murdered. As she pieces together the events and tells the police, she begins to fear repercussions. DI Winter Meadows must work out the identity of the killer before they strike again.

FROZEN MINDS (Book 2)

When the boss of a care home for mentally challenged adults is murdered, the residents are not the most reliable of witnesses. DI Winter Meadows draws on his soft nature to gain the trust of an individual he believes saw the crime. But without unravelling the mystery and finding the evidence, the case will freeze over.

SUFFER THE CHILDREN (Book 3)

When a toddler goes missing from the family home, the police and community come out in force to find her. However, with few traces found after an extensive search, DI Winter Meadows fears the child has been abducted. But someone knows something, and when a man is found dead, the race is on to solve the puzzle.

A KNOT OF SPARROWS (Book 4)

When local teenage troublemaker and ne'er-do-well Stacey Evans is found dead, locals in a small Welsh village couldn't give a monkey's. That gives nice guy cop DI Winter Meadows a headache. Can he win over their trust and catch a killer in their midst?

LIES OF MINE (Book 5)

A body is found in an old mine in a secluded spot in the Welsh hills. There are no signs of struggle so DI Winter Meadows suspects that the victim, youth worker David Harris, knew his killer. But when the detective discovers it is not the first murder in the area, he must dig deep to join up the dots.

RISE TO THE FLY (Book 6)

When the bodies of a retired couple are found by a reservoir, the police are concerned to discover fishing flies have been impaled on their tongues. After they find nothing in the couple's past to indicate a reason for the murder, they begin to look local. What will they turn up in this dark and secluded corner of Wales?

WINTER'S CRY (Book 7)

When a farmer clears some trees from a field, he unearths a corpse. Suspicion immediately falls upon the neighbouring commune, a collection of makeshift huts and tents which house a reclusive group of people. Having grown up there, DI Winter Meadows goes to talk to its members, who are wary of the police. But what he finds will have him questioning everything he knows about his past.

HARBOUR NO SECRETS (Book 8)

A young woman is found in a Welsh lake, murdered. Detectives find seaside trinkets placed in her home. Are they a message from the killer? DI Winter Meadows becomes convinced that the perp might be lurking within the victim's circle of friends. Who is bearing a grudge and who might be targeted next?

All available FREE with Kindle Unlimited and in paperback.

More fiction by the author:

BLUE HOLLOW

When a family friend is murdered, a journalist begins to probe into his past. What she finds there makes her question everything about her life. Should she bury his secrets with him, or become the next victim of Blue Hollow?

Other titles of interest:

IN THE FAMILY by Martyn Taylor

When a former gangland boss is found shot dead in his home, DI Penelope Darling knows that the investigation will take her into the nether regions of her city's criminal world. But finding the killer among the likely suspects will require keeping her eyes open to the unexpected. She'll need to have her wits about her to stop a ruthless individual from getting away with murder.

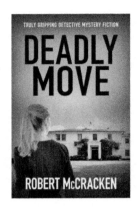

DEADLY MOVE by Robert McCracken

When hacker Thomas Brady is killed in his home, DI Tara Grogan isn't convinced that the reason was just his anti-social habit of playing music too loud. She becomes suspicious of a very wealthy businessman who was connected to the victim. But trying to pin him down is going to be a true test of mettle.

Sign up to our mailing list to find out about new releases and special offers!

www.thebookfolks.com

Printed in Great Britain
by Amazon

45039576R00158